SHORTCUTS

Advance Praise for *Shortcuts*

"A diverse cast of relatable characters teach us that kindness, acceptance, teamwork, self-reflection, and self-forgiveness can alter the future in unexpected ways."
— *Jennifer Moore, Ph.D., School of Library and Information Studies, Texas Woman's University*

"The power of *Shortcuts* is the characters. Every middle grade student will find a character they can relate to in this book."
— *Dr. Jennifer Heine, Elementary School Librarian, Judson ISD*

"Bearce's beautifully descriptive writing is a buffet of emotions complete with taste and smell! The characters are entirely relatable and intriguing as they learn to wield gifts that, if discovered, could destroy their lives."
— *Stacy Webb, Librarian, John Glenn Middle School*

AMY BEARCE

A SINGULARITIES BOOK
CBAY BOOKS
DALLAS, TEXAS

Shortcuts

Shortcuts hand drawn title by Jeff Crosby.
jeffcrosbyillustration.com

Children's Brains are Yummy Books
Dallas, Texas
www.cbaybooks.blog

Hardcover ISBN: 978-1-944821-76-0
Paperback ISBN: 978-1-944821-77-7
eBook ISBN: 978-1-944821-78-4
Kindle ISBN: 978-1-944821-79-1
PDF ISBN: 978-1-944821-80-7

Printed in the United States of America
First Edition in 2019

To my friends,
You are all fabulous.

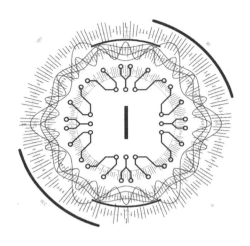

THE buzzing of the lunch bell made me jump, but I was ready for the chaos that followed. Ninety-two eighth-graders hurtled from their classrooms, sending ninety-two separate emotions gushing down the hallway like an invisible tidal wave. Anger and amusement, elation and embarrassment, warmth and worry.

Like always, I gritted my teeth at the emotional tsunami. Having excellent acting skills came in handy at times like these. I just imagined I was in a performance.

The stage is set ... The curtain rises ... And ...

You're on, Parker.

I braced myself and pasted on a big smile. Throwing my leather-fringed backpack over my left shoulder, I

strode down the eighth-grade hall, aiming for my most confident look, the one Avery called "The Fashionista." My grin promised I had exactly zero worries. My walk announced I felt confident and happy. And I did, at least most of the time.

But only a few people knew just how many *other* things I felt. The rest could never know.

I greeted all my friends as I went, waving constantly like the winner of the annual Miss Divine Pecan Pageant. (Which I actually have been. Twice. I probably held the record for the most bobby pins in an updo.)

Being small—or my preferred term, *petite*—meant I could move through the crowd without bumping into anyone, which was a good thing. I worked hard at it, too. Touching someone boosted my empathy, as if they were shouting their feelings right in my ear. School was already too loud, in every possible way: Shrill laughter and the babble of voices echoed down the white-tiled hall. Lockers clanked like a washing machine full of loose quarters. But the feelings were the hardest to ignore.

Shame! Pride! Dread! Random bits of other people's feelings drizzled down around me like rain, soaking into my heart. Today, shame was particularly gross, sticky yet acidic.

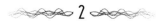 2

Stepping to the side, pretending to tie my shoe, I imagined a waterfall pouring over me and washing away all my classmates' sticky emotions. The Venerable Madam Lily did this on her late-late show, *Ask a Psychic*. Who knew a phony psychic's technique to block intrusive feelings actually worked? Well, *mostly*. Still, any help was better than none.

The water bubbled along inside me, carrying away all those unwanted feelings. Slowly, the flickering emotions vanished, until only my own remained. My stomach still felt a bit curdled from that shame slushee, though.

I couldn't sense everyone's feelings all the time, thank goodness, but sudden or powerful emotions often slipped past other people's natural walls to ambush me. Some flares of emotions were like fireworks: sudden and bright, then gone in a heartbeat. More powerful feelings slid slowly from my senses, stubborn ghosts that would rather haunt than disappear.

All emotions faded sooner or later, though. Some just needed a little help, especially on Mondays, a day full of extra zips from weekend fights and flirtations.

Today was definitely a Monday.

I let out a slow breath and pressed a hand to my belly. Okay, so my shielding could stand some improvement,

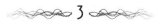

but I still had to eat. Mondays required dessert, though. I stopped by my locker to toss in my books. Today I'd go for the banana pudding. Maybe I'd even grab one for Ethan as a surprise.

Pain. Psychic claws raked down my back, out of nowhere.

I flinched but forced back the emotion from whoever had brushed past. It'd be gone in a minute. Leaning my head against the locker door, I waited for the feeling to pass. It didn't.

Disbelief. Despair.

A one-two punch to the gut.

Okay, waterfall, don't fail me now. One more time. We can do this. I steeled myself to focus, always hard during a class change, but before I managed to turn on my imagery mood cleanser, the stench of burnt chocolate and over-brewed coffee bloomed right beside me. The smell of betrayal and heartbreak.

I hid a gag. Two merciful months had passed since the last time an emotion had shown up in my mind with Smell-o-Vision. No imaginary waterfall could wash away agony like that, not when it was right in my face.

That. Was. It.

I slammed my locker shut and turned to the girl

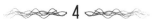

beside me. "Hey, Kayla. Are you okay?"

It was a rhetorical question. I judged Kayla's heart-break a 7.1 on the Emo Scale. Anything over a 5.0 showed up in my mind at least briefly, whether or not I was trying to tune it out. By 6.0, their pain seriously burned. But manifesting pain as a smell was rare, reserved for 7.0 and up.

Kayla looked around her locker door, with one eye hidden behind her braids. "Brad's taking someone else to the Halloween dance. I can't—" The words melted into tears.

I sighed and looked around for the boy in question. Attending middle school in a small town meant it was never too hard to pick someone out of the crowd, but Brad made it easy. Always wanting to be first, he barreled right by on his way to the lunchroom, not even looking our way.

He wasn't pushing his feelings on me, but I could suss them out anyway if I wanted. Keeping my stance casual, I stretched out my psychic sense of empathy and opened it to become a walking X-ray machine for the heart.

I wrinkled my nose and closed my gift down fast. Hatefully smug. Brad-boy wasn't worried about Kayla's tears, though he knew about them. He wasn't interested in her anymore.

"I'm so sorry. He's not good enough for you."

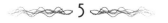

Kayla pressed her lips tight, yet the tears kept flowing.

Words were such awkward, gangly tools to accomplish emotional surgery. Even the hug I gave her—mental waterfall set to high so I could touch her without her feelings gagging me—could only do so much. I ached to make Kayla feel better *right now*. For a psychic empath, the happiness of others was truly my own.

Unfortunately, so was their pain.

Though I wished I could reach into their hearts and make everyone better instantly, my gift was a one-way street. I could look but not touch. Luckily, a liberal dose of Texas charm could smooth over the sometimes-necessary pushiness and persuasion, leaving everyone, including me, happier in the end. Win-win.

Another blip hit my empathy radar, at least a 6.1 on the Emo Scale—the Attraction scale this time. Tinted silver with long-term admiration, it came from Anthony Perron, standing across the hall, watching Kayla.

Excellent.

I said, "So Brad sucks. But you know who doesn't have a date for the dance? And who really, *really* likes you?"

Kayla wiped her nose and looked up. "Someone else … likes me?"

I pulled out my most knowing smile. "Don't look now, but Anthony's across the hall. I can tell he's totally into you. Have you read *Reading the Signs of Love*?"

The title always made me snort, but it was a real book. A dumb one, but it made for a useful cover.

Kayla shook her head.

"It's about how you can read someone's emotions from their body language. And he definitely likes what he's seeing."

Kayla sniffed. "Brad thinks I can't get another date."

"Prove him wrong. But first, let's get you fixed up."

I pushed the girl into the bathroom and busted out the emergency bag I kept on hand for exactly these situations. In a minute flat, all blotchy evidence of crying was gone. Kayla walked over to Anthony with a new, if fragile, smile on her freshly painted lips.

I gave myself a mental high five. If they gave out medals for psychic empathy, I'd definitely earn the gold these days. I'd also be the only one competing in that particular category, but that was beside the point.

A voice behind me said, "Seriously? You're still playing Cupid?"

I shrieked and spun, clutching my chest at the familiar sight of my best friend Avery. "Don't sneak up

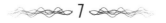

on me like that!"

Avery tossed her books in our shared locker. "Pshaw. If you'd ignore all the sob stories around you, you'd have heard me coming. Check these out."

She held out one foot wearing a green thick-soled boot covered in hot pink flowers. Fascinating choice, but one Avery could carry off, no doubt stomping like a T-Rex as she went. "And don't even tell me you weren't using your awesomeness to find Kayla a perfect match."

"Only a little!"

"Whatever. You're going to get us all busted when people figure out you're selling Love Potion Number Nine to sad-faced girls."

"As if. Brad's a hateful user, but Anthony's sweet. They'll be cute together, yeah?" I smiled, purposefully bringing out my dimples.

Avery rolled her eyes and tugged a brush through her red hair. "Yeah, they're adorable. Don't bother flashing the dimples. They don't work on me like they do Ethan."

Heat burned my cheeks, but I shrugged. "Ethan's not interested in my dimples." Or any part of me other than the friend part. Which was fine by me. Absolutely fine.

"Whatever you say, Parker. If you're willing to bend the rules, at least have the decency to fix up Todd with some awful match and make him miserable." Avery glared at her ex-boyfriend, who squirmed by like a snake.

When they broke up, Todd had told Avery that she needed to learn to relax. And sure, Avery could be intense. But when a girl was truly precognitive, things could get heavy. Like the time she had a vision of a guy getting beaten to a pulp in a locker room. He resembled Ethan, same spiky black hair, and all locker rooms look alike. But it turned out to be someone in Ohio, two weeks later.

Luckily, that kid survived, not that we could've done anything about it if he hadn't. No matter how brilliant Avery was in science—very—her visions were random, vague, and not super helpful most of the time. For logical Avery, they created lots of stress.

I understood better than anyone. I was drawn to suffering like an animal lover was drawn to the pound. I felt compelled to help people find their happiest path in life.

Even though people could suck my heart dry if I wasn't careful.

And even if people might figure out my secret sauce if I wasn't careful.

But that's why I was always super, duper careful.

 9

2

ONE last exhausting waterfall rinsed away the worst of the remaining distractions. I heaved a deep sigh.

"Better?" Avery asked, used to the ritual.

"Much. Let's go dig in. I need to fortify my strength."

The cafeteria was already pretty full. We headed to the hot lunch line, and our path took us right past Todd. Avery tightened her lips into a line, but not even a tiny zing scratched my skin. I gave a contented sigh.

The best way for me to relax was spending time with Avery, Ethan, and Deshawn. The four of us had been connected from the start when our parents met in the same clinic for a trial of a new fertility drug. That doctor disappeared fast when the drug got banned—pausing only long enough to delete his files—but the family friendships stuck, especially when our parents realized their kids not only shared similar birthdays, but similar … differences—unusual abilities that grew stronger with age.

Our four families swore to keep it secret, keeping us kids under the radar as best as they could. Though each of us had a different type of ability, all our gifts were awesome—except when, like mine, they weren't. Luckily, we'd all worked on mentally shielding emotions after I stumbled onto Madam Lily's show. Being around any of our Fab Four now was like turning off a fuzzy radio station.

I leaned closer to Avery. "I've got connections I can use. Tina Lee will spread any rumor I tell her not to. In under an hour, the whole school will know about the time Todd sharted from laughing too hard at the movies. Not my usual, but I'll go for the jugular for you."

"Yeah, no. He's not worth it, and then you'd suffer his agony too."

I snorted. "Are you're saying I gotta block better? The suggestion box is open."

We paused the conversation while we paid. At the utensil kiosk, all the forks were gone already. That's what we got for being late. We grabbed spoons.

Avery poked me in the shoulder with her own spoon and lowered her voice. "I'm saying stop the fortune telling love matches."

"Even if someone's crying?"

Avery spoke firmly. "Even if the girl beside you is weeping clumpy mascara into raccoon eyes. You're being too obvious. Being a walking science fiction movie isn't cool when real scientists could find out about us."

She'd know. Avery's mom was a prominent neural researcher. Some of her colleagues were more interested in paranormal abilities than she liked. And as much as she'd love to learn more, too, no way would she risk her daughter or her friends' kids.

Ahead of us, a table of 4-H kids burst into angry shouts about the latest steer show. I made a U-turn to take Avery the long way around.

Avery said, "Good call. That's a lot of rage right there."

We skirted the edge of the wide room. "I don't step in a cow pie if I see it waiting. Some stuff just slips in. And then it's hard to resist fixing things."

"How did your dad figure out how to, you know, keep his emotions on the down-low? Maybe we could figure out a better method for you if we studied him." Avery was always ready to study.

Shrugging, I headed toward our table in the back. I kept my voice low, but there was really no chance of being overheard in this din. "Dad? He just worked super hard, riffing off Madam Lily's techniques. He may be a plain brain, but he's still a genius." I dropped my voice to a whisper. "And he wanted a mental shield really bad."

"To spare you pain. That sweet Daddy Mills."

I smiled. "Yeah, and to spare himself embarrassment, I bet. As if I'd want to eavesdrop on my dad's mood. Some things should remain a mystery."

"Lots of things should, like people's secret feelings." Avery looked around. "You have to cut it out, Parks. I'm not kidding."

"I get it, but if I can help someone have a happier future—"

"Stop. Just no." Avery paused. "I'm the fortune teller, anyway. Don't rip off my gig. I could totally sell that gold turban and crystal ball."

"I'm picturing a purple silk tent and your own website. With live stream palm reading."

"I could definitely cash in on that business."

I bumped her shoulder. "But it would ruin your stellar academic rep."

"Truth. Plus, the boys wouldn't want to work in the

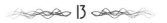

love biz, and what would they do without us?"

"Get into trouble?"

"No doubt. Speaking of, there's Trouble himself, with his sidekick, Uh-Oh."

"Which one's which?" I laughed.

Avery called a greeting to the two boys already at the far corner table. Our table.

Ethan waved, and Deshawn lifted his fork briefly but returned to studying whatever textbook he had open. Probably math, since he was already in Geometry.

They sat directly under the huge air conditioning vent. The clattering noise and faint stench of mold kept our classmates at a distance, making it a perfect place for private discussions.

Ethan leaned forward as we sat down. "Just in time to answer a very critical question. Tell me, Parkour"—I secretly loved when he used his old nickname for me—"do I have a chance with Sophie as a date to the dance?"

Avery slapped the table. "Ethan Jae-Sun Kwon, don't you dare encourage her. She needs to knock it off."

"Don't listen to Mom over there," he said. "Breaking the rules now and then won't hurt anyone. Come on, Parker. It's for me!"

"People's emotions are private." My tone was prim.

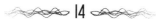

"That's not what I heard." Deshawn finally looked up with a snort, deep brown eyes sparkling with unusual mischief.

"Heard? Or *over*heard?" I used air quotes.

He chuckled. "You'd better believe I was keeping my distance from that cry-fest, but public spaces are fair game. It was worth the effort to listen in. You're a little scary, Parker. But impressive."

"Kayla was a special situation." I stuck out my tongue. "And you know what they say about eavesdroppers."

"That they learn really useful things?"

Ethan turned to Deshawn. "So, you're saying Parker would help me if I boohooed like Kayla?"

I pointed at Ethan. "Were we recorded live on camera for the whole school to see or something?" He could make things move with his mind, but he couldn't listen in from a distance like Deshawn. Which meant he was … watching me on the way to the cafeteria? Was he looking for me?

Well, we sometimes walked to the cafeteria together. He'd probably just been passing by when Kayla's pitiful scene caught his attention.

Ethan said, "You're such a sucker for tears."

"Okay, true, but this actually smelled bad." I kicked

the table leg.

"What, I stink right now?" Ethan sniffed near his armpit and burst out laughing at my face. "I kid! I tease! I know what it does to you, Parks."

A rosy glow bubbled inside for a moment. He *knew* me. "Today was really bad. It stunk like burnt coffee. I get enough of that stench at home."

"Parents at it again?" Avery asked.

"Worse than ever. Dad keeps a pretty decent lid on things these days, but Mom's still spewing her mood all over." I pushed chunks of neon orange chicken around but suddenly couldn't eat any.

Everyone else's parents accepted their kids and their honest-to-goodness psychic gifts, even Avery's parents, who divorced years ago. My parents had stayed married, but at the rate they were going, that might not last for long. None of the parenting books had a chapter called "How to Raise Your Empath Daughter When Her Gift Gives One of You the Willies."

"Aw, I'm sorry, Parks," Ethan said. "Come hang with us anytime. My parents love you. Shoot, even my grandma loves you when she visits. At least I think she does. She doesn't speak English, and my Korean's still pathetic, but I'm pretty sure she said you were awesome."

"All our families love you, Mood Ring," Deshawn said, his bass voice rumbling.

No one was teasing now. They all knew that for an empath, living in a home with a bitterly angry mother was like taking a daily poison pill.

I took a deep breath. No way would I ruin their lunch with a Parker pity party. "Thanks, but it's okay. It's her loss."

After a split-second pause, Ethan said, "Of course it is. So. Back to me, then. I'll totally blubber for you if you'll tell me if I should ask Sophie to the dance." He winked, and I laughed, grateful for the topic change.

Hands clasped against his chest, he continued, "But if you can tell she'd say no, you could spare me the humiliation before I get shot down. Wouldn't that count as one of your patented do-gooder acts of mercy?"

My necklace began to lift and jiggle.

I clamped my hand around it and glared, checking around the room. Talking in code around clueless classmates was one thing. But visible gift-using was something else altogether. "Cut it out. Anyway, you wouldn't cry—you'd just ask the next girl. Sophie's feelings are her business."

And Ethan's feelings were … maddening.

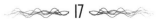

"Not if they involve me!"

I sighed, looked over at Sophie Reynolds. Super cute, with a charming little giggle. He'd have a great time with her, no doubt.

"Fine," I caved. I called over, "Hey, Sophie! Love those jeans!"

Sophie grinned back. When her gaze landed on Ethan, I took a quick peek inside the girl's heart.

"Green light. She thinks you're cool." *Of course.*

"Thanks, Parker! You're a great friend!" Pushing away from the table, Ethan jogged over to Sophie with his adorable mile-wide grin and those sparkling hazel eyes from his red-headed mother.

"Yeah, yeah," I muttered. I ignored my chicken, taking a sip of water instead.

Ethan had never asked me what my feelings were about a dance. Just as well. The two of us together like *that* would be way too complicated. Definitely a bad idea.

Ethan said something to Sophie, but the words didn't carry over the rattle of the air conditioning. For the first time, I cursed our clever soundproofing plan.

"Want me to listen in, Mood Ring?" Deshawn didn't lift his head, but his voice held understanding.

My throat tightened. "No, why would I?"

 18

When I received no answer, I looked up to see him exchanging eye rolls with Avery.

"We're friends," I insisted. "Lifelong friends. That's all. And friends feel happy for each other if they get what they want—"

There was a squeal, and Sophie gave Ethan a tight hug.

"I guess that answers that question," Avery said.

"There was no question." My voice was flat. I scooped up a spoonful of pudding and let it plop back into the bowl.

Avery pursed her lips. Deshawn frowned. Their shields were locked tight, thankfully, but Sophie's happiness radiated across the room like sunlight. She was a nice girl, dang it.

I stood up, my chair screeching along the tile and forced myself to smile. Acting chops. I had them. "Gotta go, guys. Tell Ethan congrats on the date."

"See ya, buddy." Avery's voice was faint, left behind by my speeding feet.

On my way out the door, I tossed the barely touched chicken into the garbage. Who cared, really? It was just a dumb dance.

Okay, it was only the coolest dance in the history of

 19

our school, one Avery and I helped plan, hoping to use it on our application to the high school student council next year. I could get a date. The thing was, there was only one person I wanted to go with.

When I was upset, the library called to me like a Siren. Books never demanded, never cried. They simply waited. Quietly.

I headed there now. I didn't usually mind so much when Ethan found a new girl to crush on. If it was a day ending in "y," he was flirting. But today? Today had stung.

My tennis shoes slapped faster against the floor, but before I reached the library, I turned the corner and ran into someone.

"Oomph!"

"Parker! Are you okay?" Dr. O'Malley, the new eighth-grade counselor, held my elbow to steady me when I bounced off her.

"I'm fine." I said automatically, hiding a shudder. I avoided Dr. O like blue mascara, although it wasn't easy most days since I served as an office aide during third period. The counselor was as buttoned down as her business suits and as severe as her bun. No emotions ever billowed from her. The whole rest of the front office was usually coated with stressful feelings, and the principal radiated near-constant anxiety. But when I had tried to X-ray behind Dr. O's emotional iron curtain, I couldn't. Other than the Fab Four, the few people who could block me like Dr. O were either highly repressed or very controlling. Or both.

"I'm glad I ran into you." Dr. O didn't even smile at the pun. "I was hoping you could show our newest student around. Parker, this is Mia Rodriguez. Mia, Parker Mills is social chair for the eighth-grade student council and one of our office aides. I know you'll be in good hands."

The new girl stared at the floor, hands clasped tightly together.

"Nice to meet you, Mia," I said. "Where're you from?"

Mia finally looked up. Her eyes were such a dark brown, they were nearly black, filled with misery.

Pain. Betrayal. Self-hatred.

Emotions poured from her, covered in the scent of burned meat. Emotions so powerful they almost washed words along with them like debris in a raging flood—*I hate my life. I hate myself.*

The feelings pierced my heart like a knife, and I gasped. I faked a cough to cover it up. "Sorry. Allergies."

Powerful stuff. Deep. *Waterfall, waterfall, waterfall …* I tried to wash the bad mojo away, but it was too strong, too close. I stuffed my trembling hands in my pockets.

Mia looked away. "I'm from a small town near Houston. Bent Creek."

The emotional storm shut off as suddenly as it began. To my psychic senses, it felt like a wall of granite sprung up between us, blocking the rogue wave of hatred and pain. It had been silenced completely and immediately … but I hadn't stopped it. Mia had.

3

POWERFUL emotions like Mia's shouldn't have stopped mid-flood like that, not without me flexing my empathy muscles.

"Another Texan, then," I said, a bit breathless. I'd long ago learned to manage unexpected emo-jabs, but this girl ... that was at least an 8.5 of Pure Pain on the Emo Scale, maybe higher. The worst I'd felt in ages. A migraine loomed behind my right eye. I thought of the quiet library and almost whimpered.

"Parker, show Mia the cafeteria, please. You both have permission to go to fifth period late so she can eat."

I took the blue hall passes with a nod. There was no use arguing, and besides, in the face of Mia's pain, I wanted to help. Thinking of Avery's warning, I pursed my lips. Maybe simply offering a good listening ear would be enough to take the edge off.

We set off toward the cafeteria. I had to look up to meet Mia's gaze. I often had to look up at people, but Mia was taller than most.

"Well, welcome to Divine. Just moved in?"

"Yesterday." Mia took in everything with watchful dark eyes.

I took in everything I could, too. Mia wore faded jeans, a gray T-shirt, and a denim jacket. Way too plain. Hair just hanging there? Practically criminal to waste those thick black locks, perfect for messy buns. I made a mental note—Operation Butterfly might be an easy fix here, no psychic skills required. Makeovers didn't help everyone, no matter what the movies said, but it was a basic option in my happiness shortcut toolkit. Sometimes simple was better.

"I bet being new is hard. I've lived here all my life, so I can't imagine."

"It'll be okay." Mia sounded grim.

On impulse, I reached my gift over to peek in Mia's heart to see what the deal was, but my empathy slid along a solid wall, bouncing right back off. I frowned, upped my power a bit, and looked harder. Still nothing.

It was one thing not to leak emotions much; quite another to actually block an empathy X-ray attempt. Mia was better shielded than my dad, even … more like Avery, Ethan, and Deshawn.

I noted Mia's tight muscles, clamped jaw. No, more like Dr. O with her rigid emo-silence, a natural side effect of a shut-down heart.

"Well, it's a small place, so you'll get to know everyone soon enough." I smiled, making sure my dimple popped up.

"Actually, I was born here, too," Mia said. "I guess in a way, I'm actually coming home. Sort of."

"Get out! What brings you back?" The noise—and emotional waves—from the cafeteria grew louder.

"I'm, uh, living with my aunt for a while. She teaches Latin American studies at the university here."

"Oh, you'll have to meet my besties, then. All of us have a parent working at the university. My dad teaches psychology."

Mia looked like she wanted to say something, but by this point, the roar of the cafeteria was impossible to ignore. Once inside, our noses were assaulted by the cafeteria's peculiar perma-smell of fried foods and ammonia.

Chatting to keep things light and relaxed, I showed

Mia the various line options. ("Skip the ham rolls. Totally gross. The desserts are really good, though.") Ten minutes of lunch remained when I returned to our table with Mia in tow.

Ethan and Deshawn were pouring over sheet music. Avery was throwing fries at them, no doubt just to irritate. Sophie still sat at the other table.

I beamed. "Hey, everyone, this is Mia Rodriguez, from Bent Creek, Texas. She's new here. Mia, these are my people. The guy in the Led Zeppelin T-shirt is Ethan Kwon, an awesome drummer. His band's called Kinetic Threat, and they're fantastic."

"Aw, Parker. You're going to make me blush," Ethan said.

"He's also an attention hog, so ignore him when he acts up."

He fell from his chair, groaning as if he'd been stabbed. Yeah, the boy could definitely be a star on stage if he wanted it. A giggle escaped me unwillingly, and Mia gave a small smile.

I cleared my throat. "Deshawn Boothe here is a math whiz who runs like the wind, and this is my best friend Avery Portman, who's going to study brains one day. Y'all, keep an eye out for Mia, okay? I'm showing her around."

Deshawn and Ethan pulled out a chair for Mia, already chatting her up. This wasn't my first rodeo at helping out a new kid, and my friends always pitched in. My attention zeroed in on Avery, though, who hadn't yet said a word. She sat ramrod straight, motionless. Her eyes were wide pools of blue, pupils shrunk to tiny pinpricks ... and she was staring right at Mia.

Uh-oh. I kicked Ethan's foot under the table and rolled my eyes in Avery's direction.

After taking a second look at Avery, Ethan exchanged a glance with Deshawn and jumped to his feet. "Mia, hey, sorry we gotta go, but nice to meet you. Avery, come on, the bell's about to ring."

He hauled Avery to her feet, and she waved goodbye. The movement looked stilted and nothing like her usual—*ohh*. Ethan had waved Avery's hand goodbye, using his telekinesis to move her hand like a puppet's.

I raised an eyebrow at him, and he gave the tiniest shrug. Clever boy. More than a little creepy and definitely risky, but I understood why he did it. Caught in a vision, Avery could barely stand on her own. It must be a bad one—she usually had enough warning to get out of public before she zoned out.

Deshawn and Ethan left with Avery between them.

Mia stared after them with a little furrow between her brows. "Is she okay?"

I had the same question. "Avery sometimes gets an aura before a migraine. They'll get her to the nurse if that's what's going on."

Mia began eating. "I'm sorry to hear that. She looked pale."

"Redheads often do. She hates it."

"She's really pretty, though. I like the boots."

I gave an approving nod. "Avery's got style. She wants to be a neurologist but weeps at the thought of wearing scrubs. She makes half her clothes herself."

Mia pursed her lips before saying, "Applause. I can't sew a button."

"Me either. She's also super smart. I'm just thankful for my one A in Drama. What about you? I can set you up with clubs and stuff, depending on your thing."

"I paint. And draw. I think I've got art last period. I hope so, anyway." She unfolded a printed class schedule and squinted at it.

"Oh, cool, I'd love to see some of your work!"

A flash of sharp pain screeched against my skin but was gone just as quickly. *Not totally repressed after all,* I thought.

"I'm not unpacked yet." Mia examined her schedule as if it held the meaning of life.

Avery's warning to stop interfering flashed again through my mind. Mia's level of pain really needed professional help anyway. But still ... pain was pain. And happiness was my specialty.

I tapped my fingers on the table. "Let me see your schedule."

The piece of paper looked like it had been stuffed in someone's shoe for a week. Sweaty fingerprints smeared the ink in several places.

I pretended not to notice. "Good news! We've got history together after lunch, so I can walk you there when you're ready. I won't see you the rest of the day, but I'm free after school."

I'm not trying to fix Mia, I told myself firmly. This was being neighborly.

When Mia didn't reply beyond a half smile, I asked, "Are you living in the Glade?"

Forest Glade was the biggest apartment complex in Divine. Not too pricey and within walking distance of campus, it had a high concentration of professors. I'd lived there all my life, along with two others of the Fab Four. Avery and I even shared a wall—it made life bearable when my parents fought.

"I think so?" Mia shook her head. "I can't keep it all straight."

"I hear that. Don't worry. We'll take care of you."

Mia definitely needed a friend. The fact that she didn't bleed emotions easily was actually a bonus, with that kind of intense unhappiness inside. Surely I could come up with something that would help without being obvious—a simple, easy plan that even Avery would approve of.

On the way to history, hardly officially late yet, we passed Elizabeth Frenneli putting up a poster next to the stairwell. I stopped and squealed. A spooky castle sat on a cliff, a bolt of lightning glowing behind it. Jagged orange letters announced the Halloween costume dance.

"Oh my gosh, Elizabeth! Did you make that?"

At the girl's shy nod, I crowed, "You have such a gift! Good thing we have you on the dance committee!" Good thing I'd sweet-talked her into it. She'd been wasting all that talent.

"A costume dance? For Halloween?" Mia asked.

I quickly introduced the two girls and went on. "It's

gonna be the best! The eighth-graders always throw the Halloween dance, and our class is going to make it the best ever. It's still a month off, but a month is practically like tomorrow. You've got to get the perfect costume, and then there's all the maneuvering for a date. Speaking of, got a date yet, Elizabeth?"

If I recalled correctly—and I usually did—Elizabeth had liked Rob Harris for years. Which is why I'd made sure he was on the dance committee, too. Two birds, one stone: a truly gross phrase that happened to apply perfectly.

Elizabeth blushed. "Rob asked me already."

Bingo. "Awesome!"

"Yeah, but …" Uncertainty flickered, a sensation like a small poke in the ribs. It was low on the scale, but it marred the perfection of my work here.

"He wants to go as Tweedledum and Tweedledee." Elizabeth's cheeks grew pinker.

I whooped with laughter. Mia smiled but didn't join in. Anyone who didn't guffaw at the image of tiny Elizabeth in a giant striped belly costume needed a serious pick-me-up.

Luckily, Rob's bad idea was a small fly easily removed from the ointment of my perfected plan for Elizabeth. "That could work, I guess," I snorted, "but I think I'll have a chat with him about tweaking that idea. How adorable would you be as Alice if he was the Cheshire cat? Can't you see it? Same theme, different style."

Excitement and relief rose off Elizabeth in soft waves.

I winked at her. "Don't worry. Let Auntie Parker talk to your boy and straighten him out. And go get yourself a cute Alice dress."

We left behind a happily whistling Elizabeth putting up more posters.

"Does everyone really dress up?" Mia asked.

"They'd better. Our committee is working our tails off to make this happen. You can come, right? Because everyone's going to be there, trust me."

Mia shook her head. "I'm not much into dances. Or dressing up."

"Well, we'll have to see about that." I raised one eyebrow in challenge.

Beyond Mia's tall frame, a patch of red hair bobbed past the corner. Relief was followed by a dying need to get in the loop. Thinking fast, I said, "Hey, I'm going to check on Avery real quick. Keep going straight. History's last door on the right. Here's your pass—I'll be right behind you."

Without waiting for a response, I raced the opposite

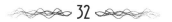

way to where my friends inched along the hall with the last of the lunchtime stragglers. Catching up quickly, I demanded, "What did you see, Avery?"

"You're not going to like it," Ethan said. His eyes weren't dancing like usual.

"Seriously," Deshawn said, shaking his head.

"Can you tell me now?" No one was within twenty feet of us.

"I think it'd better wait until after school," Avery said. "The guys are walking me to the nurse to lie down. I can't think straight right now."

"Are you kidding me?"

"It's going to take some discussion." Avery's face was paler than usual, more fish belly than cream.

"Okay, then. No worries."

"Just—be nice to Mia, okay?"

I tilted my head. "I'm always nice."

Avery shook her head. "No, I mean, be her friend, a real one. More later, but trust me. It's important. Mia needs to be happy here."

The tardy bell rang—lucky I had a pass—and the others turned to leave. Ethan reached back and touched my elbow. "I'll let you know when and where we're meeting later, okay?"

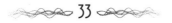

I smiled, alarm melting away at his touch. Avery's visions were only vague warnings of what *could* happen, not guarantees. They didn't always come true. The future was constantly changing—it's part of what made Avery's gift so tricky. Precognition only showed the most likely outcome based on someone's current path. Change the right behaviors, change the future.

But as I slid into a seat next to Mia in history class, I couldn't stop thinking about the hollow look on Avery's face.

4

HISTORY went swimmingly. Mr. Bransford's love of black and white documentaries kept the mood of the room calm (possibly asleep), even though Mia chewed her nails the whole time.

I watched her closely. New friends were great, but being close to Mia would be like cuddling an electric eel that could shock me at any point. As much as I'd love to help her, I wasn't sure I was ready to sign up for that.

On my way to drama, I dropped off Mia in the art room, relieved to see the girl's face light up. A good ending to her first day. I could use one of those myself.

For my monologue assignment, Mr. Beller had given me one of the most overdone scenes of the most overdone play ever, *Romeo and Juliet.* Challenge accepted. I'd been preparing all week. I was going to own it.

On the auditorium stage, I closed my eyes for a moment against the spotlight. Heat washed over my face, along with the scent of sweat and power that was all theatre. Real life fell away. I was Juliet, longing to see my Romeo. I was about to learn his death was all too real.

My eyes flashed open. Words poured easily from my mouth.

> *"O comfortable Friar! Where is my lord?*
> *I do remember well where I should be,*
> *And there I am. Where is my Romeo?"*

Past experience of being exposed to people's true hearts made it easy for me to imagine Juliet's: the hope turning to fear, the growing ache of loss until agony crushed her heart in its fist.

In the spirit of the monologue assignment, I skipped Juliet's brief exchange with the friar offering to take her away. The friar didn't matter anyway. This scene was all about Juliet. I took a deep breath to bring it all for the next, brutally sad moment.

> *"What's here? A cup, closed in my true*
> *love's hand?*
> *Poison, I see, hath been his timeless end."*

I looked toward the audience, including my classmates in the moment. The glare of the spotlight hid them from my sight, but I could feel their emotions pressing against my empathy like dark clouds descending all around a glass house.

Good. I didn't want to block them now. Their feelings were the best stage director. Focusing on the roil of mourning in my stomach, I bent over an imaginary Romeo in hopes of stealing poison from his lips. I whispered, *"Thy lips are warm."* My voice broke on the last word, and I choked back a sob.

The sound echoed in the silence, and to my mind's eye, the dark room began to glow.

Sparkles of sympathy. Flickers of pity. Delicious suffering. Wishful longing.

My audience hated that sad declaration almost as much as they loved it.

Luckily, those flashes of sadness didn't sting. They never hurt during performances, not like real life. Emotions invented for a show lacked the punch of the genuine article, more of a whisper than a scream. Occasionally, a scene might dredge up a memory and trigger real pain, but the physical distance between the stage and audience kept that muted, too.

I allowed a tear to tremble on the edge of my lashes, enough to sparkle without spilling down my cheek and ruining my make-up, which is harder than it sounds. I pulled out the stage knife from my pocket, lifted it high. It glinted in the lights.

Reading and responding to my audience's shifting moods was a lot like an intricate dance—requiring precise attention to detail without missing a beat. I tilted my head as if hearing someone coming, breaking the heavy moment. Relief from my classmates flowed like an incoming wave. It wouldn't be there for long.

"Yea, noise? Then I'll be brief. O happy dagger,
This is thy sheath. There rust and let me die."

I aimed the plastic dagger at my chest, let my eyes drift shut, and held the pose. I felt Juliet's hope destroyed, let the grief swell in my body until it burned. Juliet didn't really die from a knife. She died of a broken heart, and hearts were my specialty.

The audience's anxiety peaked—*now*—and I plunged the collapsible stage knife against my chest. My sharp cry shattered any thoughts of a happy ending.

Even without a dead Romeo onstage, I had them in the palm of my hand. No doubt I'd snag the lead in the spring play. The trick was making the moment feel so real inside myself that it looked authentic to others.

Like now.

I allowed myself to sink slowly to the stage—come on! I was dying!—and finished in a limp pool, knowing I was the one bright spot in a field of darkness.

There was a moment of pure silence, the best sound in the world to an actor, before my classmates burst into applause. Their emo-cloud disappeared into harmless mist as it always did when the curtains came down and real life came up.

I curtsied. Bubbles of perfume-scented admiration floated by. A few digs of jealousy stung. Oops. I'd left my gift wide open, actively listening in on the mood around me. I concentrated and, a heartbeat later, the room was just a room, with no hint, color, or smell of emotions in the air. Now only the strongest feelings would touch me.

I whisked off the stage and dropped Juliet's sadness as easily as taking off a heavy cloak. My family might not be full of rainbow ponies, but at least it wasn't Juliet-level.

Ethan stood in the wing of the stage. My heart skipped a beat. Why was he here? He didn't do theatre. Not that he couldn't if he'd wanted to, but drumming was his passion.

"Hey, Avery said to meet in her room at 4:30. Her phone died, so don't bother texting."

"How bad is it?"

"Don't worry, Parks. No matter what, we'll get it all worked out."

His smile was like the sun, drawing me into his gravitational pull.

Too dangerous, that feeling. *Keep it light, Parker.* "Thanks for the heads up, but you'd better not get caught skipping class, mister."

He flashed a hall pass—who knew what reason he'd concocted for it but I was sure it had been convincing— then he smirked and stepped toward the stage exit. "And by the way, nice moves out there. I'll be your Romeo any day."

"You do know Romeo dies, right?"

"What a way to go, though." He walked backward with a wave and a ridiculous wagging of eyebrows.

"But then who would Sophie go to the dance with?" I hollered after him. He'd make a mighty fine Romeo, of course, but if I joined all the other girls in the Ethan-Hallelujah chorus, his head might swell too big to fit in the room.

He called back, "Oh, she changed her mind. Turns

out her best friend already set them up on a double-date with a couple of freshmen football players. Can't compete with that."

"Ouch. Sorry it didn't work out." I managed to keep a straight face.

He shrugged and grinned. "Win some, lose some. It's probably just as well. She's nice and all, but she's not my Juliet. Gotta head back to class." He spun and left.

I stared after him, flat-footed. What did he mean by that? His shields were as solid as they came, not that he ever shared emotions on accident.

He wasn't going to the dance with Sophie.

After class, with an hour to kill until the meeting, I took my time getting ready to go home. My mind drifted again to Ethan. Maybe we could go together to the dance after all. I imagined swaying in his arms, leaning close ... then shut down that daydream with a sigh. No use wishing for something that would never happen.

I soaped my face. Stage makeup wasn't required for class performances, but it gave an edge. And I had to get an A. It was more than wanting—needing—to prove myself. That single shining A from drama class on my report card was one of the few things that lightened my mother's disappointment in me. I scrubbed harder at my makeup. My eyes stung. The lousy soap must have gotten in my eyes.

An image of Mia popped into my mind, a total downer with her sadness, her obvious pain. A tragic figure, like Juliet. But Juliet's life would have been way different if she'd had a friend. Someone to cry with, to tell her it'd all be okay, to bring some fun in.

I turned off the bathroom lights on my way out, ready to hear what Avery had to say. Whatever it was, Mia deserved a happier ending than Juliet. Everyone did.

Stepping into our apartment, I braced myself. No emotions battered at me, which was a hopeful sign. The first thing I did was check the blue table by the door, where my mother stored her little purse. The table was empty. Good.

Kicking the door shut with my heel, I dropped my book bag and headed to the kitchen. My dad stood at the stove, stirring a pot. The pungent aroma of canned chicken soup filled the air.

"Hey, Dad. Home early today?"

He jumped but turned with a smile. "I had about a thousand papers to grade, so I decided to work in the comfort of my own home with some soup instead of the cramped office where the AC is on the fritz."

"Again?"

"The budget's tight these days."

I snorted. Psychology and sociology were at the bottom of the pecking order for sure at Koblaire University, which prided itself on its hard science departments. Despite the school's small size, famous neurologists and surgeons frequently spoke to classes. Any one of them would love to get their hands on my brainwaves. The university wouldn't have a budget problem anymore.

"How about your day? You look tired," my father noted. He reached into the fruit basket on the counter and tossed me an apple.

I snatched it out of the air and plopped down at the kitchen table. Having a shrink for a dad had its ups and downs, but it sure saved time. "I showed a new girl around today, which was fine, but she's obviously got issues."

"Oh?"

"Yeah, she's really down. I mean, she didn't say that, and I couldn't even read her—weird, right?—but she let stuff slip a few times. Just getting a smile out of her was like pulling teeth."

My father looked to the ceiling as if he'd find the right

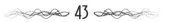

words up there to say. Finally, he said, "I appreciate that you want to help people. You've got a good heart, Parker. But just because you can feel someone's pain doesn't make it your obligation to fix it. Actually, you don't even have the right to interfere in their lives, much less a responsibility."

"But see, Avery got a vision. I didn't hear it all yet, but she said I had to be friends with this girl, Mia. I'll be careful, don't worry. I already got 'the talk' from Avery about not being so obvious. Knowing stuff I shouldn't and all that."

He tapped the spoon on the edge of the pot before turning around to face me. "That's not what I mean. Listen to your father here. No one wants to feel unhappy. But vision or no vision, if you smooth over all their problems so they never have to struggle ..." He sighed heavily, ignoring the dripping spoon in his hand. "You're taking away an opportunity for them to grow. Do you see? You're not helping them."

I furrowed my brow. I understood the words he was saying. They were English. They were in order. But the concept ...

"Uh, no. Relax, Dad. I'm just saying some fun would do the girl a lot of good."

He returned to stirring his soup. "Not every problem is solved with a dose of fun. And some grief can never be fixed, only carried."

"Maybe, but a smile never hurts anyone." I winked at him and crunched into the apple with gusto.

"You always make me smile, at least."

His smile was one of my favorite things about him, slightly goofy, but warm and authentic, like the man himself. I preened like a peacock, and he chuckled, as I intended.

But his smile faded. "Just remember, people have to feel their pain in order to heal it."

The front door opened and closed. His shoulders tightened, and a flicker of pain scratched down my arms.

I narrowed my eyes. "I don't see how you can say that. In your situation, I mean."

His gaze flitted to the hallway and back. "I'm sorry, Parker. I'm trying to shield, but I can't always react fast enough—"

My mother swooshed in. "Shield talk again? You know, just because she has a special sensitivity, Tom, doesn't mean you should cater to it. She'll have to learn to cope. Normal people won't ever be able to hide all their feelings from someone like her."

The word *her* dripped with scorn. A sharp stab to my heart made me cringe.

My father paled. "You could learn to shield, too, at least a little, if you'd—"

"We aren't all mental geniuses, Mr. Psychology Professor." Bitterness shrouded her like a veil.

"I would prefer that we speak about this later." He managed to sound both polite but firm.

"And I would prefer you not undermine my authority with our child."

My mother's self-righteous anger swerved to panic lined with regret, like always. She simply couldn't block her strong emotions.

I didn't look on purpose. Conflict just shoved emotions in my face without asking. "Mom, Dad, I respect both of you—" I began, but they talked right over me.

"I've told you I'm willing to work with you on this, whatever it takes."

"Nothing can help, Tom. I just want us to be normal. I don't think that's so terrible."

"There's no such thing as normal, believe me. It's a fact."

"The fact was, we couldn't conceive. Maybe we weren't meant to, did you ever think of that? But we intervened and ended up with a—"

Fury rose like a black cloud from my father. "Parker, go to your room. Now."

I stumbled to my feet and fled, choking on the stench of burned coffee and soured milk.

Waterfall, waterfall, waterfall. Their pain faded, but mine grew worse. It was tons harder to wash bad feelings from inside my own heart than to wipe off the feelings of others.

I sat at my desk, staring at a history textbook I didn't see. My trembling slowed as the minutes clicked by. It wasn't like this situation was new.

Coming to Divine for my dad's job had been a supposed brief detour that had led to a dead end for my mother, who'd been a buyer for an upscale retail store. But psychology jobs at top universities were rare, so she tried to settle down and enjoy motherhood with her bonus round baby. Led PTA and baked cupcakes, smiling her trademark smile, Hollywood gorgeous.

I'd learned a lot about acting from my mom, who could entertain a crowd while drowning in sorrow inside. But now, Mom said life in Divine wasn't enough. She wanted to go somewhere with a future for *her*.

But Divine's slow way of life wasn't the real problem:

me and my friends were. As our gifts had grown stronger, so had my mom's fear, hidden so deep down she couldn't even recognize the emotion for what it was. I knew, though. I couldn't help but know.

So, if I was going to be friends with Mia, something would have to be done about the girl's obvious misery ASAP. Life at home was plenty full of unfixable pain without adding a walking pit of despair at school, dragging me down.

I opened to a fresh page in my pink journal labeled PRIVATE! With careful cursive, I wrote "M.'s Happiness Prescription," adding some flourishes. Usually, the idea made me smile. I liked helping people and thought I was pretty good at it. But now, a feeling crawled through me like ants. Not hunger, not pain, not humiliation ... what was it?

Discomfort. That was it. Naming the right emotion felt like putting my finger directly on a faint bruise. I didn't like ignoring my dad. As a psychologist, he knew stuff, no matter what my mother said, and he obviously didn't want me to meddle with people without permission. Mia had definitely not asked for any help. I crossed off my doodle and ripped it up.

If Avery said I needed to befriend Mia, befriend Mia

I would. I'd just have to chill on the whole helping thing. No subtle plans, no sneak peeks, no fixing her up fast with shortcuts to happiness. We'd have to make friends like everyone else in the world did. Surely that couldn't be so hard. Normal people did it every day.

5

AVERY'S words were flat. "You have to use your gift to fix Mia. Do your sneaky-peeky thing with her and work your magic manipulation on her. Fast."

My jaw dropped, and I stared wildly at my friends in Avery's room, waiting for the punch line. But no one laughed.

"You just told me I had to stop that! No more interfering in people's lives!"

"That was before."

"Before?"

"I've never had such a clear vision, Parker. It came on me so fast. I saw she's homesick, that she's furious and heartbroken. Something she does at the dance next

month exposes us, shows the world our powers ... but I couldn't see exactly what happens, of course. Because my visions suck." Avery shuddered.

I scooted closer. "Hey, take it easy. Freak-outs happen all the time, right?"

"This is way more than a few sobs. Mia has some kind of third-degree meltdown at the Halloween dance and somehow puts us in danger," Avery said. "One giant mess of sadness, regret, and anger. Then things get really bad."

"What kind of bad?" Thankful for my friend's shields, I waited without their emotions to warn me what was coming.

"I'm talking locked-up-like-lab-monkeys kind of bad."

"Here? Not even my dad worries about that anymore. It's a small town," I protested.

"We're in a small town that happens to have a near-Ivy League university with a top-rated neurology program. The department just got a grant, my mother told me. Want to know what for?"

Deshawn popped his knuckles. They sounded like gunshots. "I don't suppose it's about advanced human abilities?"

"Close enough. One of my mom's colleagues found old notes from that fertility doctor, tucked away somewhere in the department. They seem legit. There's stuff in there about 'unexpected changes in the fetus.' My mom couldn't cover it up in time."

"I thought he burned all his notes before he took off?" Ethan wasn't smiling.

"We thought so too. Maybe someone stole some of them first. I don't know. But the notes are there now. And so there's been some discussion about the drug that caused all the malformations and miscarriages—and us."

"It's not like the doc knew anything about us for sure," Deshawn pointed out.

Avery said, "They aren't talking about psychic gifts right now. That's a big leap for most scientists anyway. But my mom says that they've found cases of super intelligent kids born from similar trials in other towns and want to study them. Savant kinds of genius. We're the next logical step, if there's even a hint we're something special."

Ethan shrugged. "Plenty of people already claim to be psychic. It muddies the waters if anyone does try to find us. Why come after us when lots of folks actually want the attention?"

"Sure," Avery said, "but enough people in town remember we were part of that whole fertility trial mess, even if our personal files were destroyed. And if they find us, they'll test us until they prove we're the real deal."

Avery's point was valid. None of us doubted that the chemical cocktail used by the fertility doctor had done something unusual to us. And apparently, the same or similar drug had been used elsewhere, too. It made me wonder how many babies were exposed to that drug before it was banned.

"Why not just keep her away from the dance?" Deshawn asked. "Wouldn't that solve it?"

"It wasn't about the dance." Avery rubbed her eyes. "I think she'll explode no matter where she is, but it gave us the time frame. Though maybe at the dance we'll have a better chance at predicting her actions. Or stopping them."

Ethan leaned forward, steepling his fingers. "Fine. So Parker needs to work out a happy plan. She's got that business down."

"How happy are we talking?" I asked. "There's only so much I can do with raw materials."

"I'm not saying Mia needs a personality transplant or anything. I think she just needs to start feeling at home here. Accepted. She's got to let go of whatever bad stuff she's holding onto, or else they'll find us. I don't know how the two are related, but they are." Avery bit her lip.

I swallowed. "Even you? I thought with your mom watching your back—"

"All of us. But there's one they'll want the most."

She turned her gaze to Ethan.

He ran his hand through his spiky black hair with a smirk. "Everybody wants me, baby."

My fear grabbed me by the throat. *Not Ethan.* I slapped his arm. "How can you joke about this? She's saying we're in danger. That you're in danger most of all."

He shrugged, stretching his arms behind his head. Even with panic beating in my chest, I couldn't help but notice the muscles bunching beneath his T-shirt. Stupid thing to notice.

Ethan said, "Avery's visions are warnings, not promises. We've changed things before."

"Nothing like this. Nothing this bad."

Deshawn pointed at Parker. "Tell that to Kane, who *didn't* break his leg and miss his chance to go to State, mostly thanks to you."

Ethan learned forward. "Parker, if anyone can make friends with this new kid and make her happy, you can. I have faith in you."

His gaze roamed across my face and, for once, no

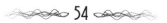

jokes lit his eyes.

Heat bloomed along my cheeks. I hoped the blush didn't show too much. "Okay then. To make her happy, I've got to know what's causing the problem. She's pretty blocked off, but the best treatments for stress or depression deal with the root of the issue, my dad says."

"Look at you, sounding all smart," Deshawn teased.

"She is smart," Ethan said.

The blush burned hotter, but I kept my voice cool. "Helping people with what's bugging them is like figuring out a giant puzzle. But Mia has mental walls that are hard to get past, and when I *have* felt her heart ... It really hurts. Digging around in there's going to suck. Plus, her walls could collapse without warning, and I can't even imagine what that would feel like."

Avery offered me a piece of chocolate. "I'm sorry, Parks. As if you need more pain."

Deshawn stood and paced Avery's little room. He flicked the mini-blinds and peered outside, letting in a stream of sunlight. "It'll be good for you, Mood Ring. You run away from pain or fix it up real pretty, but one day, you'll have to face it and deal."

"Easy for you to say. Eavesdropping from a distance doesn't hurt you or anyone else." I pushed my bottom lip out in an exaggerated pout.

Deshawn gave a bitter laugh. "That's what you think. Knowing things that you shouldn't causes problems all on its own. Why do you think I run track?"

"Because you're like a cheetah on speed?"

He laughed again, this time a much happier sound. "Nah, I love football, and I'm pretty good, but it's too tempting to listen in on the other team's huddle. I don't want to win by cheating, and that could get us all busted, too. But for track, all I gotta do is sprint. Just me, running. Simple. No time to listen to anything but my own breathing."

"I never thought about that," I said, eyeing him appreciatively. I'd always known his heart was gold, but I hadn't realized just how wise he was for his years. He'd given up football in the peewee leagues.

He shrugged. "You've got to work with what you've got. What I'm saying is, if you'd stop being afraid of what you might feel from others, maybe you'll be happier, too."

"I'm plenty happy." I tipped my head sideways. "Happy is my middle name."

He didn't offer his usual grin. "If you say so."

"Well, I say so," Avery said. "If anyone can help Mia, Parker can."

I shook my head. "She's a tough case."

"Don't sell yourself short." Avery patted my arm.

"Is this where I manfully refrain from making short jokes?" Ethan asked.

I smirked and started pacing. "Focus, y'all. She's really shy. All kinds of shut down. That'll make it hard to come up with the right plan for her."

Ethan reached over and took my hand. "I'll help you if you need it. Take it one step at a time."

I couldn't even move. *Stay calm,* I warned myself. He was just being supportive.

"We all will," Deshawn added. His bigger hand covered both of ours.

"All for one and one for all." Avery put her hand on top.

"Weren't there only three musketeers?" Ethan asked with a quirking smile.

I tossed my hair, summoning my acting skills to pull visible courage around me like a costume. "Whatever. It doesn't matter. We're better than some old dudes with kabob skewers for swords. Don't worry, y'all. I've got this. Mia's gonna love us, and by the Halloween dance, she'll be happier than a kid with a bag full of chocolate—the good name-brand stuff, even."

Ethan snapped his fingers. "The Draconids Meteor Shower is tonight. You should take her to the party at the hill, see if you can work your buddy magic."

"I figured I'd use tonight to make some plans first. Last time, the meteors were underwhelming."

"The party only happens once a year, though," Deshawn added. "You could use it as a way to introduce her around. We can all go, watch your back."

Avery nodded thoughtfully. "Not a bad idea."

"Tonight could work," I mused. "Super short notice, but that means she won't have time to wiggle out with a lame excuse. It'd at least get her out of the house and meeting people."

"Exactly," Ethan said.

"Okay, then," I said. "Let's do it. See you tonight."

With one last hug to the still-shaken Avery, I headed to my own apartment. Deshawn lived in a nearby subdivision, so he turned right to head out the main door, but Ethan followed me to the left, walking me home even though it was fewer than a dozen steps. He lived two floors up.

At my door, Ethan stopped me before I could head inside. "It's probably best if Deshawn and I meet you at the hill. We don't want to scare her off."

"The crowd alone might do that."

"Yeah, everyone'll be there. Maybe she'll even meet a special someone to distract her."

I shot him a suspicious look.

He lifted his hands up. "Not me. I'm not interested in locking lips with anyone who could destroy me."

I crossed my arms, trying not to feel pleased that another girl was on Ethan's no-kiss list besides me.

"I'll still have to figure out what stuff she likes. Do a little detective work. Not everyone puts having a boyfriend or girlfriend at the top of their list, you know."

"True. Some people seem to be a natural at it, though." He lifted one eyebrow at me.

"Hey, I haven't gone out with that many people. Unlike some I could mention."

"Are you kidding? There's a daily parade of dudes strutting through this building, hoping to get a chance with the infamous Parker Mills, actress and future sorority girl."

I laughed and a lock of hair slid over one eye. Before I could do anything, Ethan pushed it back for me. His palm was warm against my skin before he tucked his hand in his pocket. Had his touch lingered a moment at my ear?

My head felt full of helium. If I didn't remember to breathe, it might just float away.

He took a half step back. "Hey, if I don't give you a hard time, who will?"

Just friends. He was teasing, like always. Tomorrow, he'd probably ask out another girl. Still, I couldn't resist smiling back. "Stargazing. Tonight. I'll bulldoze my way into Mia's apartment and sweet-talk her into joining us. I'll see you at the hill."

"Wouldn't miss seeing you in action, Cupid."

I blushed again. I could feel the burn. Stupid blond blush, the bane of my existence.

"I'm not signing her up for any speed dating yet. I'll just be hanging out with her, trying to be her friend."

"She's lucky," he murmured, barely audible.

My knees went a bit weak. *Stay cool, stay cool.* His scent of cinnamon gum and fresh-scented soap filled my awareness. I cleared my throat but couldn't think of any snappy, silly answer. Ethan knew me better than anyone but Avery. So why didn't he know I'd been dreaming of him for years?

He leaned back, eyes twinkling. "Problem, Parkour?"

A new thought occurred to me with a tingling, thrilling dread: maybe he knew more than I thought he did. What if he already guessed I wanted to go to the dance with him?

"No. Just, uh, thinking," I managed to say, which was true. My mind was already jumping ahead like a skipping stone, leaving my worry behind. My words came faster. "The dance is obviously in this vision, and we can't ignore it. Everyone's talking about it, even you, goober that you are, so maybe my job is to make sure she has a great time there. She said she doesn't dance, but whatever. The right person could change that in a hot second. And I'll know it when she sees the One."

I imagined Mia smiling, dancing with the perfect date. *Yes.* My breath caught and a delicious zing twirled in my chest. My doubts faded. This was my thing. It's what I *did*.

Everything would work out fine.

He nodded, lips easing into a slow smile. "I'm sure you'll figure things out. If it involves the heart, you've got the pulse."

Talking dates with Ethan made me twitchy. Too close for comfort.

"So long as she doesn't sit home crying in her ice cream all night. That could be the trigger I'm supposed to prevent. Haven't you seen any horror movies in your life?"

I continued over his laughter. "But fun, party, dancing—that's all easy stuff that can boost her mood. And in the meantime, I'll find some other options, if the date and dance thing doesn't work out."

"It sounds like you've got this locked up already. Speaking of dates. Question. Does having a date to a dance really mean so much to a girl?" The question hung between us. He tilted his head, as if observing a new, strange creature.

All the air froze in my lungs. Why did he want to know? After only the smallest pause, I said, "Depends on the dance. Depends on the date. Depends on the girl."

Ask about this girl.

He held my gaze for an endless moment but said nothing. With his solid shielding, I had no way to know if he *liked me* liked me, or if he was playing around, or if he just wanted the inside scoop on girls from a prime source. No way would I risk utter humiliation by asking.

A door slammed down the hall, and we both jumped. The hushed moment snapped. A slow, devilish grin spread across his too-cute-for-comfort face. "Good to know. Later, Parkour."

"Later." If my voice was faint, surely it was only from exhaustion. Not from a ridiculous hope.

6

A couple of hours later, I stood outside Mia's door and put on my game face. I had this. The girl was going to have a great time. She really, really would.

"Knock knock!" I called and rapped twice on the door. Mia lived on the same floor as Ethan, but at the opposite end of the U-shaped building.

The door swung open to reveal a tall woman, hair in an elegant topknot.

"Hello, Parker!"

"Dr. Lopez! I didn't realize you were Mia's aunt!"

"Too bad I didn't know you were coming by. I'd have made some cookies."

We both laughed. Dr. Sofia Lopez used to fuss about all the kids in the complex making too much noise but then secretly handed out cookies when parents weren't around. Cookies had been lacking in recent years, but the woman's stern expression melted into the same bright smile.

Dr. Lopez swung open the door. "Come on in."

"Thank you! Tonight's the meteor shower—"

"The Draconids, yes. The party at the hill has been an annual event since I first started working here."

"Then you know Mia's got to go! Rip that new-girl bandage right off."

Dr. Lopez spoke softly, so her voice didn't carry beyond the room. "I like the way you think. My niece is a sweet girl, but she's having a hard time." She lifted her voice. "Mia! Parker's here!"

I stepped inside. A vase full of fragrant roses sat on the table, and whatever they'd had for dinner lingered in the air with scents of cumin and roasted corn. My own apartment never smelled so good.

"She's in her room—why don't you head on back? First door on the left." Dr. Lopez winked.

"Thank you, ma'am!" Without missing a beat, I crossed the small living room and poked my head in the tiny room at the start of the hall. "Hey, Mia."

"Oh! Parker! I didn't know you were here." Mia stood

behind an easel across the room with a brush in hand. The painting itself faced away from the door. She slipped out from behind the canvas and wiped her hands off with a stained towel.

The tiny room was stuffed. A bed, neatly made, was topped with bright orange cushions. A pile of books towered on the desk next to a laptop. Art supplies were stacked everywhere, with trays of charcoals, pastels, and paint tubes taking up most of the space. Mia must be serious about the Picasso business.

Maybe she'd even have an online portfolio. Most artist-types around our school did. But I'd done a quick search online and found a big fat zero on Mia, which was more than odd. It was intriguing.

Mia blushed. "Ah, come on in. If you can find a spot."

I could always find a spot. I moved a few pillows to sit on the bed. "Wow, you've already gotten your room cleaner than mine. You must be organized."

"I just wanted to get moved in."

"I can only imagine. I've had the same room since I was born, full of who knows what at this point. Avery's bedroom is even worse, with her creepy design mannequins and plastic brain diagrams." I gave an exaggerated shudder.

Mia cracked a smile. "Avery's the redhead, right? Hope her headache went away."

"Yep. She's feeling better, thanks. She always bounces back."

Mia began piling one sketchbook after another in her arms, clearing a space on the little chair by the desk. "Uh, sorry, there's not a lot of room. Let me move these, and you can sit in an actual chair—"

A sketchbook toppled from the top of the pile and landed open at my feet. I scooped it up—to be *helpful*—and happened to take a quick look at the top sketch. A super cute guy. No one I knew, though. Blond hair. Light eyes. Sort of an arrogant expression. Across the page from Arrogant Boy was a woman who looked far too much like Mia to be anyone but her mother, with the same long dark hair, soft brown eyes, and Audrey Hepburn cheekbones.

Mia snatched the book out of my hand. Our fingers brushed, and a shock of betrayal laced with fury and terror ripped through me. *Ow.* I jerked my hands back like I'd touched the wrong end of my flat iron. Riding on the emotion came an image of the arrogant boy, clear in my mind's eye, like he was standing right in front of me, in flesh and blood. He looked beautiful, but … unkind.

Scornful. The image faded, and I took a deep, quivering breath.

Smells and sounds linked to emotions were thankfully rare. Mia had already shown her emotions ranked high enough on the pain scale to generate a horrible stench. But this had been like ... seeing a clip of a memory, a regular 3-D experience for a split second.

Empaths didn't see things like that. Or who knows, maybe they did if the feeling was strong enough. It wasn't like I had anyone to ask about it. Maybe I'd imagined it? How many times had my mother complained about my overactive imagination? Too many to count.

Mia shifted her weight, tucking a lock of hair behind one ear. "Sorry. It's just my sketches are sort of private, you know?"

"No sweat. I know how artists are, believe me." I made a mental note to look up local art contests Mia could win. Hard to sit around moping with a giant trophy reflecting your face. Band, track, basketball, art ... the hobby didn't matter. If I helped someone up their game, it always upped their attitude.

Mia slid her notebook onto the desk with a casualness that didn't match her trembling hands. "I was surprised such a small school had an art class. But glad."

So bland chit-chat it was. No problem—I could work most any topic to my advantage. "Yeah, the university here has its benefits. I've taken summer acting camps all my life. We're practically swimming in theatre productions, art shows, you name it. Ooh, I'll have to take you to the next art show hosted by the university. That'll be fun!"

Mia nodded but couldn't seem to find a verbal response. The poor thing was so uptight, she might just explode before anyone could help.

Such pain. I'd forgotten how much it hurt to purposefully open myself to other people's pain. My best friends all kept their raw emotions to themselves. I could commiserate with all my fellow Fab Four members without living their painful moments. And with plain brains, I worked to make sure their lives were smooth. If I couldn't fix them, I avoided their negativity. The impossible exception was, of course, my mom.

But Mia was a sinkhole of sadness that I would now have to spend lots of time around. I'd better get those happiness shortcuts started today.

I studied the room for clues. A dozen more sketches were scattered under the desk, lots of them images of Arrogant Guy. Mia certainly was focused on her subjects.

All those sketches, plus the betrayal I'd felt, was painting a pretty clear picture to me.

"Bad breakup?" I asked, gesturing to the pile. A bad breakup often called for a good fix-up, and I excelled at those.

"You could say that." Mia's tone was clipped. She began cramming the loose sketches in a cubby of her desk, lips mashed into a thin line.

Okay, then. Time to back away from Van Gogh over there before she chopped off an ear. I slapped my hand on my forehead. "Oh! I almost forgot!"

I hadn't forgotten, but it leant a feeling of spontaneity to the moment. "I came by to grab you because tonight's a once-in-a-lifetime opportunity. Well, once this year, at least." I described the annual stargazing event held at the top of what passed for a hill in the area. "The meteors should be starting up soon. They're really something. You've got to come."

"Oh, I don't know. I'm sort of in the middle of this." Mia gestured at the canvas.

"No problem. I can wait for you to clean up. Already got an assignment for class?"

Mia picked up her brush and dipped it in the blue paint on her palette. "Oh, uh, no. I'm finishing something I started before I moved. Sometimes I can't think about much else until I finish. So, I don't think tonight's going to—"

Dr. Lopez stepped through the door. "Mia, mi'ja, this is the meteor shower I was telling you about earlier. Where I met your Uncle Max, bless his soul." She shimmied and gave a wink. Mia flushed with an "Oh my God" under her breath.

Dr. Lopez chortled loudly. "If you go, I can't tell embarrassing stories in front of your friend."

I giggled and added, "It'll be just for a little while. It's like five minutes from here. After a few shooting stars, if you're done, I'll walk you home, promise."

Persuasion was my strong suit. Avery always said that used car salesmen could take lessons from me. But given Mia's mental blocks, I was glad to have unexpected help today.

"Dr. Lopez, tell her. It's a big deal here."

"It's true," her aunt said. "You can clean up later."

Mia stood by her easel. Blue paint dripped down the brush, touching her fingers, but she still didn't move. Another jab of Mia's fear punched me, this time shaded with the scent of acrid smoke.

Sympathy pushed me to give the girl a break. A

small one. "How about I meet you on the front lawn in ten minutes? You can get ready without me breathing down your neck. And I promise—we'll leave if you don't have fun."

Mia nodded, too quickly. "Sure. Okay. See you down there. My aunt seems to think I'd better." She gave a little glare to her aunt, who laughed. Her aunt's relief lit up the room like a spotlight, so this must be the authentic Mia, not the polite one I'd been talking to all day.

I took the chance of adding, "You know if you don't show, I'll just come back and drag you there, right?"

"No doubt." Mia included me in her small glare but reluctantly smiled.

Progress for sure. I slipped out of the room, tossing Mia a thumbs-up.

At the front door, Dr. Lopez whispered, "Don't let her scare you off." Sadness floated out from the professor like a cloud, coated with love and concern. "She could use a good friend like you."

Yep. That's what I'd heard. Avery was really never wrong.

"You can count on me, Dr. Lopez. One happy niece, coming right up."

Satisfied, I paused outside the closed apartment door

and rinsed off with my mental waterfall. Mia's mood took three washes to get rid of.

As I headed down the hall, I skirted past clumps of kids gathering to walk to the stargazing party. Lots of kids from school lived here—which still didn't mean much in a town of 40,000, tops.

I waved at everyone I passed. At least six of the boys sent zings of interest my way. It put a bit of pep in my step. Ethan might not see me like that, but it was nice to know I wasn't invisible to everyone. I'd focus on the positive. Tonight was a night for fun.

I raced down the two flights of stairs and strode along the hallway with determination in every step. Grateful to pass up my own door, I knocked three times on Avery's, taking a deep hit of the scent of cinnamon and apples that wafted from the apartment. Everyone's home smelled nicer than mine. I'd have to fix that. I *would* fix that. Positive thoughts. Anyone could use a diffuser or buy flowers. Or cook a frozen apple pie.

"Hey, I thought you were getting Mia tonight." Avery swung open the door, munching on potato chips, wearing pajama bottoms and a sweatshirt—her staying-in clothes.

"No way," I protested. "We all agreed to this. She's

meeting me out front in a few minutes." I pushed past Avery, swept into her bedroom, and jumped onto the bed full of stuffed animals. This evening would require finesse. I was absolutely not going in there without my best partner in crime.

Avery closed the door and sighed. "Look, you'll be focused on Mia, Todd and I broke up, like, two weeks ago, and frankly, I don't want to freeze tonight. That vision took it out of me today, and it's supposed to get down to 55 degrees already. This rear's too cute to fall off from frostbite." She did a little shake with her lower half.

I giggled but said, "I know that vision sucked, but didn't you just tell me we were all in this together? What if you get another update from the great beyond when you see Mia tonight? Even the boys are going as secret backup. Are you going to let them out-psychic you?"

"As if they could." Avery pshawed.

I gave sad puppy eyes and puffed out my bottom lip. "Pleeease? We *neeeed* you."

Avery was silent. Then she sighed. "Why can't I ever tell you no?"

"Cause you looove me!" I crowed and wrapped her in a tight hug.

Avery swapped out her clothes in record time, adding

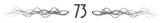

her signature knee-length velvet coat.

Mia was easy to find out front, despite the milling students meeting up with their own friends. Her black coat set off the silky darkness of her hair. I reintroduced the two girls, and we set off walking. Thankfully, Avery didn't zone out this time. Now it was Mia who said not a single word. Whatever tiny bit of trust had begun in her room had evaporated. Back to square one.

I chatted a mile a minute and looked at Avery meaningfully to say *See what I mean?* By the time we reached the hill, Avery was talking just as much to prevent any awkward silence. It was one of the things I loved most about Avery—she really did bounce back fast.

It was crowded up at the hill. Love, desire, bitterness, disappointment. Pushing past people, I felt emotions raining on my skin like soft sleet. *Ping, ping, ping.* Thankfully, it was low key enough to ignore. Mia wasn't sharing anything, though, not even a whisper. It left me a bit lost.

I'd just have to improvise.

7

THE stars were taking their sweet time to die. Mia, Avery, and I had waited for thirty minutes. So far the meteor shower was a no-show. Talk about annoying. And Ethan and Deshawn might have planned on being backup, but so far, they were as absent as the falling stars.

Avery had been right about the temperature. The tip of my nose was turning numb. The sky arched in a deep black bowl above us, perfectly cloudless. At least the meteor shower would have a perfect backdrop if it ever got started.

Mia checked her phone. I didn't need psychic empathy to know the girl was about to take off. I cast about for any distraction. A blond guy was staring at us from across the hill. No, not staring at us. Staring at Mia.

The boy was one of the few new transfers into our grade. Josh Remmel. He wasn't someone I'd forget, with those dark brown eyes and beachy white blond hair. His nose was a little crooked, as if he'd broken it before. He wore shorts with a sweatshirt. I wasn't sure if that made him tough or an idiot. His expression required no X-ray.

I always researched new people before considering them as possible matches, but this was an emergency situation, more of a Rainy Day Hair Frizz Shellacking Job than a careful updo.

I nudged Mia on the shoulder. "Hey, a cutie is checking you out at one o'clock."

Mia looked up from her phone and met Josh's gaze. A soft gasp escaped her lips.

A jab of shock hit me, followed by a mental boom like a thunderclap. A rush of tangled emotions came with the mental noise—shock, fear, hope, interest, and … something I couldn't quite place before the rush cut off to leave Mia as emotionally silent as before.

A gust of wind blew Mia's hair across her face, hiding her expression and any clues it held. But something about Josh had surprised Mia and triggered a whole landslide of messy emotions. One of those flashing feelings had been interest. Lots of it.

The answer to our problem appeared to have landed on my doorstep on a pair of mighty fine muscular legs.

"Well, well, well," I murmured to Avery, raising an eyebrow. "Good possibility for the dance, yeah? For Mia?"

"If she passes, sign me up."

"We've got a month. Plenty of time. Shoot, going with him might make *me* happy if she won't take him," I said.

"It's worth a shot. It's what you do best."

"Truth. You take him, I'll get her. Meet up in five."

The words volleyed back and forth swiftly, culminating with a discreet pinkie shake before we set off on our respective missions.

"Mia! Look, here's the perfect spot!" I squealed, stepping closer.

The girl jumped. No one ever expected me to be so loud, but actors had to project to the back of a room. I had good lungs.

Mia's gaze flicked between me and Josh. Avery was already smiling up at the blond boy in her most charming way. For a moment, a hint of wistfulness shimmered from Mia, the way heat waves hovered above the streets in August. Then it was tomb-silent again.

I sat down on the grass. "So. *Josh.* You know him?"

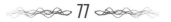

"J-J-Josh?" Mia's thick, dark eyebrows knitted together, a very Frida Kahlo look. She could carry it off, too.

"Blondie over there? He's new this year, too. Did you meet at a new student orientation or something?" I jerked my thumb at him. He was looking past Avery to Mia.

Mia burned with a blush again. "No, I haven't met him."

Faint embarrassment from her trickled along my skin like condensation on glass. I leaned forward and opened my mental shields to seek deeper, but my gift was immediately overrun with a rush of insecurity from the skinny girl to our left and the panicked confusion of some guy tripping over his own feet. Love, fear, anger, jealousy—they all crammed inside me, demanding to be heard, turning into a blurred surge of unrecognizable feelings.

I pushed back mentally, struggling to wash everything else away. Understanding Mia was hard enough without random emotions blaring like a wrestling match in the background.

Mia stared at the ground, but she must've snuck a peek at Josh again through her lashes. A stream of emotion poured from her like music blaring from a radio suddenly plugged in. Wistfulness, definite interest, and luminous hope flowed just for one short moment, but it was enough to confirm my plans.

If I could maneuver the two of them together, Mia would be a happy camper in no time. Crisis averted.

A glance over at my bestie sent a little spark through me—Ethan and Deshawn had finally arrived, carrying an old blanket. They were talking with Josh, too. Excellent. All hands were on deck.

I casually caught Avery's attention with a quick jerk of my head. It was a tiny movement, but like clockwork, my girl knew what to do.

Josh, Ethan, Deshawn, and Avery wove through the crowds toward us. Ethan sent a wicked smile that sped my pulse. They passed Sophie, but he didn't look twice beyond a relaxed wave.

I hid a smile. This night kept getting better and better.

Mia looked up again in time to see Josh standing right in front of her. A warm blast of air raced past us. Someone must have started a campfire on the other side of the hill, perfect for later.

Ethan jogged the last few steps and slid into an imaginary home base at my feet. "Score!" he yelled.

"You weirdo, you're supposed to say 'safe.' Get up. You're getting dust on my boots." I pulled Ethan up, and he bowed deeply, still gripping my hand. For one breathless moment, I thought he was going to kiss the back of my hand in a courtly gesture, but he dropped it instead. My heart dropped along with it, but I shook it off and smiled.

Avery spoke with a cheery tone. "Everyone, this is Josh! He's new."

I didn't miss Mia's frown directed at Avery's delicate hand on Josh's arm. Avery didn't miss it either: her smug, I'm-secretly-laughing dimple popped up. She pulled away her hand and took a casual step back from Josh. Clockwork indeed.

Mia blushed and focused on the stars like they were the most fascinating thing around when clearly, the most fascinating thing was standing right in front of her. Romance wasn't for everyone, but it looked like there was interest from both parties, even if Mia felt out of her comfort zone for now. No doubt dancing with Mr. Mighty Fine Legs would be worth a little sweat from her up front.

I said, "Hi, Josh. You're not the only new kid here, FYI." I gestured at Mia.

Josh's smile grew, his eyes warm as he gazed at Mia. "Nice to meet you …"

He paused, waiting for Mia to fill in the gap. With her name. That she obviously suddenly couldn't remember. Her eyes glazed slightly—visible panic—and she turned tomato sauce red, shining right through that gorgeous olive skin tone.

At this point, she might spontaneously combust. Maybe that was the way Mia would bring national media attention down on us all. Death by embarrassment. That would certainly suggest something unnatural was afoot in our little town.

"This is Mia," I smoothly stepped in.

Mia just stood there staring at Josh like the Tin Man caught in a monsoon.

My smile faded. If these two got together, it could work wonders, but playing matchmaker could backfire in a hurry if the right feelings weren't there. I knew this from hard-won experience. I put my hand on Mia's shoulder and imagined stepping inside that buried heart. I had to know.

Then Josh smiled at Mia. Her eyes met his, and sudden nerves and, well, *interest*, exploded from her again, singing through my fingers. Fear was still there, too. But there was that odd feeling again … wistfulness tinged with hope and heartbreak. A feeling of home.

That was it. Josh made Mia think of home.

The sensation cut off. I dropped my hand, confused. Why all the complicated emotions? He was a stranger. I took a closer look at Josh. He looked familiar.

Blond hair. A bit floppy. Angular cheekbones. Where had I seen that face before?

It struck me like a stiletto stomp to the foot.

Arrogant Boy. From Mia's sketchbook and the memory flash. They weren't twins, but the resemblance between Josh and the pictures was uncanny, despite the different colored eyes. Who was that other guy? Whoever he was, maybe Josh could be Mia's home away from home.

"Nice to meet you," Mia said after a billion years, her voice as chilly as the air.

I hid a sigh. Before my frustration could fully bloom, Ethan said, "Hey, Avery. I heard Todd's not coming tonight. Something about all his underwear being sewn shut?"

I burst out laughing.

"I don't have the foggiest idea what you're talking about," Avery said primly.

Ethan's eyes twinkled. "Too bad. Because Deshawn and I came up with some other ideas for you."

"Omigod, let's sit down so I can take notes. Later, y'all!" She gave me a hug and whispered, "You've got the bait. Now hook the fish. Come over tonight and fill me in." She pulled Ethan and Deshawn with her to a nearby empty spot and laid out the blanket. Ethan looked back and waved a fast goodbye.

Josh's grin suggested he and Ethan might be peas in a pod, nothing like the arrogant expression of the other blond. Still. Just in case, I'd oversee this relationship by hand. Usually, once I picked out the right match, the rest happened on its own. That was the beauty of it. But Josh and Mia stood staring at each other, saying nothing. The moment was getting awkward.

Fortunately, at that moment, a brilliant light blazed through the sky. Oohs and ahhs filled the air, and we all followed the glow of a meteor speeding its way to earth.

"So beautiful," I murmured.

"Like falling fire," Josh replied.

Mia shook her head. "That's how they look, but, really, they're just rocks burning up in our atmosphere. They're flashy now, but in the end, all that brightness turns to dust in a heartbeat. Rocks on Earth last a lot longer."

What? My eyes widened at the unexpected speech.

Josh hooked his thumbs loosely in his shorts pockets. His gaze remained steady on Mia. "Maybe. But everything's made of stardust. The rocks up there and down here. You and me. Everything's beautiful in the right time and place. Whether you choose to create beauty along the way or sit in the dirt and do nothing—that's up to you."

Mia stiffened and turned away, tossing her long black hair over her shoulders. "Whatever. Gotta go. Catch you later, Parker."

"Wait up—I'll walk you home!"

I had a feeling there'd been a whole other level of conversation happening, and I'd missed it. But I knew one thing for sure: I had to get Josh and Mia together somehow. The interest was there. The chemistry was definitely there. They just had to ease past this initial weirdness. When it came to smoothing over rough patches, I was better than an all-natural face scrub with coconut sugar.

Mia let me accompany her home but pretty much said nothing the whole way back. Her one depressing speech must've used up all her words for the day.

I shrugged in response to Dr. Lopez's questioning expression. It was too soon to tell how helpful tonight had been. Mia was a tougher nut to crack than expected.

After slipping on my favorite PJs—hand-crafted by Avery—I waited for my best friend's return. Less than thirty minutes later, a double thump sounded through the wall, and I ran next door for the debriefing.

Avery opened the door and laughed at our matching pajamas, neon-orange flannel with tiny pink hearts. "Great minds do think alike. Now I just need to sew the boys a set, too."

"You make the most comfy clothes, and comfort is required after a night like that."

"Come on in. I've got the perfect addition to flannel."

As we passed through the living room, we waved at Avery's mom, nose deep in research papers.

"You girls have a good time?" Dr. Portman asked, still immersed in her reading.

"Uh huh!" we said without slowing. We headed to Avery's room, busted out the dark chocolate—thank heavens—and got to work.

"So, what do you think?" I closed my eyes in delight at the bitter sweetness of the candy.

Avery whistled a long breath, reclining elegantly

on the bed like an ancient Roman. "What happened? I thought you were going to play matchmaker?"

"I did! No idea why it was a total fail. Any visions?"

"None. Maybe Josh was steaming up my receptors! Did you see his muscles? I hear he's a dancer. Ballet."

"What? No way." I tipped the desk chair back on two legs, considering the marvelous implications.

"Oh yes. Are we sure Mia likes him? I saw sparks, but no fire."

"She likes him alright. She barely lets anything past whatever wall she's got, but once or twice, she couldn't keep her interest to herself. It's huge. I think he reminds her of some guy from home. They'd be perfect together. Who could be sad dancing cheek to cheek at the best dance ever with a guy like that?" I dropped the chair back down with a thud and smacked the desktop with my palm.

"Maybe. But she seems wound tighter than Principal Macy. Even your awesome self may not be enough. And I don't want to see that vision in real life. Not even kidding."

Avery had gone pale. It made me very glad to not be precognitive.

"It's only the first quarter of the game. Don't worry,

Ave. I've got lots of tricks up my sleeve, but she's going to miss her chance for the best one if she doesn't snap out of her funk fast. Josh won't stick around forever."

"Did you X-ray him?" Avery laid her head back on the pillow and closed her eyes.

I sighed. "Trying to read Mia took all my focus. But it didn't matter—he was super obvious about it."

"He's definitely into her, yeah."

"Hmm. Here's a thought. What if I got Josh moved into history class with me and Mia? They'd be stuck together every day, with me right there to make sure things go well!"

"If you can make it happen, you'd have an excuse for study dates and everything."

"*If* I can make it happen? There's a reason I signed up to be an office aide this year, you know. Third period, baby—no homework and access to student files. They love me in there." I arched my neck like a confident supervillain.

"I meant *when* you make it happen. Naturally."

"That's right, oh ye of little faith." I threw my last chocolate at her.

Avery caught it with her mouth and ate the treat with great gusto before saying, "I believe in you, I do.

I just wish my visions were more specific. Science. Science is specific. Psychic stuff is so messy. So totally unpredictable." Disgust shone from her eyes.

"Hey, don't worry. Psychic stuff is also totally awesome. Like, because of you, we already know key intel. We'll figure it out."

"Just get it done, Parker, before the Halloween dance. Make her trust you, set her up with Josh, whatever. Make her laugh and chill the heck out, or the only way we'll ever get out of this town is inside an FBI van with no windows."

spent a very productive third period sneaking in some research on Josh's file and setting up all the paperwork while the lead receptionist enjoyed a big box of chocolates, a gift from *moi*. Even as a student aide, though, I couldn't finish the job on my own. I needed one specific person's signature to make my plan work. Of course, I'd come prepared.

"Hi, Dr. O'Malley." I set a plate of brownies in front of the eighth-grade guidance counselor. Store-bought, but hey, better than burned.

The woman stared at the bounty before her and looked up with one eyebrow raised. "What do you want, Parker?" Dr. O wasn't the kind of lady who engaged in small talk.

"Josh Remmel needs to be moved to fifth period history. The registrar has approved it and entered the data already, but she needs your signature, too."

I'd hoped to bypass the requirement for Dr. O's approval. Ms. Baylor, the registrar, owed me big time for helping her step-daughter make the cheerleading team. It had taken tons of patience to train that girl to master a standing back tuck. But apparently, some basic paperwork was too much to ask for in return. I hid the glare that wanted to surface at the thought. But that's why I always had a Plan B. Brownies covered a multitude of sins.

Dr. O's eyebrow rose higher. Slightly miraculous.

"We do not accommodate any student's dating wish list, not even for our social chair."

I laughed, bad mood fleeing. "Oh no, I'm not into him. I mean, he's cute and all, but no. Josh is having scheduling conflicts with some major projects due in his current history class and his extracurriculars with dance competitions. His mother is concerned."

Well, no one had asked for a change, but there was a note in his file from his mother that he'd be missing the last day of exams due to a competition, which was the day of his current history class's semester exam. The explanation was close enough. Practically not even a lie.

"We have an empty seat in my class. It's a perfect win-win." I flashed my best grin.

Dr. O did not grin back. My confidence began to fade like a cheap dye job.

I'd pondered Mia's situation all last night, staring up at the little glowing dots on my ceiling, left over from childhood when I was into stars, and my mom was still mostly happy.

Darkness let people admit hard things. The hard truth was that Mia was seriously shut down. Moving was tough, no doubt, and new friends and a date to the dance wouldn't hurt, but … she needed more. A lot more. Therapy, friends, goals, accomplishments she could be proud of.

The thing was, we didn't have time for more. A month was nowhere near enough time to fix a broken heart and ruined self-esteem. But it *was* enough time for a fun distraction that might help in the long run, too. A boyfriend wasn't a cure-all, no, but a good crush sure could keep a girl's mind occupied—and be a lot of fun.

I had done some research in my dad's professional psychology journals last year. In real research studies, teenagers who said they were in love had higher mood scores. And in brain scans, love-struck people got a rush of feel-good hormones kinda like a hit of cocaine—no kidding—even if the couple broke up soon after.

Science didn't lie. Dopamine, serotonin, and adrenaline created euphoria. Those hormones could come from other things too, yeah, but if Mia really liked someone, she'd be caught up in the moment here and now, not focused on the sad past, at least not until after our deadline. We'd keep working on the big stuff, but in the meantime Mia would feel better, and what wasn't to like about that? Getting things rolling with Josh was the easiest, fastest option on the table.

Heaven knew Josh would be near impossible to resist with a smile like that if he was a decent guy. And I'd be right there to make sure he was.

Dr. O leaned back. "I haven't received any complaints from him or his mother, though I suppose the request is logical." But still, she didn't say the magic words.

Why the big deal? It wasn't like Josh would learn less with a different teacher. One way to find out.

Keeping my expression calm, I tried to X-ray the counselor, focusing hard to work my way past the mental blocks built from severe repression. Though I'd never gotten any emotional impression from Dr. O, I'd admittedly never tried to look very hard. Something about the woman reminded me of a boa constrictor.

Using my gift, I imagined seeing beyond the navy pant suit, past the too-thin ribcage, into the woman's tiny, tiny heart. A wall stood in my way, but I pushed harder ... and for one moment, I felt something. Not much, but a hazy glimpse of suspicion, self-righteous satisfaction, and ... was that ... the burning pinprick of obsession? Uncertain. A heavy darkness wove through all of it.

My mind stuttered to a halt. My plans poofed away, and all I could do was blurt, "I promise he'll be okay. I'll watch out for him." *Let him change classes. Let him change classes. Cooperate, dang it.* Dizzy with nerves, I braced a hand against the table and steadied myself.

Dr. O blinked and smiled. Her mental walls snapped shut and this time, I let them. Chilled, I hoped Dr. O wouldn't ever smile again. There was a definite gross fakeness to it. Maybe it was time to retreat and try a different angle later—

The counselor said, "We certainly want all our new students to feel at home. I'll approve that change for you."

I grabbed the signed slip and fled the room while things were going my way. If I never had to feel inside Dr. O's heart again, it would be too soon. But I'd gotten what I wanted. The exchange had been weird, leaving me a little drained, but who cared? It worked. I gave a fist pump of triumph.

At lunch, I gleefully explained my plan to the rest of the Fab Four.

"That's it?" Deshawn asked, voice lower than usual. "Throw the two of them together until they go to the dance? That's the big plan? What is this, some fairy tale? Or did we time travel to 1950 when I wasn't looking?"

I squirmed. "That's not the *whole* plan, of course. I'm working on her art stuff, too. But I can't even tell you how often I've seen someone with a crush forget all their other problems for a while, even shy people. It's almost like magic, I swear. And she likes Josh even if she pretends she doesn't. I figure if she hangs out with a guy who treats her right and makes her laugh … It won't fix the deeper issues, I know that, but if we can make it past the dance deadline, we're in the clear, right? And then we can focus on other things that take longer to set up."

"Works for me," Ethan said, mouth full of pudding.

Avery chewed her lip. "I don't know. It doesn't seem like enough right now. And you're conveniently forgetting those same studies pointed out the emotional downside to breakups and risks of dating the wrong person. Not to mention, the prefrontal cortex is still developing in the impulse control and decision-making departments until our early twenties, so she might not make the best choices. And if Josh isn't going to play—"

I hurriedly cut off the neurology lecture. "Oh, don't worry. I'm setting other plans in motion as soon as she warms up to Josh a bit. I've got oodles of ideas." I actually didn't. But I totally would.

"Good to know," Avery said. "I've been trying to get another vision. Meditating and stuff to see, you know, if the future's changed already."

I raised my eyebrows. Avery never sought out the "psychic garbage," as she put it.

"And?"

"And nothing. Nothing. Nothing." She hammered her fist against the table, making me jump.

"Whoa there, Ave. It's okay. I've got a good feeling about Josh. It'll be a piece of cake."

"If you say so," Deshawn said. "I was listening in on the hill when Mia said the bit about the stars. That girl's got problems."

"Well, duh. Speaking of problems, question about Dr. O: Have you guys ever noticed that her emotions are really ... flat? Like, she smiles but isn't actually happy?"

"I think most of humanity's like that," Deshawn said. "You should hear what people say when they think no one's listening. Depressing as all get-out."

Ethan snorted.

"Well, she makes me feel weird. So, watch your back around her, okay?"

Avery said, "If you say she's off somehow, I believe you."

"No kidding." Ethan nodded.

"I'll listen in now and then, if it'll make you feel better," Deshawn added. "Eavesdrop in her office to see if she's saying anything weird we should know about."

"That'd be awesome," I said, the uncomfortable itch inside dissolving instantly.

Mia finally walked into the cafeteria.

"Hey, here comes Mia. Everyone act normal."

Ethan burst out laughing.

I joined in, thankful for my friends. As long as I had them, no problem was too big to be solved.

Finally, fifth period history. The moment I'd been waiting for all day.

My chat with my friends had left me fizzy like a

shaken-up soda. Now I'd get to play matchmaker, a role I unabashedly loved more than anything. I didn't even mind the sadness from Mia that flared like a solar wind when she walked into the room today. Joy could combat grief any day, and Operation Cupid was about to commence.

Mia sat across the aisle on the left. The seat behind her was empty. For now. History class was going to get spiced up, and Josh was the jalapeño pepper.

I fidgeted and stared at the closed door. No Josh. The clock's minute hand seemed to move backward. Mr. Bransford's voice droned on and on.

Near the end of the period, the door finally swung open, much to my relief. I'd begun to worry that Dr. O had changed her mind.

Josh stepped in, and flashes of attraction rippled through the room. Typical. I rolled my eyes.

"They told me I'm switching classes," Josh told Mr. Bransford. He handed over a yellow slip and scanned the room. His gaze snagged on me but stuck on Mia. Oh yeah, he remembered her.

I zeroed in on Mia, but it was like listening for the flute in an orchestra full of brass and percussion. Any hints of emotions from her would be soft, delicate, and fleetingly fast.

At first, Mia seemed to feel nothing. Then her eyes clicked together with Josh's, and pink stole over her face. A racing thrill sparkled from her before she slammed her gaze back down. The sensation cut off.

Too late, chickadee. The guy would have to be blind to not see the way Mia's body unconsciously angled toward his, the way her cheeks flushed every time she looked at him. She should never play poker.

The teacher reviewed the information and waved his hand toward Mia. Her back stiffened.

"You can sit behind Mia, last seat in the second row."

A wave of panic flooded from her. I could almost hear words echoing through the emotion: No. *No no no no no … not him!*

Dread curdled in my gut. Skipping the funky smells and going straight to audio had to be an 8.9 on the freak out scale. Had I made a mistake? Was there something about this guy I didn't know? His emotions weren't flashing at me, but nothing in his warm smile suggested any threat.

"Welcome to class, Joshua," Mr. Bransford added.

"Just Josh." He flashed a grin and strode down the aisle. Toward Mia. Whose emotional output doubled.

Panic, fear, desire, and hope whirled around the girl before stillness rose through it all like the hush before a storm. Tension prickled my skin like physical static, but Josh didn't seem to notice. He filled up the entire room with his presence. Ballet dancer, I recalled. Yes, the boy had stage presence, something I knew a thing or two about.

Several girls shamelessly craned their heads to get a better look as he strolled past them. Mia's expression darkened as she noticed, too. So she *was* interested.

I gave Josh a cheery wave as he slid into his seat. I took a quick X-ray of his heart but picked up nothing. He acted too jovial to be repressed. Maybe he just had no baggage. Wouldn't that be a relief compared to the thousand-pound suitcases Mia carried around?

He sat behind her, back straight in his seat. Beneath his cargo shorts, his legs were long like a colt's, and his feet nearly touched Mia's under her own desk. Mia very carefully did not look back during the remaining ten minutes of class.

Lucky for Mia and her happy future, persistence was my middle name, along with peppy and party.

"Mia, why don't you catch Josh up on the assignment?" I said. "It's the neighborly thing to do, but I've got to get to drama early today, so I can't."

"Oh, I couldn't, I ..."

"You took the words from my mouth, Parker," Mr. Bransford interrupted. "Thanks for always looking out for your classmates. Mia, please fill Josh in."

I gathered my papers as if I were in a rush but managed to stay put and eavesdrop anyway. I noted Mia's dismayed expression and Josh's pleased one. People were starting to pack up. *Come on,* I thought. *Talk to him!* Not for the first time, I wished I could do more than just feel people's emotions. If I could *make* them feel happy, all this tap dancing could be avoided.

"Page 47," Mia blurted. "The odd questions."

Josh bent his head to write it down, and a lock of blond hair fell over his forehead. Mia happened to glance over her shoulder at him just then.

Focused so hard on Mia, I was hit with the most tangible memory I'd received yet, a small slice of a live-action scene with the boy with blue eyes, his blond hair sliding over his forehead. It played like a movie in my mind's eye. Fingers twirled through the fallen hair and pushed it back. Mia's fingers. The hair was soft as corn silk. A jolt of sudden heartbreak shattered the image.

I tried not to reel. My hands instinctively clamped on

the desk hard enough to leave indents in my skin. The pain helped clear my mind. *Keep it together,* I commanded myself. *Breathe.* Hiding my shock took every ounce of control I had.

"So, we're studying—" Josh began to ask Mia, but the bell clanged.

Mia ran. Truly, she sprinted, sneakers squeaking as she pushed out the door like a fire raged behind her.

Josh looked at me, eyebrows high. "Did I say something wrong?"

I discreetly unpeeled my fingers from the desk. "I don't think it's you at all. She's hard to get to know, but she seems really great so far. I'd hang in there if I were you."

He grinned. "You don't have to tell me twice."

At least one person was doing what he was supposed to.

9

MIA resisted Josh with superhuman strength the rest of the week, which was, admittedly, a blow to my plan. I still believed that Operation Cupid was the most likely solution, but the unexpected failures over the last few days were exactly why I always mapped out multiple shortcuts to happiness.

Mia was gone a lot over the weekend, avoiding me like garlic on a first date. She returned from yet another errand on Sunday carrying a bulging rectangular something that looked like a flattened briefcase. The girl staggered on the front steps of the apartment building, surely about to dump whatever was stuffed in the thing.

I jogged over from where I'd been lying in wait, pretending to read on the bench outside our building.

"Hey, let me help with that!" I took one side and lifted.

"Thanks," Mia said, using her free hand to brush away hair from her face.

As we huffed our way up the stairs, I asked, "What the heck is this?"

"It's my portfolio. My aunt had me work with a professor this weekend, getting some pieces ready for my Pre-AP art class application." Mia unlocked her front door and rushed in with me on her heels. We plopped the portfolio on the table.

Art was supposed to be the window to the soul, and here was a chance to open the curtains over Mia's. Plus, this was perfect timing to find a good portrait to enter into that university contest next month. Operation Van Gogh was now up and running.

"Oh wow! I'd love to see some of your work, Mia!" A five-hundred cash prize, blue ribbon and a trophy ... Who wouldn't smile at that? Better to only tell her if she won, though. Maybe I could sneak a piece into the competition. All surprise-like. A teensy bit unethical, admittedly, but losing left most people raw inside. Mia didn't need any more emotional exfoliation.

"Oh, I don't know," Mia said. "My art's, well, personal." She scrunched her shoulders in a shrug and ran her hand along the black portfolio with the unthinking motion of a pet lover petting their favorite cat.

"Don't you show other people in class?"

"Well, yes, but those are other artists—"

"Please? You can come see me perform a monologue in exchange. I promise, I'm already a huge fan." I offered up my most winning smile.

With a sigh, Mia gestured at the portfolio. "Fine. You're pretty stubborn, you know that?"

I laughed. "That's what they tell me."

Lifting the cover felt like opening a giant book of fairy tales. On top was a landscape. Beautifully flowing watercolor captured the dark bulge of a thunderstorm over a plain full of waving wheat. I swore I could feel the heavy weight of the impending rain on my skin. The scent of rain practically bloomed in the air. My arms broke out in goose bumps. "Mia, that's incredible."

"The colors are too muddied."

Mia needed a few lessons on the value of tooting her own horn. If not you, then who? That's what I always said. But I needed a portrait for the competition, like the sketches I'd seen on that first day.

I eagerly reached to see what treasures waited beneath the top painting, but I paused. No emotions blipped, but

Mia's stiff posture set off alarms. Art was personal. That's what Mia kept saying. That was both good and bad at a moment like this.

"May I?" I waited.

I could feel the NO in the air but doubted Mia would say it out loud.

"Uh, okay."

Excellent. Still, I didn't move the top watercolor. It'd be better not to bulldoze this. I met Mia's eyes. "You know, I put myself out there for performances, but your artwork can be seen by anyone, anywhere, for always, once you share it. I bet that's hard."

"It can be."

"It takes guts, for sure. Thanks for sharing with me. Really."

Mia relaxed a little, and my hesitation evaporated. I carefully sorted through the pages. Sketches flipped by. More watercolors. Photos of oil canvases too big to put in the portfolio, and even some kind of giant mural on a building wall. Many of them shared the same theme: wild landscapes with threatening clouds hovering. Power radiated from the very page.

I sighed. "You are so talented, Mia. I can't imagine being able to do this."

 105

"Thanks." The word was almost inaudible. Mia wandered over to the living room window. "You know, if you want, I can help you draw something sometime. Go over some basic techniques, maybe with a still life." She bit her lip. "I mean, if you wanted to."

"That sounds like fun. Though you may regret it. I can't even draw a stick figure."

"I think you'll surprise yourself. People who can pick out good outfits like you have a good eye for art."

"Aww! Thanks." I bowed at the waist with a flourish and made Mia grin. That was the nicest thing she'd said yet. Progress, one tiny step at a time.

Mia made no move to collect the portfolio, so I kept going. I'd almost forgotten my real purpose in looking through the vivid images.

But I turned past the last photograph and came to a small stack of portraits. *Yes.* Pencil sketches and pastels. An image of Mia stared up at me from the page. Remarkably, eerily exact, Mia even caught the way her own eyes overflowed with secrets. I whistled low and turned the page.

A jolt ran through me. A woman was drawn in charcoal, soft lines, but clear. I'd seen her before—it was the same woman from those sketches in Mia's room.

"This must be your mother?" Had to be. The same hair. The same eyes.

Mia looked over at the image. Immediately, burning pain raced through me from head to toes. No memory or scent, thank goodness, but it hit 6.5 on the Pain Scale, at least. I bowed my head under the weight of it. This pain was exactly why I meticulously plotted out ways to make people feel better and avoided people I couldn't fix.

"Yes, she died five years ago."

"Five years?" I blurted. And Mia was still in this much pain? "That must have been really hard."

Mia's eyes were black with emotion. "Thanks. Losing someone is … never easy."

A huge ball lodged in my throat. Trying to make Mia happy by dangling a cash award for her art or gold trophies suddenly felt trite. Ridiculous. The girl was in dire need of so much more. She deserved more. If only there was time …

"I'm so sorry, Mia. Really." For so many things I couldn't even explain.

Behind that picture was one final piece of art. Did I risk it? I moved the image of Mia's mother out of the way and there he was—the arrogant blond boy. His eyes were cold somehow, even in pastel, and his sneer made me wince.

I readied my gift to slip past any opening in Mia's wall. "And this guy? Who is he?"

I suddenly smelled summer flowers and a musky cologne too strong to be a good idea. A flicker of the boy flashed again in my mind. He was laughing, but spite wove through it, not mirth. The mood shaded the scene the color of ashes.

Another wave of pain rolled through the room, reverberating inside my heart. Thunder boomed outside. Loud. Insistent. Real thunder, I realized, not a memory from Mia's art. I struggled to look away from the mental video clip until it clicked off on its own.

"Oh, that's just a guy back home." Mia's words tripped over each other. She turned back toward the window. A stabbing panic reached past her into me, and with it came the smell of rain, the touch of cloying heat. An image of towering black clouds flickered in my mind, jagged orange lightning crawling through the darkness. Terror laced through the memory like the lightning through the clouds.

Code red! Waterfall, waterfall! Taking a deep breath, I imagined that horrible fear washing away from me. I didn't want any memories tied with those feelings. They faded fast, at least, and I took a deep breath.

Thunder growled through the room again, real thunder.

"It's late in the season for a thunderstorm." I joined Mia at the window.

Half the sky was robin's egg blue, but black clouds crowded the other side of the sky. If Mia's sudden terror stemmed from the coming storm, she'd have a lot of trouble being happy here in Tornado Alley.

"We should go somewhere without windows. Storms like that can be dangerous." Mia's voice shook.

I patted Mia's hand and looked right into her eyes. "Don't worry. We know how to deal with even the worst storms around here."

Mia's lips were tight. "Maybe. But I'd feel better not looking at it."

"Let's go to the kitchen then. No windows."

"Thanks. We can have a snack or something."

"I'm always up for food." I closed up the portfolio. It looked like Mia used her art to express her pain, which was a great therapy tool. I'm a big fan of therapy—even had my fair share of it—but it made entering Mia's work for that contest a no-go. I couldn't parade Mia's pain around for the sake of a trophy. First of all, it would definitely backfire. A shortcut to happiness that added complications wasn't a shortcut. Besides, losing a parent made even first prize count for nothing.

Operation Van Gogh was a bust before it even got off the ground. Dangling a date for the dance suddenly seemed like a dangerously weak option for Mia, too. A bit of flirty fun wouldn't be enough, not against this kind of grief. My friends and I would offer the steady support of friendship, but nothing could take center stage as fast as caring for the right person. Love lifted the spirits in the face of pain.

And I knew, *knew* in my empathetic guts, that Mia really did like Josh. He didn't have to be her one true love to be helpful. If Arrogant Boy had soured her on humanity, going out with such a sweetheart might help her enjoy life again, at least enough to not freak out in a few weeks. That's what I had to focus on for now. Mia just had to accept that she deserved any kind of happiness at all.

As the new week began, I swore to do everything and anything I could to help Mia feel at home. This was only her second week, and she needed to know she was welcome here.

Monday was a school holiday, so I took her for coffee and pie at Charlie's Diner and suggested shoe shopping afterward—and got turned down. Tuesday, the quiet girl picked at her lunch, morose as a friggin' tomb, dang it. Wednesday, she'd skipped lunch with us altogether to work on her art. And all this while I had been at my most charming.

I'd walked Mia to school each day since she'd arrived. I'd made sure Mia sat with my crew whenever she wanted, even though that meant no more code-talk about gifts. I'd invited her over after school. What more could the girl want before she considered me a real friend and loosened up a bit? A blood sacrifice?

"I don't know what else to do," I told Avery as we walked home on Wednesday. Mia had stayed late to work on her portfolio. "Operation Van Gogh's still off the menu, at least for now. Operation Butterfly won't get us enough mileage thanks to all that natural beauty, and she's already a top student in her classes. Not even having Josh sitting by her with his cutie-pie self is making her happier, and if that doesn't do it, I don't know what will." Panic spoiled my sense of achievement over getting Josh into history class. I was failing like last season's fashions at the Oscars.

"Then you'd better kick things up a notch," Avery said. "I've tried to reach out to her, too, but I'm getting nowhere at all. That girl's got more problems than my math book."

That was one way to put it. Mia was like one of those airplane black boxes. There was a lot going on inside, no doubt, but no one would know what until I learned the trick to open her up. Until then, I worried I was spinning my wheels. It was messing up my personal problem-solving track record, and as the dance loomed closer, Avery grew more skittish. It all put me on edge.

Arrogant Boy clearly haunted Mia. Whether or not Josh would be effective as a happy-influencer depended on who this blond dude was to Mia. Time to find out. Snooping was part and parcel of being a solid do-gooder. Given the time crunch, I'd have to expand my search and use all the gifts I had at my disposal—which included my posse of psychic besties.

Thursday afternoon, I told Avery at our locker, "We need a meeting of the minds. Today."

"Your place?"

"Yeah, Mom has a thing today for dinner, so everything should be quiet."

"Cool. I'll tell the boys. 4:30ish?"

"I'll have snacks."

"They'll be on time, then. Smart."

When the time rolled around, Deshawn appeared first at my door.

"Hey, come on back. Did you run here top speed or something? I thought you were coming with Ethan."

He rumbled with good humor. "I'm timely, what can I say? He was late."

I offered him the chair at my desk. It was rare for the two of us to have a moment alone. Not that we weren't friends, but Deshawn had his track friends he literally ran around with, and he spent more time with Ethan than either of us girls, especially once we hit middle school. Maybe I could ask Deshawn to ask Ethan ... no. I wouldn't. Couldn't. But I could ask about *Deshawn's* love life. That would be much more fun.

I smiled in the way I knew made my dimples pop. "So, D-Man, decided who you're taking to the dance? I know a few who'd love to get asked by you."

He snorted. "No, thanks. I'm going stag."

"What? Why?"

"We've got a job to do. And I'm too busy to be going out with anyone, anyway. If I want to get a scholarship in track, I gotta start now."

"Your mom still bent out of shape you want to focus on sports instead of academics?"

He rolled his eyes. "She gave up on that dream a long time ago. She even admits I'd have a better shot at a full ride if I stick with track and keep my grades high, too."

It was a smart plan. Deshawn had wisdom, not just brains—one of the many reasons I admired him.

"What about you?" he asked.

"What? What about me?"

"You have a date yet?" His eyes twinkled.

I forced myself to look unconcerned. "Not yet. I'm taking my time."

"Don't take too long." He squeezed his lips like he was trying not to laugh.

"What does that mean?"

"Just sayin', maybe worry about your own backyard before you keep mowing everyone else's."

A knock came at the door before I could demand an explanation.

Deshawn tilted his head. "It's Avery. She's griping to herself, so I'm thinkin' she's had a hard day."

With a last glance at Deshawn, I headed to the door.

Avery staggered in, her skin waxy.

"Are you okay?" I pulled Avery into the bedroom.

"You look awful. Deshawn, get her a drink, please."

He jogged to the kitchen.

"You don't look so hot yourself," Avery muttered, lying on the bed. "Aren't Thursdays usually good days for you, with Friday so close?"

"Yeah, well, I came home to my mom and dad fighting full volume before Mom stomped off to her dinner thing. And then Deshawn dropped some of his cryptic advice. What's your excuse?"

"The vision. It started coming back every night this week. I can't sleep. But it hit me again when I tried to take a quick nap after school."

"Why's it doing that?"

"Wish I knew. The dumb part is it's getting clearer, like a camera lens moving into focus, but I still can't see what makes Mia do whatever she does to ruin us. It's exhausting."

"Sounds like it. Sorry, Avery. I'm doing everything I can. I know y'all are, too, though I don't think she's going to trust the guys with anything serious. She barely talks to Josh, and that's someone she's actually attracted to."

"Hmm. She might've put me on the no-friend list when I was super friendly to Josh that first night. I'm trying to be her friend, too, but looks like this is mostly on you. Sorry. Make her laugh. That's what happy people do, right? You'd know for sure you're on the right track. Has she ever laughed that you've seen?"

"No." I scowled.

"How sad. We've got just a little over two weeks until the dance. Once the decorations are up around the school, the clock is ticking. We're running out of time."

10

DESHAWN came back with a glass of sweet tea, Avery's favorite. She sat up and took a sip. By the time Ethan finally arrived, she had color back in her cheeks.

The four of us barely fit in my room, especially since I never bothered to clean up. Who had the time?

Ethan sat propped up in my bed in his favorite White Stripes shirt. Eyeing the food piled on the desk, he said, "Chips and soda? I'm shocked. Where's my whole-grain granola?"

"I guess that just means more for us."

Ethan floated the whole bag of chips over to himself with his telekinesis, but Avery snatched it out of the air and ripped the bag open.

"Saw that coming a mile away," Deshawn said.

I said, "Settle down, y'all. Avery. Tell them about the repeating vision thing."

After Avery filled them in, I told them about the mystery around Mia's past. "I can't make her feel better until I know what she's hanging onto. I know she lost her mom five years ago, and that's rough, but there's something else going on for her level of Emo-Scale pain. I normally do my own snooping, but time is of the essence here. Deshawn, I need you to do some eavesdropping."

"I said I'd help, Mood Ring. Where and when?"

"No time like the present, right? You can work from here. Mia lives in the building. I need to know if she's hiding anything big. She's too good at blocking her heart, and when she lets stuff slip, it's so strong that I can barely hang onto my cool, much less push deeper."

He frowned.

I gave an impatient sigh. "You're not being a stalker or anything. It's for our safety."

"Fine. Hang on." He closed his eyes, tuning into the far away sounds.

"Has Mia told you anything useful about herself?" Ethan asked.

"Not much. She's a total clam. Josh could definitely

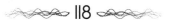

118

make her relax, but she's resisting it. Avery thinks a key turning point is if she laughs, but that's a long way off."

"What's Mia's aunt's name?" Deshawn interrupted.

"Dr. Sofia Lopez."

After a minute or two, Deshawn spoke. "I hear them. I recognize Mia's voice. There's no TV on or anything. It's just the two of them. Sounds kind of like a fight. The aunt's saying, 'You need to give yourself some grace, Mia. It wasn't your fault. It was a freak act of nature.' And Mia's saying, 'No, it's because I'm cursed …'"

His eyes snapped open. "Cursed? That sounds like a bigger problem than we can fix."

"Keep listening," I urged. "It's not nice, but eavesdropping beats getting our lives destroyed."

"So her aunt just said, 'Mark wouldn't want you to suffer like this.' Mia whispers, 'He would. He hated me. Before the … accident, he said I should die.'" Deshawn shook his head, but his eyes remained closed.

He continued passing along the conversation. "Now the aunt's talking again. 'He was confused. Scared. I'm sorry about what happened to him, but life goes on. I just want you to be happy.' Now Mia's answering back, 'But if you're happy, you've got something to lose and it hurts when you do. And hurting causes … problems.'"

He opened his eyes and clamped his hands on the sides of his head.

"What does that mean?" Avery asked.

He cleared his throat, lowering his arms. "I think it's pretty clear. She doesn't want to feel anything. Not pain, not joy—nothing. She's got everything on lockdown because that guy was a hater or something."

"One guy did this to her? She didn't say anything about loving him or anything like that."

"I don't know, but I can't keep listening. It's too private. Sorry, guys, but it's not right."

"No wonder she's so hurt," I mused. "Mark must be that guy she's always drawing. Mia's aunt said something about an accident. Do you think Mark got hurt in an accident, and Mia blames herself? Maybe he even died or something?"

"That would definitely make someone miserable," Avery said.

I tapped my pointer finger against my lips. "She'd already lost her mom. Then she loses this Mark guy. She's afraid to feel things, to be happy. Maybe she thinks something bad will happen if she lets herself care for someone. Maybe that's the problem, deep down, that I'm supposed to help her with."

Silence descended.

"That's a tall order, Parker, even for you," Ethan said, serious for once.

"Look, I can't give her a new mom. I wish I could. Her aunt has potential to be a mother figure for her, and maybe that'll help. But I know I can work with a new boyfriend for now. Plus, moving on could help close that door for her over the long haul, too. I already tried looking up stuff about her, but maybe we can find something about this Mark guy from her old town. She said it was Bent Creek. Search them together."

Avery opened a new tab on her tablet, and her fingers tapped on the screen. In a few moments she said, "From May of this year. 'Fourteen-Year-Old Mark Abels in Coma from Lightning Strike in Front Yard.' Yikes. Talk about bad luck. The odds of anyone being killed by lightning are like 165,000 to one. I imagine the odds of ending up in a coma from lightning are about the same."

"How do you remember that kind of stuff?" Ethan demanded.

"More to the point, did he ever wake up?" Deshawn asked.

"Not sure," Avery murmured. "There's no follow-up article I can find online, at least."

I wanted to pace, but there wasn't room. "Hmm. I will say, though, even in the drawings, he looks mean. Like, a scowling, snotty kind of dude. Not what I'd draw if I loved someone. But maybe I can get her to tell me what happened, now that I know just enough."

"If anyone can, it's you," Ethan said.

"I'll take that as a compliment."

"Oh, I meant it as one."

Avery rolled her eyes. "Okay you two. Parker, keep pushing. She obviously blames herself for whatever reason. We'll support you as best we can, but I'm not sure even yummy Josh can outweigh something like that in her past."

Ethan made loud gagging noises at Avery's description of Josh but added, "And it still doesn't explain why she'd be a danger to *us*. We've got nothing to do with that guy."

"Don't underestimate the effects of love. People can do some pretty extreme things when they're hurt by someone they care for." I'd seen people's hearts swell four times their regular size thanks to a new love. It transformed everyone. But when they fell out of love, it could change them just as much, like an apple sitting in a desert—all the sweet, juicy goodness evaporating right out.

The front door slammed. "Hello? Anyone home?"

At the sound of my mother's voice, my shoulders tightened. My mom was home early. Heels tapped closer to the bedroom door.

"Parker, is that you?" My mother peeked around the doorframe. Her smile grew pinched, but she nodded hello to everyone. Hopefully no one else noticed the whiteness of her knuckles as she grasped her purse like a lifeline. Flickers of nerves sprayed against me like ice.

Before I could say a word, Avery's eyes glazed. She stiffened and stared into space like she was watching a movie no one else could see. Which, I assumed, she was. The worst time for a vision ever. My mom would know what it meant. She'd seen the show before and hated it more every time.

My mother took two steps back, horror stamped on her carefully made-up face. Pure fear swamped the room with a stench like skunk road kill.

Before I could get a mental waterfall going, three words blared through my mind, carried on my mother's terror, as clear as if they'd been whispered in my ear. A first.

Unnatural.

Dangerous.

Mistake.

I ducked my head at the last word, the emotional blow

hitting like a punch to the face. My mother stammered an excuse—always some stupid excuse—and backed into the hallway, slamming the door shut. We all flinched, and Ethan took my hand. My chest ached.

Avery groaned. "I'm so sorry, I couldn't stop it."

"Well?" Deshawn asked.

"It wasn't even worth the damage. We already knew there was more than one possible future."

I tried to not snap. It wasn't their fault my mother hated me. "It's okay, Avery. Give us the deets."

"It was pretty murky. I'm pretty sure I saw Mia dancing with Josh, though, which is a positive sign. Maybe the future is tipping the right direction now."

"That's super awesome!" My lungs began working properly again. They felt expansive, even. Better to focus on what I could affect than what I could never, ever change. The Cupid plan could work. This was proof.

Avery continued, "I also saw your mother on a dance floor, laughing. She's what triggered the vision, I think. So it looks like your mom could find happiness one of these days, too. It's a potential future, anyway, if things play out right to make it happen."

"I hope so." I sighed. "We could all use a little more happiness."

"That look on her face," Ethan said, his voice almost a growl. "It's like someone gave her a diamond, but she wants to trade it for a freakin' piece of glass. What's her deal?"

I almost said, "She wishes I'd never been born." But I bit back the words. My mother wished *none* of my friends had been born. We all stuck in her craw, indigestible and irritating.

But I didn't say a word of any of it. It was one thing to suspect someone truly hated what you were. It was another to have it officially confirmed.

"I'm fine. She's an idiot. Sorry she gets so freaked sometimes."

"You're not a freak," Deshawn said softly.

Which wasn't what I'd said, but it was what my mother felt. I stared at my bedspread. The purple dots on the fabric wavered through my tears. "You've eavesdropped on my parents before, haven't you? Like you did with Mia and her aunt?"

He gave me a measuring look. "Only twice, a few months back. Just to make sure your momma wasn't getting out of hand. It's not just daddies who hit their kids."

"Anything you need to tell the rest of us?" Ethan

asked the other boy, eyes narrowed.

Deshawn pointed at him. "Look, you know I wouldn't listen in on y'all without a good reason. And I haven't. Your parents are so mushy together they might make me throw up anyway."

"Truth," Ethan acknowledged, the question in his eyes fading.

"And Avery's mom is chill. But even my parents noticed the way Mrs. Mills has been acting. My mom talked about it with your dad at work, to check. I wanted to make sure you were safe."

I gulped. They'd been that worried? And he'd checked on me. I thought I'd feel violated, but that'd be like throwing stones in a glass house, wouldn't it?

"Thanks, then," I said. Deshawn had stricter ethics than the rest of us combined. If he said he only listened in once or twice to make sure I was safe, that's all he did. Invading private spaces made him feel squeegeed. "I appreciate you watching out for me."

"That's what we do."

"Yeah, we do. And it's okay, just so you guys know. She's not violent or anything like that. She just thinks I'm a freak."

"Well, technically, we're all freaks, aren't we?" Ethan

said and paused. "But we make freaks look good." He grinned impishly and waggled his eyebrows.

I giggled. The burning sensation faded, thank goodness. If everyone's laughter sounded a little forced, at least I didn't have to feel their lies and pretend not to. Not with them.

I squared my shoulders and lifted my soda. "Here's to the freak show. Let's get this done. I'm tired of worrying about being turned into a lab project. Besides, I wouldn't look good in a white straightjacket."

"Scalp electrodes would ruin my hair, too," Avery added.

"So. One happy Mia, coming up. Josh is going to be a happy guy, too, so bonus joy."

"Well, we'll hope for the best," Avery said.

"Parker always does her best, so there's no need to hope," Ethan said firmly, sending my heartbeat wildly fluttering.

"She *is* the best," Avery corrected.

"We all get the highest of fives!" I sang, a wild surge of affection for my friends pushing away the lingering stench of my mother's fear. These three people loved me and watched out for me, no matter what. And I'd do anything to protect them. Anything.

Helping Mia find love again—at least the hope of it—could keep the bad vision from happening. It might not be a perfect or complete solution, but I felt certain now it would work. And if that happy ending needed a little help to arrive, I'd pull out every last trick in my very thorough playbook.

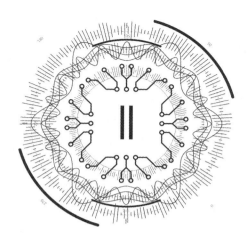

GIVEN the new intel, I doubled down on Operation Cupid the next day.

Moving Josh into class had turned history into Mia's daily gauntlet. He sat like a giant sun behind her each day, no doubt burning her back with his gaze. She fidgeted and tapped her pencil. Blips of emotion shot from her occasionally—wistfulness, confusion, hope, followed by fear, like some strange marching band song on repeat. The two of them had to get to know each other better somehow—soon. Josh looked ready and willing to treat her right if Mia would give him a chance.

This Friday, the group assignment was "Leadership in the Home: Who's in Charge?" We were supposed to ask each other about our home situations. This was probably an invasion of privacy, but since it worked to my advantage, I shot my hand high and chirped, "Mr. Bransford, Josh can work with me and Mia since there's an odd number in class, and he doesn't have a partner."

"Good idea. Thanks, Parker," replied Mr. Bransford. The dour glares from the other girls and their petty jealousy fumes amused me.

I couldn't have set it up better myself—and for once, I actually hadn't. The questions would likely bring up some pain for Mia, unfortunately, but it would also give her a chance to get to know Josh. That was key. Only trust would allow Mia to let go of her fears.

"Who is the head of your household at home?" I read the question to the two others, one grinning casually, one striving not to look up from her worksheet.

Mia remained silent. After a heartbeat, Josh answered. "I live with my mom," he said. His voice was deeper than his frame suggested.

"No father at home?" I asked. Mia snuck a quick look at him. Surely it wasn't that she was curious. I hid a snort. *Here kitty, kitty …*

"Nope. He took off years ago."

Now Mia looked directly at him. "I'm sorry."

I kept my own mouth zipped. I was fading right into

the background, yessiree. Nothing to look at over here. I slid lower in my seat.

He shrugged. "No big. What about you, Mia?"

A sudden flash of Mia's mother, her smiling face, made my throat tighten. The swift jab faded quickly for me, but I was pretty sure the pain was a needle that pierced Mia's heart daily. Some pains never went away.

Not to mention the pain from whatever that jerk Mark had done to her. The need to console burned inside me. A real friend would offer comfort about the accident, but I couldn't. For the first time, I began to understand what Deshawn meant when he said it was hard knowing things you shouldn't. The best I could do for Mia was try to cover that old, hidden pain with new, better experiences.

"I live with my aunt right now." Mia's lips pressed tight. I didn't push.

"Where'd you move from?" Josh held his pencil at the ready, but that wasn't a question on the form.

"A little town outside of Houston."

"And will you go back one of these days?" Josh pushed a little more on his own.

"I don't think I'll ever go back," she whispered and snapped her mouth closed.

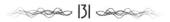 131

"Not go back home? Like, ever?" His brown eyes were intense. Their gazes met, and I felt an arc of attraction flare between them. Mia gulped and fiddled with the edge of her paper.

"Yeah, my mom passed away when I was nine, and my dad, well, he sort of dumped me here."

Josh looked indignant. "He didn't want you with him?"

"Seriously, what kind of garbage is that?" I said. My plan to stay out of their way flew right out the window. "I mean, my home's nothing to sing about either, but that's awful."

"Things are easier for him without me, I think. Anyway, I'm glad I left, even though I miss parts of home a lot." Wistfulness floated around her for a moment like a wreath of smoke, spreading to me.

"Why would you miss home if that's how things were?" Josh asked, which was good, since I couldn't speak.

Mia's mood held a powerful mix of pain, fear, and longing. The emotions carried with it the rhythmic hum of cicadas late on a summer night when the air cooled and darkness fell. The faint citrus scent of her mother's perfume wrapped around her, keeping her safe.

I shivered and came back to the present. Mia's

mother. Mia's homesickness was based on a reality that was long gone.

"Oh," Mia finally spoke. "Well. My mom was … really special. When I was at home, our house reminded me of her all the time."

"I get that," he murmured, gaze steady and soft with sympathy.

She rambled on. "But my aunt's really kind, and I like it here okay. No one back home believed I was … I mean, that my art was worth anything. I don't miss that." The words tumbled out, and her gaze flipped back and forth between me and Josh, expression guarded.

I kept my mouth glued shut. Relief bubbled up, though. Mia was already feeling more accepted here.

Josh said, "Glad to hear it. I feel the same way here. It's cool. A male dancer gets a lot of grief in some places. Being in a college town has its perks."

"You dance?" The surprise was clear in Mia's voice.

"Ballet."

"Oh. Wow." Her eyes were wide.

Ballet took a lot of strength and self-discipline. Oh, man, Mia didn't stand a chance against this guy. I had to hide a smirk behind my hand.

"So. Mia. Got a date to the Halloween dance?" Josh

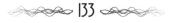 133

asked. "I hear it's a big deal. Costumes and all that. Sounds pretty cool."

My ears perked, and I began shuffling papers in my folder, to give them the bit of privacy I could. I wanted to do a little dance. Josh was already working his magic. I snapped my psychic attention to Mia without turning my head, honing in as deeply as I could. Avery's vision could change as soon as today. *Say yes, say yes, say yes.*

Mia's spine stiffened, and a dozen feelings flickered from her. They were all as insubstantial as ghosts. Pleasure, pain, pride, panic ... like some children's show teaching emotions via the letter P.

Mia set down her pencil. "What?"

"I said, do you have a date to the dance?"

"I'm not going. I don't dance."

He tapped his pencil twice on the desk. "Too bad. I think you'd be good at it."

The bell rang. He slid out of his seat, gave us both a wry salute, and strode out of the room.

"Hoo boy!" I crowed, giggling at the dumbfounded expression on Mia's face. "Girl, if I were you, no way would I let that one slip by!"

Mia blew out a hard breath. The edges of her papers ruffled, and she slapped her hand down on them with perhaps a wee bit too much force.

"A guy like that is bad, bad news."

"Are you kidding me? What on earth do you want? A supermodel who gives all his money to orphans? Did you hear him? Ballet. He's better than chocolate! Better than *Belgian* chocolate."

"Too much chocolate gives you diabetes." Mia flounced out of the room, cramming her papers into her bag as she went.

"Methinks the girl doth protest too much," I murmured.

The situation was serious, but this was too much intrigue to not enjoy. Mia needed fun anyway, not a bunch of tears and self-pity. That Mark guy was an anchor dragging the girl down, tied to her by some moldy, tangled rope. Time to cut the rope.

And Josh was the knife.

Josh versus Mia ... I was putting my bets on Josh. And when it came to setting up couples, I could play the odds as good as any bookie.

On the way out of school at the end of the very long week—TGIF had never been truer—I was ready to get home and scheme up some more Josh-Mia run-ins. Something for the weekend, maybe …

Dr. O'Malley came around the corner, not a hint of emotion preceding her, of course. The clack of her heels echoed in the empty hall.

"Hello, Parker. Running late?"

"You know me, Dr. O. Always got something going on." I tried to breeze past the older woman, but the counselor put a hand on my shoulder. I froze.

Boa constrictor. Boa constrictor.

"You do know, I hope, that if there's anything you ever need to share, I'm here for you as well as for any other student, such as Mia. Or your other friends. Avery. Ethan. Deshawn. I think you have a lot to offer each other, but sometimes you need an adult to help with complicated issues. And that's exactly what my job is: to be there for students like you."

The words raised my hackles. "I'm fine, ma'am. But thank you." Time for the dimples. Charm. Smile. I twirled my hair to play dumb, an easy trick more useful than it should be.

"Well, I've noticed you seem to have taken it upon yourself to help Mia settle in, which is very kind of you. But some problems are too big for students. No matter how *special* they may be. Do you understand?"

Coldness trickled down my spine. Did I understand? I surely hoped not. Because it sounded like Dr. O had some idea about what I could do. What we all could do.

"But of course, if any student could help Mia feel at home here, I'm sure you could."

A split-second flare of emotion made me blink like a camera flash in the darkness. Smug. The hint of obsession remained, buried beneath it. And her smile … I wouldn't be surprised to see canary feathers plastered all over the counselor's face.

My knees went weak, but I summoned a wide smile. "Thanks for thinking of me, Dr. O'Malley, but we're all just fine." Alarms shrieked in my mind, but I forced myself to walk a slow measured pace until I hit the sidewalk. Then I raced home.

12

I needed to tell my dad right away what Dr. O'Malley had said, but my mother was already in the kitchen with him.

No matter how great things ever were at school, home was always a swift kick to the teeth. I could make my friends and even enemies happy at school by pulling this string or that, but I'd long-ago resigned myself to living in the dark cave of my mother's unfixable regret. Staying quiet seemed to be my only option to keep things from getting even worse.

Tonight, critical information burned inside me, but I silently sat at the kitchen table with my textbook open as if it actually mattered. Meanwhile, my mother stared into the refrigerator mournfully.

"We should just go out tonight. Do you remember that tiny little hole in the wall you used to take me to in Manhattan?" Mom pushed around a few half-empty jars of pickles and olives. "It was Thai, right? No, wait. Korean. Too bad we don't have any good places like that here."

My dad's irritation shimmered briefly before he pushed it down.

I gripped the bridge of my nose. I didn't have the patience for this tonight. Not after Dr. O's weird comment. Maybe I could get Dad to come to my room ...

"Maybe we can find a place here you'd like just as much," he said.

My mother drank deeply from a glass of wine and scoffed, "If wishes were fishes, Tom, we'd be living in New York City."

"I think that goes 'we'd walk on the sea.'"

"Oh, that's right. You always know the right answer."

"I never said I knew more than—"

My mother's voice rose. "I know what you think about me—what all your professor friends think—"

Cringing, I slapped my hands against my ears, wishing I could push away all the horrible feelings. The bitterness. The shame. It made me gag. Literally—I gagged, loud, right there at the table. So gross.

"Stop it!" Dad yelled. "You're hurting Parker!" He slammed his hand against the table, something he'd never done before.

I jumped in my seat. He wasn't helping. Rage blossomed from my mother in response, bleeding like a severed artery. It poured all over me, turning my vision red. My strongest waterfall wasn't enough to push it away.

I locked my jaw against a scream and bowed my head. Why couldn't my mom change? Be happy for once, at least for a few moments? But she wasn't cooperating, and the worst wasn't over yet.

Mom glared, turning her pretty face into a distorted monster mask. "*Parker, Parker, Parker!* It's always about her feelings! What about my feelings, Tom? My talents? My dreams? You never nurtured any of those."

"I can't believe you're acting this way—"

"Oh no, you couldn't bother supporting me. You were too busy protecting her, and I just can't—" Her voice broke.

I looked up in alarm, concerned for her even now. Instinctively, I peeked with my gift, like checking for a pulse.

The disgust and hate on my mother's face was a slap to my own. And with my gift on full seek mode, the toxic emotions struck me full in the heart, an arrow tipped with poison, sending a pulse of pain through every fiber of my being.

Something inside me snapped.

My chair clattered against the tile floor as I leapt to my feet, fists clenched. I screamed, *"Stop it."*

Two words. That was all I shouted. But inside, I was completely focused on my mom, wishing with all of my soul: *Be happy! Don't feel this way anymore.*

My empathy exploded from me like a sonic boom, leaving me shaking on my feet. My gift wasn't seeking information now. It was delivering a message, a command to change.

The emotion blew out from me and poured into my mother's heart. The ragged pain from suspicion, heartbreak, and disappointment ... It was wiped away in an instant, like a sand drawing erased by a wave. All that remained was peace. For me, it felt like letting out a breath I'd been holding too long, leaving me hollow inside, but in a good way.

Mom stopped speaking, mid-word. Her jaw snapped shut. She blinked twice at the open refrigerator and then smiled at me. "What was I saying? What would you like for dinner tonight? I feel like we need some music here."

She reached over the sink and turned on our old radio, ignoring the dust on the buttons, and began shaking her hips to the beat. She pulled out some wrinkled zucchini from the fridge, tossing them on the rarely used cutting board.

I stared, my stomach twisting. My dad stood frozen, too, jaw dropped.

Omigod, omigod, omigod.

Had I really pushed emotions into my mother? Controlled her feelings? What did that mean? I hadn't even known that was possible.

Then again, why not? Empathy that allowed me to truly see someone's secret feelings was also supposed to be impossible. And there was no denying something big had just happened.

Joy and happiness sparkled inside of my mother now. I could see it from here. The new feelings had pushed out the resentment and darkness that had lived there for so long—nearly fourteen years was my guess.

The sudden absence of her unhappiness tasted like peach pie, literally. Sweet contentment floated in the air now, with a delicious hint of cinnamon.

"These veggies look pathetic," Mom announced. "Let's go out to dinner! I'll get on my party dress." She waltzed out of the room.

Dad turned slowly, as if he might break. "Did you do that, Parker?"

"Uh. I don't know? I was wishing for her to stop being so mean—"

He blew out a long breath. "If you did this, if this is a new aspect of your gift ..." He rubbed his forehead. "I've wondered if this might happen one day. Honey, you've got to be careful. If you start changing people, if that's actually what happened, there could be serious, unintended consequences. Dangerous ones."

"But how can you say that? She's so much happier now! Just look at her. Listen to her! She's finally happy. You'll be happy now. We all can be!"

"For now. She's happy ... now. But we don't know how long that'll last, or how much she'll remember with such a sudden change."

My mother began singing as she came closer to the kitchen. Dad swallowed hard. "How do you think she'll feel if she realizes you manipulated her mood? Given how scared she is of your gift as it is?"

"I—I don't even know how I did it anyway. I might

not be able to do it again even if I wanted to."

But boy, did I want to. The thought hit me like a thunderbolt: Mia wouldn't be unhappy anymore, not if I could help it. This was the solution I'd been waiting for.

Dad knelt by me and whispered, "I hope you can't. You could be caught so easily if you go around doing this. There are scientists—real, actual scientists, not flakes—who write about stuff like this, Parker. Paranormal psychology. Avery's mother and I have talked about it. People who work *here*, looking for real examples of what they believe is theoretically possible, a science fiction-level reality. Projection is what it's called, to push feelings into others. It's like giving people drugs, Parker, altering their mind without their permission. It's not right, even if you get away with it. You can't turn a caterpillar into a butterfly overnight. It's not natural. Can you see that?"

"Yes." The word came out like a question.

I mean, wouldn't a caterpillar be happy to skip the whole dissolving-in-the-chrysalis step and go straight to the butterfly? How was it any different than my father talking sense into a client or a doctor prescribing an antidepressant? Except it was faster and cheaper, of course.

And more powerful. More effective.

"I'm serious, Parker."

"I know. And I've never done anything like it before, I promise."

Although … was this projection-thing so different than what I did already? For years, I'd improved lives with a whole host of shortcuts to happiness. I bent over backward, made arrangements, built connections, created gossip, sought out hidden strengths, and used every possible option to make things better. This was just one more tool in my collection of techniques—one that could seriously boost my results. Granted, it was risky, like Dad said. Dangerously powerful. I could think of it like a nuclear weapon, maybe. For critical moments only.

His eyes were dark. "I'm glad to hear it. You must never, ever do that again, Parker. It's not fair to anyone."

Guilt burned as I nodded. He didn't understand, though. Avery's vision couldn't be altered without my specific involvement. I'd told him about the vision, but he hadn't seen Avery's expression. This wasn't business as usual. So, a compromise: I'd never use it again … once the dance was done, and my friends were safe.

But until then, I had to figure out if this was a one-time deal or something I could master. And if it was a new part of my gift, I definitely had to practice and get more subtle. If my dad knew right away that something odd had happened, someone else would be able to figure it out, too.

Dr. O sprang to mind, her eyes following me like a cat's. With all the unexpected drama, I'd nearly forgotten.

"Dad? Dr. O said something strange to me today. Like, stranger than usual."

"Oh?"

"She hinted that I might be out of my league helping Mia. But it also sounded like she was encouraging me to make Mia happy. She even used the word 'special' to describe me, in this way that gave me shivers. I mostly can't feel her mood at all, but I sensed this weird sort of obsession last week. And today I got a flash of smug self-righteousness. Her smile was like she knew something I didn't, you know? It made me feel gross. And scared."

"Scared?"

I ransacked my mind for the proper emotion. "Anxious. Uncomfortable. I wanted to run. Like she might know my secret, even though that's impossible."

He straightened in his seat. "This is the new counselor at the school?"

"That's the one. And actually, now that I think about it … There was this moment a couple weeks ago when I really wanted her to do something, and she wasn't going to. I felt dizzy and drained, and then she agreed. Maybe that was my gift, making her agree."

Fear filled his face before he composed himself. "You were lucky that you didn't do to her what you just did to your mom. People would have noticed. I'll look into her. Maybe one of my colleagues knows her. If she's got even a inkling of an idea about you, Parker, it's imperative you don't let your gift slip around her, at all. Don't even wish hard for things you could affect. No one can find out about you, especially with this new level to your ability. It changes its value exponentially, from an X-ray machine to a weapon."

I said, "I'm more of a peacekeeper, Dad. Don't worry."

"Not everyone is. That's what scares me."

I knew that every Saturday morning around nine, Ethan checked the mail after his morning run. I timed my mail check accordingly. Always easier to ask a favor in person. Dimples didn't carry across phones nearly as well.

"Hey, Ethan." I smiled, thankful the mail room was empty. "Got a minute?"

"For you, Parkour? I've got all day." He winked.

The boy flirted with everyone. Plenty flirted back, too, thanks to that messy black hair, golden skin, and the most jewel-like hazel eyes I'd ever seen. Today he wore a tattered Rush shirt that was nicely fitted. Very nicely. Luckily, he was telekinetic, not telepathic.

"I need a tutor," I told him. I watched his fingers deftly spin his mail combination and grab the waiting stack of mail, even though he could have done it all with the power of his mind alone.

Slamming the little door shut, he rubbed his hands together. "This gets better and better. How much do I get paid?"

I slapped his arm. "I'm serious. A strange thing happened."

He raised one eyebrow.

This couldn't wait, and there were no code words for this. I pulled him around the corner to the stairwell that ran along his side of the building. I whispered, "I changed my mom's feelings yesterday. Like, mid-stride, she went from furious to happy."

His gaze darkened, flitting across my face. "That's new."

"New as in, never dreamed it was possible kind of new, yeah. Freaked my dad out, but I can't help thinking …

If I can do it again, I can make Mia happy, right? Stop the bad vision in its tracks."

A faint flush touched his cheeks. "Can you affect everyone's emotions?"

"That's the question, isn't it? My mom, well, my mom has no shields to speak of, and I was feeling, um, some really strong emotions myself."

"I'll bet," he murmured.

I pressed on. "But you have the best shields of any of us, so I figured if I could affect you, I could definitely work on Mia. I don't want to risk it on her first and get caught—it was too obvious with my mom. But later on, she didn't seem to remember it at all. This morning, she was back to her usual complaining self. I didn't fix her again. My dad told me not to."

"Is he on board with you using it on me? For the sake of the team?"

Wincing, I said, "I don't think he understands the severity of Avery's vision. Also Dr. O was really weird yesterday, and he's scared about what she might be up to."

"The counselor? Dang, I knew she was weird. She watches me way too close."

"She knows you like to break the rules."

He flashed a grin but shook his head. "I think it's

more than that. Deshawn says she's been on the phone a lot, but it didn't seem like she was talking about school stuff."

I frowned. "Maybe I can do something about her, too, if I get this new thing down."

"In the meantime, you need someone to practice on, I take it?" He widened his eyes like he was afraid.

I laughed. "I get that it's creepy to make someone feel something they don't. Like you making Avery wave her hand. I swear I'm not interested in making anyone into a love slave—"

"Aw, that's too bad."

I rolled my eyes. "But I've been working hard to get to know Mia, and so far, I'm sucking wind."

He snorted. "As if. Everyone likes you. You know her history's rough. It's not about you. Why don't you relax?"

My heart did a little jig right there in my chest. Everyone liked me. Did he mean he *liked* me?

I cleared my throat. "Well, she and Josh are stalled out for reasons that defy understanding, but if I could change her feelings, it would put the ball in our court finally."

"I can't believe you don't have her wrapped around your little finger yet." He quirked the smile that always

made my heart thump.

I jokingly tossed my hair, feigning coolness. We'd been babies together, but I'd had a serious crush on him since fifth grade. With his shielding, he was super restful company. And man, it felt good to be around someone so fun, someone with zero guilt about being psychic. He was a walking, talking glass of sweet tea in a blazing Texas summer.

"You know how it is. Lovey-dovies are my favorite thing."

"You're the biggest romantic I've ever met."

"That a problem?"

"Not for me."

We stared at each other, silent. This was the perfect moment. In the movies, he'd lean over and kiss me, tell me that he was a romantic at heart, too, and ask me to the dance. Crisis of souls and fighting parents did not erase the very real excitement of attending the biggest party of the year.

Ask me to the dance. Ask me to the dance ... Ask me.

"Fine. I can help you," he said. "Dinner, my place. Tonight." His voice seemed lower than usual.

"Still doing Saturday night pizza?"

"Always. Six o'clock. We can work from my room

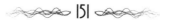

without any interruptions." He kindly didn't mention my parental units. He added, without smiling, "We'll have the whole evening after dinner, alone together."

Alone together.

He didn't ask me to the dance, but he'd asked me over. Alone. "I'll be there."

I'd better get my own emotions in order before arrival. Or else things could get messy.

13

filled Avery in on the new situation before heading over to Ethan's. All Avery could say was, "Wow. You're sure you did that?"

"Assuredly."

"Well, take it easy, Parks. Like your dad said, that's pretty major stuff."

It was pretty major ... especially if I could do it again.

My steps grew lighter as I ran up the stairs to Ethan's. Mrs. Kwon opened the door, brushing her red curls off her forehead. Her hazel eyes lit up—Ethan's were the exact same color—and she offered a hug. "It's good to see you, sweetheart!"

I held her tightly, taking in her scent of jasmine perfume. Mrs. Kwon would never think her son was a mistake.

"Come on in! Where have you been that you couldn't spend Saturday nights with us? We've all missed you!"

Was that a special emphasis on the word *all?*

"Summer just got away from me, I guess, and school's been so busy. Sorry, Mrs. Kwon."

Ethan walked up. "Ready to buff up your weaksauce gift?"

I stuck my tongue out at him.

"You kids be careful, now. Emotions can be tricky, yes?" His mother's smile was as mischievous as her son's, as was the sparkle in her eyes. A knowing delight radiated from her—she was pleased with this match for her son, which was flattering, if a bit premature.

I gave a meaningful glance at Ethan and rolled my eyes. "Emotions are definitely wild cards."

He snapped his teeth at me, forcing warmth over my face. His mother chuckled and patted my cheek before walking off.

"Thanks for embarrassing me in front of your mom."

"You've got to be used to it by now."

I had to smile in response to his grin. That smile combined with his permanently tousled hair gave him a rakish appearance, a ridiculously good look on him. No doubt dozens of other girls had already told him so, I reminded myself.

We gulped down a couple of slices of pizza while chatting with Ethan's parents.

"How's school, Parker?" asked Mr. Kwon.

"Full of adventures. How are your classes going this semester?"

He grinned. "The freshmen are moaning about how hard my classes are already."

Ethan laughed. "Economics is cutthroat. They might as well get used to it now." Like father, like son, in so many ways.

Mid-meal, Mrs. Kwon asked, "So, Parker, is your mother doing better these days?"

I nearly choked on a pepperoni. "Uh, she's okay?" I bet I was redder than the pizza sauce.

Mrs. Kwon patted my hand. "Your mother never did know what to do with a gifted child, but I'm hopeful she can learn to relax into it, like your father."

The comment made my shoulders tense. I glanced at Ethan—had he told what I'd done to my mom? He gave a subtle shake of his head, and I let out a slow breath of relief. Ethan thankfully directed the conversation elsewhere.

In the meantime, his parents' steadfast love flowed around me, a balm to my heart. Their affection and concern was a rose-colored mist curling around everything in the room.

A heavy knot in my belly faded. Parents who both adored their kid. Living in peace. How nice would that be? And it was within my grasp now.

Ethan closed the door to his bedroom. The bed was still covered by the faded red bedspread he'd had since second grade. Band posters hung next to the window. An old photo of the two of us still clung to his crowded bulletin board. The sight of it pinched my heart.

"You know your parents are worried about us, right?" I asked.

"Don't need to be an empath to see that. They want to have a parent powwow soon, I hear. But I have total confidence you're going to save the day. Especially with this new thing you've got."

"I'm glad one of us is sure." We sat cross-legged on the bed, facing each other. The twin mattress sagged, tipping us toward each other. He smelled of his favorite cinnamon gum. "Okay, break it down for me. How am I going to do this?"

"Tell me more about what happened. Details."

"I just did it last night—I was so … upset …" I stared at the back of my hands and doggedly continued. "All I could think of was how much I wanted my mom to stop fighting, to be happy, and suddenly, she was. It was like her brain got replaced with someone else's."

"Wild."

"Yeah. My dad was *not* happy about it."

"Huh. His wife's finally stopped griping, and now he's got a problem with it?"

"*Right?* That's what I said."

"Parents are weird." He shrugged.

"Truth. The thing is, my mom has no shields, right? Zippo. But Mia's got some kind of natural block going on, so I might not be able to send emotions into her at all, even if I figure out how I did it."

"So let's try it. You know what my shield feels like. I'll make it thinner, let you in a bit. Still there, but more like a plain brain's block. You try to send me an emotion, and if I keep out your sending, you try to make me feel it anyway. No peeking inside, though, deal?"

"Who, me? I don't snoop."

He snorted. "Yeah right."

"Not on y'all, I don't. I've never even tried to X-ray you." And I hadn't. I'd only thought about it. His shields were like a steel wall anyway.

"Okay then. Let's do this."

Ooh, the temptation. Make Ethan feel something? Like, oh, maybe make him want to ask me to the dance? Or even … kiss me? I'd kissed someone before and hadn't been impressed, but I had a feeling kissing Ethan would be different.

But no. There were ethics, and a girl had her pride. I only wanted to go with someone who wanted to take me to the dance, and double that for kissing me. I could make him feel super peaceful, maybe, like I did with my mom. Happy, peaceful, singing with delight. That seemed harmless and was the same thing I'd need to do with Mia.

He closed his eyes. Dark lashes swept over cheekbones that were too chiseled for my comfort. I closed my eyes, too, and imagined radiating peace. I tugged on the peace and sent it his way, like a puff of steam surrounding him. One happy hippie, coming up.

I focused as hard as I could. *Waves of gentle peace. Contentedness.*

I cracked an eyelid. He sat stoically, not even a small smile. "Feeling anything?"

"Nada."

I sighed and tried again. Minutes passed, but nothing changed.

"Don't tell me you're actually trying to infiltrate my emotions right now. Because, Parkour, that's pathetic. Come on now."

"I'm trying," I muttered through gritted teeth. I wiped my palms on my jeans. It would help if he didn't smell so good. We should've met at the library.

He took my hands, and my breath tangled in my chest. I hated myself for freezing like a newbie onstage. This was just Ethan, my friend since forever.

"You need to relax, not work so hard. You've got this."

His palms were warm, ever-so-lightly callused from his drumming. I'd held those hands many times before, but in recent months, he'd been too busy holding drumsticks or other girls' hands. His touch felt both familiar and different. Full of new possibilities.

Staring at his closed eyes, I imagined us together, how we could be as a couple. I sighed. He was smart, kind, and funny. And he knew me better than anyone but Avery.

A player, though. He dated lots of girls, never sticking with one for long. If Ethan and I dated and had a bad breakup, I wouldn't just lose a boyfriend. I'd lose a second family.

But seeing him like this—so solemn, so helpful, so mature ... It was like the world had tilted. I couldn't help wondering. What would it be like to lean forward and press my lips against his?

My heart rate spiked and a shot of emotion raced through me, clear to my fingertips, which were still touching Ethan.

He gasped, and his eyes flew open. "How did you do that?"

I yanked my hands out of his. "What did I do?" My voice squeaked.

"I felt a shock, almost a physical shock, and it was like ..." He stopped and licked his lips.

I raised my eyebrows and waited. Ethan wasn't usually short on words.

"Like ..." He tried again and failed. He shook his head. "Have you ever woken up one morning, tired and grumpy, and then realized, oh yeah, it's Christmas morning! And there are gifts under the tree for me!"

"Uh, no, doofus. I always remember when I'm gonna get gifts."

He laughed but ran his fingers through his hair in agitation. "Gotcha, but Parker, for real, have you ever felt that? That unexpected happiness?"

I hesitantly nodded. That was exactly what I'd felt a moment ago.

"It was like that. An average day shot through with a sudden burst of possibility. Thrill. Excitement, you know? I knew it wasn't coming from me, so you'll have to work on that—you were way too obvious. Even a plain brain might figure it out, but hey, you did it! You *did* it!" He rubbed his head. "But once you pulled away, it didn't stick around like it did for your mom. And it gave me a headache. I wonder why? Do you have one?"

Stunned, I shook my head.

"Hmm. I think you'd better not use this on anyone else until we tweak this better, but it's a great first step! Way to go!" He gave me a slow round of applause.

I wanted to feel excited, but discomfort flooded me. I'd somehow blurted out my real feelings for him after all. He just didn't know it yet. *Dear God ... Don't let him figure it out ... please please please.*

"What were you thinking about?" He leaned forward, looking at me like I was a puzzle to solve.

Of course, he'd ask that now. I slid off the bed and wandered near the window. "Oh, you know. How awesome it was to see, uh, my mom so happy. The possibilities, you know?"

Was it my imagination, or did he look a little disappointed? As if he'd wanted to hear I'd been thinking about … him? It wasn't that far-fetched, I told myself. What guy didn't want to be the subject of a girl's dreamy hopes? Even a girl who was just a friend.

Excitement spun up in me like a motor revving. Best friends could become something more, right? It happened all the time in the movies. He didn't seem to care that Sophie couldn't go to the dance.

An idea jumped into my mind, fully formed, and the words popped out before I could stop them. "I had a thought just now."

He looked at me quizzically. "I'm all ears."

I sat back down. *Breathe,* I reminded myself. I could do this without spilling all my guts. Casual-like. I was a master at matchmaking—why not try a match for myself? Just dipping one toe in, not jumping full body into a potential boiling lake of humiliation. I could act like it was just for fun. It would be fun.

"You said Sophie told you no about the dance, and I don't have anyone else I'm planning on going with. I was thinking we should go together."

Hope fluttered in my chest. We could wear adorable

matching outfits. Little Red Riding Hood and the Big Bad Wolf would be fantastic.

"Oh. I'm sorry, Parker," he said, voice totally serious.

My heart stopped. Each individual cell in my body seemed to clench.

"The DJ for the dance just invited the band to play a couple of sets. He saw our last show and thought it'd be cool to have kids from the school perform, too—to spice things up for Halloween. I thought you knew. I figured I'd just go stag. I can't really *go* to the dance if I'm performing at it, you know?" He smiled, but only one side of his lips lifted.

Flames of humiliation seared through my blood. It took a minute to gather enough breath to speak. He'd told me no. He'd done it nicely, but the fact was he'd turned me down.

"Okay, sure, no problem, I get it, and I'm sure you'll do great and—" I babbled.

He was rambling, too. "Hey, I mean, I'm glad you asked and if I—"

"It's no big deal," I kept on, hating myself for my run-away mouth. "I can ask someone else. John Stadin, maybe, or Nick Diaz. No big deal."

I did have a list of guys I knew would go with me—

one of the benefits of being a psychic empath in middle school—but I had no intention of asking any of them. If I couldn't go with Ethan, I'd just go alone, but no way would I admit that to him.

Ethan blinked. "Well, I'm sure you have a long list to go through, and we should probably call it a night. Been a long day." He stood abruptly and stretched.

I cocked my head, heart hammering. "But I still need to practice more. Today."

"You sure?" His words were strangely clipped.

He was the one who turned me down for the dance, for crying out loud. And he'd already asked someone else before that. "Of course."

"Okay, then. Let's get to work." Sitting back down, he reached for my hands again. This time, his grip was loose and cool.

I wished more than ever I could take an X-ray of what the heck was going on in his heart. Why did he have to be so confusing compared to every other human in the world?

New determination filled my bones. I was going to master my gift, push it to all it could do. Then I could work on making my own life even better, with or without Ethan holding my hand along the way. But first, I had to fix Mia's life so the rest of my friends could live theirs in peace.

I bent my will toward him, ignoring a twinge of discomfort. Practice made perfect.

AFTER my success with Ethan on Saturday, I'd done a little further testing, incognito-like. I spent Sunday wandering the halls of my apartment complex with my gift set on high. Negative emotions stained the air like heat spots seen through infrared goggles. This time, I tried to make them go away.

Small things. Easy items, hard to catch if anyone felt anything. I sent away a bad dream from a toddler about to wake screaming in his stroller. I skirted by the laundry room and turned an older girl's secret weep-fest into a dance party with concentrated effort.

By the time the school week rolled around, I was ready to expand my test subjects to trickier, longer-term problems. My dad would be so upset if he knew my plan, but it wasn't like I was using my gift to benefit myself. This was all to help others. That was like the complete opposite of selfish. The fact that it had made my day feel better too was simply frosting on a very generous and unselfish cupcake given to others before they even asked.

But I didn't mention it to the rest of the Fab Four. I'd tell them later, once I had clear results.

Arriving at school that Monday, I felt like I was walking in six-inch heels for the first time. Pride and delight warred with a hope that I wouldn't fall and break my face. The first bell rang, but I didn't cringe at the onslaught of emotions. This time, I flipped through them like a card shark in search of a hidden ace. And found it.

Darla Sutters. She held a note in her hand, trembling. The silent scream from her horror echoed in my brain, dragging along the nose-burning scent of ammonia. Today was also progress report day. Since I had science class with Darla and had watched her flirt with Aaron Turner all month instead of paying attention, the issue here seemed pretty clear. Perfect.

I strolled over. "What's up, Darla?"

"My parents are going to kill me, that's what."

"Seems pretty extreme."

"I got called into the counselor's office this morning

first thing. I'm failing two classes, Parker. *Two.* Science and math."

"By a lot?"

"In math, not too bad. But science? I forgot that stupid periodic element project, and now I'm toast unless I crush the next test. I hate Ms. Conway's class. She's so hard. I don't think I can do it."

"Ah." Normally, I'd try to find Darla a study buddy who also needed help. If that wasn't enough, I might help her talk to the teacher and see if any make-up work could be arranged.

But now? I focused and sent a wave of energy toward Darla, curling like mist and sinking into her. Compared to working on Ethan, this was easier than throwing my hair into a messy ponytail. Darla had no shields at all.

Confidence. Surety. Self-respect. I sent the positive feelings so far into her that they pushed the fear and anxiety right out. There was only so much room in one heart, and I made sure Darla's was stuffed to the brim with happy juice.

Darla's eyes brightened, and her frown faded. Her shoulders lifted back. She took a deep breath and broke into a smile. Then as she stared at the note, she laughed. *Laughed.*

"I don't know why this had me stressed," Darla said. "I can deal with that test. No prob. I can boost my grades before report cards are out. I feel so … ready!" She sounded like she belonged in front of a podium of a self-esteem workshop. "Thanks, Parker, for listening. You've been a big help."

It was hard for me to keep my victorious smile discreet, even with my prime acting skills. I patted Darla on the shoulder, making sure to send a final oomph of happiness. Then I coasted down the hall, feeling light enough to fly.

That. Was. Amazing.

Mia stood at her locker, fumbling with the lock. She'd conveniently been assigned one directly across from mine, another bonus of being an office aide. I paused and pondered. Was it time? Was I ready? Maybe. Maybe not. Better safe than sorry. I tucked away my projection and called over, "Hey Mia! I missed you this weekend. Did you have a good one?"

"Could've been better." Mia shrugged.

"Oh?"

"My art project isn't turning out like I wanted."

I was severely tempted to push confidence in the girl at that very moment. *Patience*, I told myself. "I'm sorry to hear that."

Mia crossed the hall. "It happens. All I can do is keep at it." Her lips tightened. "And I will. What about you? I saw tryouts for the talent show are this week. Are you doing anything for it?"

"Wouldn't miss it. I've got a killer monologue planned. I'm going to be Electra, and it's going to be awesome."

From the neighboring locker, Kayla leaned over, saying, "You're so brave to get up there, Parker."

"You want to try out?" I asked, turning on my X-ray machine. Wistfulness, fear and something else—was that uncertainty? Laced with embarrassment.

Kayla giggled nervously. "Oh, well. Yeah, but I can't. I mean, I like to sing, but I'm not good at it." Her tawny skin blotched with a flush.

Mia said, "I wouldn't want to be on stage either."

I snorted in disbelief.

"We're not all actors, you know." Mia shook her finger at me.

"Harumph," I said. "What's there to be afraid of?"

"Total lifelong humiliation?" Kayla said. Mia nodded emphatically.

It was too hard to resist such easy pickings. "Okay then. Kayla, if you could sing anything, what would it be?"

I sent the new part of my gift soaring, pouring confidence into Kayla by the scoopful. The poor girl deserved a shining moment of glory.

Kayla said, "I want to sing 'I Dreamed a Dream' from *Les Mis*. Really belt it out!"

"Then go for it," I told her—and commanded Kayla's heart. *Take risks. Sing your heart out.* Boldness flooded the girl at my insistence.

"You know what? You're right. I should just do it!" Kayla whooped and ran to the sign-up clipboard hanging on the wall. She scribbled her name on it and then grinned broadly. "Ooh, that felt great!"

Mia watched with raised brows but seemed amused as we all headed down the hall to class. It took me a moment to realize that Mia was talking to Kayla on her own. Talking, like a friend. I smiled.

That was progress. Not the kind of kick-butt progress we needed with a little less than two weeks to go now, but still. If Mia was opening up a little, it would make my next step in the plan easier. Easier, but not easy.

Kayla's goal was simple, with a straightforward solution. Mia was complicated. She was a whole step up, like boss level to Kayla's intro level. I would need a lot more practice to master my gift before trying to fix Mia.

I focused every day, tweaking that person, shuffling another in a different direction. Stopping fights, boosting happiness. I kind of forgot to feel bad about disobeying my father. I might have even begun walking with a slight strut. Not that I'm proud, but I'm being honest.

At Ethan's house on Tuesday, for the fourth night in a row, I'd made excellent progress. We'd thankfully eased past the awkward dance discussion and were closer than ever. Admittedly, manipulating the feelings of one of my oldest friends—that was kind of gross. But it was for a good cause, and I only helped him relax and feel carefree. Well, more carefree than usual.

After my projection sessions, he often got a headache, probably from his shields resisting my influence. But my power was definitely growing. He stayed goofily happy for at least an hour tonight after I'd let go of his hands. I regretted losing the excuse to touch him.

He lay stretched back on his bed, one arm thrown over his eyes. "Think you're ready to use it on Mia now?"

"Soon, yeah. If she won't go to the dance with Josh once I flood her with carefree joy, it's just a lost cause."

He opened one eye, peering up from under his arm.

Clearing his throat, he said, "Did you ever end up asking someone else to the dance? John or Nick or whoever?"

His breathing remained easy.

My own chest felt constricted, but I flashed a casual smile. "I decided it's best if I go without a date. If it all goes downhill, I need to be free to work without making excuses to some plain brain about why I'm distracted."

He smiled briefly. "Makes sense" was all he said and then let his arm flop across his whole face again.

Of course, Ethan would be a perfectly safe date. No lies required. The best date. But he'd be performing and really, how could I begrudge him that? I could see how much joy drumming brought him, not with my gift, but from the way his face lit up when he played.

He lifted one hand, and his phone floated to him.

I sighed. "Don't you worry you'll do that by mistake some time? Out of habit?"

"Don't you ever worry you'll let someone's secret feelings slip?"

"I'm not that dumb."

"Are you calling me dumb?" He sat up, eyes twinkling, but there was a hardness there that was new.

"Uh, n-n-no. Of course not. But out of all of us, you've snuck your gift more than anyone, like when you pull my

chair out for me or make my necklace jiggle."

He waved his hand in dismissal. "People only see what they believe is possible. Don't worry. It's not like I'm going to send a car flying across the sky."

I giggled at the image. "Could you, though? Can you lift something that big?"

He frowned. "I don't know. I've never tried to lift anything that heavy."

"You should try!"

His eyebrows shot up. "What, you're encouraging me to push my gift?"

"Working on this part of my gift has been incredible, Ethan. And I'm realizing I've never actually encouraged you in yours. You could do so much, and we have no idea. Same thing with Deshawn. How far away can he hear? What are his limits? We've tried so hard to hide our abilities that we've never really celebrated them."

"Speak for yourself," he said and gave a smirk. "You're actually not the only one who's been practicing."

He flicked a single finger at me.

A lightness filled me, and the bed seemed to shift. "Whoa! What are you doing?"

He grinned, winked, and slowly raised his hand. "Rise!" he intoned dramatically.

I rose off the mattress. My hands scrambled to find purchase on the bedspread, but I was still rising. *Unbelievable.* My jaw dropped, and he burst into laughter.

"Ethan!" I yelped.

"Trust me, Parkour?"

I couldn't speak but managed to nod. His eyes narrowed, and I rose further, an inch at a time, until I floated about a foot above the mattress. My bones felt hollow, like a bird's. Nothing supported me but Ethan's gift. Who knew how it worked, but who freaking cared?

"Oh my gosh! Ethan!" I squealed. "This is amazing!"

He dropped his hand with a flourish. I lowered back to the mattress until the soft comforter touched my fingers.

He let out a gusty sigh. "It's hard to do. That's as far as I've ever lifted a big item—"

"You calling me big?"

He snorted. "Please. I've seen bigger mice. But it's not the same as flipping drum sticks, you know?"

I could feel my beaming smile practically splitting my face in half, but I didn't even care if I looked like a lovestruck puppy. Not after that. "It's awesome. Really."

"Thanks. So. Dateless to the big dance. I never thought I'd see the day when the Parkster goes to a party stag."

"I'll still have a killer costume. Just you wait."

"I'll be waiting. Don't worry." He gave his flirty smile.

I actually hadn't seen him using it on anyone else lately. A different kind of bubbly lightness filled me now, and I felt like I could float all on my own.

I imprinted that sensation onto my brain, hoping to remember it forever. It was exactly the kind of positive emotion that could turn the tide for Mia. The rush of a crush would stage a coup in her brain and hijack her heart at least for a little while. We had eleven days left until the big dance. It was time to focus on the big game now.

15

AT lunch the next day, I sat with the rest of the Fab Four. For once, I was glad Mia was busy during lunch again.

Looking around first, Deshawn said, "I've been listening in on Dr. O, like you asked, Mood Ring. I don't have much dirt on her, but I can tell you she's been watching you like a hawk."

I shuddered. "How? Is she talking about me?"

"It's not what she says. It's what she doesn't say."

Ethan pointed his spoon at him. "Explain."

"She's on the phone a lot, so I'm only hearing her half of the conversation. But today she was talking about students who might need 'intervention,' wanting to see some kind of records from their health history. She

described someone who seemed a lot like you, Parker. Wish that woman would update to tele-conferences or speaker phones. But she hung up fast when the principal came into her office."

I shrugged. "She doesn't like the principal. You can tell."

"No one does," Deshawn said with a snort.

"The teachers do," Avery countered.

"You mean you can *tell* Dr. O doesn't?" Ethan asked, air-quoting the word "tell."

I shook my head. "No, I don't get any feelings from her, as a rule. Anyone can see it in her body language. But if Deshawn hasn't even heard her use my name—"

"Nope, but I'm hearing some stuff related to you from other folks." He flipped his book closed and looked steadily at me. "Seems like our Parker's been using her new gift more than she's mentioned."

My cheeks burned, and I sat straighter. "You've been spying on me? I thought you said you only listened in twice. Past tense." I wondered for a half-second if I could make him feel … disinclined to want to use his gift on me.

Ethan put a hand on my arm. "Hey. If he's listened in on you, there's a reason, right, my man?"

"I haven't been listening in at her place."

Now Ethan slowly turned his head and fixed his gaze at our friend. "And where, pray tell, have you been tuning in?" A glow along his own cheeks turned his skin from golden to bronze.

"Chill out, man. You know me better than that. I've been following up on some of Parker's recent projects, a few she's forgotten to mention to us."

"I'm not hiding anything! We've just been busy!" I protested.

"What kind of projects?" Avery asked with a frown.

"Darla, for one."

I pshawed and leaned back in my seat. My relief at not having my mom brought up was surely only because that was too personal for the lunchroom. "That's child's play. You knew I was working on this. We don't report every time we use our gift, for heaven's sake. Like we want to hear every time Ethan cheats in shop class?"

Ethan blew a straw wrapper at me. "Hey, I can single-handedly fix four tires at the same time, if no one's looking. That might be my only claim to fame one day."

"Uh huh," Deshawn said. "The point is, y'all told us Parker's managed to affect Ethan's mood, but I don't see any long-term changes. But that Darla girl? She's different. I've been listening in over the last few days to see what happened after you did your thing, and that change is sticking."

My heart kicked into high gear, and I dropped my fork. "Even at home?"

"I don't know about that; I've only listened in at school. I've got standards, man. But the thing is, it shows you're ready. You've been waiting, afraid to use it with Mia. But girl, she's as sad as ever, and you've got the skill now. Stop messing around. It's time for you to use it for real."

I looked around the table. "You think?"

Avery and Ethan nodded. "You've got this."

"Okay, then. Wish me luck. And thanks, Deshawn. Sorry I sort of bit your head off. I think the pressure's getting to me a little."

Deshawn smiled, a little sad around the corners. "No worries, Parks. We've got each other's backs. That's never gonna change."

In history class, I was mentally armed and ready for battle. I imagined smoothly making Mia happy, relaxed, bursting for a new adventure. The feelings were at my fingertips. Now I just had to spin them loose at the perfect time to make them worth the risk.

Mr. Bransford closed the door as the tardy bell rang. "We have the history fair coming up. Now, stop groaning. It's your chance to research people who've changed the course of human history. You'll create a presentation about your chosen history-changer, due in two weeks."

"Beyoncé changed history," Clara Bell offered.

"Dream on," Mr. Bransford said dryly, making the class laugh—except Mia, of course. "You must choose a scientist, an inventor, an author, or someone else outside the entertainment industry. I want your selection by Friday."

"Sports?" Thomas Mazer asked.

"Nope."

The students grumbled.

"And you'll have partners."

Now he had our attention. Certainly, he had mine. Half the girls in class looked at Josh, who seemed not to notice. Mia did, though. I would bet my best pair of boots. It was written all over her glowering expression.

"Yes," Mr. Bransford continued. "Partners. Partners I will assign." Groans again, louder.

I threw my hand up in the air. "Sir, I think Mia and Josh and I should be a team." On impulse, I sent a quick flash of cooperation and agreeableness to the teacher. Easy peasy.

He blinked. "And yes, we'll have one group of three. Good idea. You three seem to work well together. You can do this project as a team." He paced to the back seats and handed me a sheet of paper. Despite the glares from the disappointed girls in the room, no one seemed to think anything was out of the ordinary about his decision.

Mia looked over her shoulder at Josh, and a wave of pleasure and excitement spun out from her, spiced with nerves. It only lasted for a split-second, but it was enough to catch.

I beamed. "Perfect!"

Josh smiled. "Sounds good to me."

There was no more ideal set up than this. I had to get Mia to take some chances, and it had to happen right now.

Using my hard-won skills, I carefully reached past Mia's natural block. I felt like I was tiptoeing past a guard dog, but I slowly pumped up Mia's feelings of curiosity, of excitement. I muted the nerves. It was like juggling fire. It almost hurt my brain, this delicate dance of gift-using. My lungs prickled.

Mia let out a loud sigh. She sat facing forward, but I could see her shoulders dropping.

"Ready to—" I began, but Josh wasn't listening.

He tapped Mia's chair. She turned halfway toward him but let her hair slide over half her face like a shield. "What?"

"Did I beat you up in a past life or something?"

I closed my mouth. Scribbling busily on my paper, I carefully kept every atom in my body focused on the pair across from me.

"Don't be ridiculous." Mia sounded prissy. But not afraid, so that was a good thing. I boosted Mia's confidence even more, slowly, so slowly, like pouring honey from a jar.

"You might sound more convincing if you actually turned around and looked at me."

I tried to imagine calmness flowing into Josh but working two of them at once appeared to be beyond my control. He didn't show any impact at all, so I focused again on Mia, who sat up straighter and glanced again behind her.

The plain white paper in front of my eyes wavered. I saw the blond boy, Arrogant Boy. Mark Abels. And I heard whispered words, not just a few like with my mother, but a stream of words flowing smoothly alongside the wistfulness and melancholy.

I can do this. He's not Mark. He's just a boy who looks

a lot like him. But they aren't the same. He's just another beautiful boy.

Sweat broke out along my neck. Goose bumps raced down my back. Hearing someone's secret self-talk, conveyed through their feelings like a freakin' live podcast? If this became a regular feature, I'd be more like a telepath. Way more powerful than my current abilities. More invasive, too. My potential value as a lab rat just went way up.

Panic ripped through me, but I kept my mental ears and shields open. This new development of my gift was freaky, but it at least would make it easier to help Mia.

I added new emotions to Mia's attempts at positive self-talk: confidence, optimism, liberation. I focused hard. *New days, new ways. You can do this.*

Mia turned until she faced Josh head-on. His spine was ridiculously straight in his seat—ballet—but still his feet were under her chair. He was all long-legged like a wild horse and could probably dance better than Sergei Polunin, the bad boy of ballet himself.

A rolling wave of attraction zipped along my skin, and I had to hide a smile even with the stress levels sky high. That zing was from Mia, for sure. Dopamine and adrenaline had to be working their mind-blowing magic right now.

Josh pressed his advantage while I silently cheered him on. "Seriously, Mia, if I offended you somehow, I'd like to know so I can apologize. I don't make it a habit to insult people the minute I arrive in town. I save that for when we're good friends." He quirked a smile.

"No," Mia said with a touch of impatience on her face. "It's not about you. I'm shy and being new makes … everything harder." But hope breathed through her with a sigh, like an opening door in a stuffy room.

Josh was bringing out more emotional response from Mia in five minutes than I usually did all day. I focused even harder.

"You're not the only new kid, you know. At the stargazing party, I thought maybe we could hang out sometime, but then you've acted like you hate my guts since then." The tips of his ears turned red. Adorable.

I tucked a strand of hair behind my ear to get another good look through my peripheral vision. Mia lifted her dark eyebrows, but she didn't pulse discomfort. She shimmered with … pleased pride mixed with a touch of guilt? Maybe astonishment? So, I held my peace and let their little drama play out further. Shoot, this was better than reality TV.

"And why would you be shy anyway?" he doggedly continued. The boy had persistence. "You don't have anything to hide."

An impish smile touched Mia's lips for a moment. It was totally unlike her, and I couldn't stop myself from staring right at my newest friend, spinning up the dial on my receptors as high as they could go. The constant clash of emotions in the room threatened to swamp me, but I pushed away everyone else's feelings with an imaginary wind. I swore I could even feel the wind playing with my hair, it was so real, and it left only Mia's emotions lingering behind.

Something dark bubbled like a witch's cauldron inside Mia. There was a feeling of laughter, but it wasn't happy. And then it was gone, and she was the sweet, quiet girl she'd always been. I blinked.

"I don't know what you mean," Mia replied.

She was lying, had to be. With that kind of emotional response, there was plenty more to the story. What had he said right before that strange darkness rose up? *You have nothing to hide.* And it amused her bitterly.

Mia definitely had secrets: Mark's coma for one. But why would that cause such dark amusement? It didn't make any sense.

Josh scoffed, waving his hand at her. "Can you believe this girl?" he said to me, before looking back at Mia without waiting for a response. He started ticking points off his fingers. "I mean, you make A's, you're beautiful, you're an artist. If anyone's got the right to be full of herself, it's you. But you're not. Not at all."

A rosy hue tinged Mia's cheeks. Her relaxing posture suggested a softening, some kind of melting. There was no trace of the bitter humor left inside her.

I held my breath. *Acceptance. Trust. Playfulness.* I blasted it, no longer hesitant at all. If Josh got hit with a bit of it or not didn't matter—he was already on the playing field. It was Mia who had to get off the bench.

Mia only fidgeted with the edge of her paper. He leaned forward with a sigh, his brown eyes wide. "Look, I've been around for a couple of weeks now, but it feels like I just got here."

"I know what you mean. I feel out of place still, too," Mia admitted.

"Still? Really?" I blurted, affronted.

Mia jumped slightly, like she'd forgotten I was even sitting here. Until I opened my big mouth.

"I mean," I corrected, "I feel like you've fit right in." I doubled down on the empathy sending.

Mia spoke quickly. "I'm glad you think so. It's just …
It's so different here."

"It's a big change. I get it," Josh said.

"It's always hard to be the new kid."

"But you've got Parker here and those others you
hang with."

"I got lucky. Parker was asked to show me around,
and she's been great." She flashed a smile at me.

"Glad to help," I murmured. The affirmation was
touching—I'd pull it out later to soak in the awesomeness
of the moment—but this convo needed to stay between
Josh and Mia.

"You really have."

I smiled but didn't say anything else. I did, however,
pulse a wave of boldness. As hoped, Mia's attention
was drawn back to Josh, like two magnets seeking each
other out.

"You should have lunch with us sometime," Mia
said to him, then bit her lip. But she didn't take it back.
Excellent.

Josh grinned. "That'd be awesome. I don't mind
telling you, even with the dance studio, I still haven't met
many people. It gets old fast, being alone."

"Yeah, I hear that." Mia sighed. "But for now, we'd

better pick a time to meet and research our topic. I want to choose the best person. Someone unusual. I need an A in this class."

"How about we meet at Charlie's Diner tonight for dinner? We could grab some food while we work. Parker, what do you think?" Josh offered. He angled his body so everyone was clearly in the discussion. The way he asked the question put me in the driver's seat of arranging the dinner.

Ballet Boy was fast on his feet in lots of ways.

"Good idea. We can get started ASAP. You in, Mia?" I chirped, spreading a bit more peace and love through the air. I might not fully understand how this part of my gift worked, but if it landed on the other kids in the class, so much the better. The whole school could use some more happiness, for that matter.

"Uh, I don't know." Mia hemmed and hawed.

"We need to get started on our project," he said to us. "And we have to eat, anyway."

Mia's expression suggested she might throw up any food she tried to eat at the moment. Her feelings whacked me on the side of the head, all but shouting in my ear. *Go! No! Go! No!* Good gracious, the girl needed to find her balance.

"It's a big grade," I reminded her, feeling only a touch of guilt. For Mia, maintaining good grades was also important to her happiness, so tonight would be a win-win.

"We only have two weeks to do the whole thing," Josh added. His arms crossed over a delightfully well-developed chest.

"I can do an hour tonight. Two, tops." Mia's voice was breathy.

His answering smile was the kind that welcomed everyone else into his happiness.

Mia warmed in response. By the end of class—thanks, Mr. Bransford, for creating the most boring lesson in the world—Josh even got Mia to grin with him at the ridiculous length of the lecture. When it came time to navigate the crowded hallway between classes, Josh took a step closer to Mia, sheltering her without seeming aware of it. Their shoulders brushed together. She didn't step away.

Something like hope and relief shimmered from her, faint but definitely there. It tasted like maple syrup.

I smacked my lips and hid a smile. Those two needed some time alone, pronto. And I needed to get out of this hall. This crowd was roiling with anticipation, distress, and desperation. Big test nearby next period, probably. I rubbed a hand across my forehead. All this focused work seemed to have amped up the volume from everyone else, too. I brushed against Josh and Mia in my haste to scoot by, and for a moment the floor seemed to dip under my feet. All the emotions bouncing around me simply … disappeared.

I jerked to a stop. The silence was staggering. Then a group of tall kids jostled me, and the cacophony of emotions bombarded me again as loud as ever.

Ow. It took all my strength not to clap my hands over my ears. I frowned, letting habit carry me forward. What was going on now? My gift had better not go on the fritz just when I needed it the most. Tonight was going to be key.

After school, I stopped by Mia's locker. "You're serious about going to dinner tonight, right?"

"Yeah, but don't expect me to be happy about it."

"Why on earth not?"

"I just want to fit in here, you know? Do my work, paint. Keep things simple. But Josh isn't simple, and he isn't the kind of guy who's easy to ignore."

"Why ignore him? He's nice and funny. He's definitely

upfront with things, always a bonus. Not to mention gorgeous."

Mia tightened her arms around her books without radiating any emotion. Whatever channel had opened to Mia's heart was slammed shut again.

"Being gorgeous isn't everything."

"I say again: nice and funny and honest."

Mia said nothing, and I sighed.

"You know," Mia said suddenly, "I really appreciate all you've done, but I know you've got lots of other friends. Please don't feel like you need to keep hanging with me out of pity."

I laughed. "Oh, I never do things I don't want. At least, not often."

Mia scanned my face. "It's just … I was thinking, after talking to Josh, that really, I was pretty much an assignment for you. The counselor told you to help me out."

"I showed you around that first day because she asked me, sure, but I stuck around because I genuinely like you. You're my friend, Mia!"

As I spoke, I realized it was one hundred percent true. Mia was shy and held a lot of grief inside her, but when she did finally talk, she was thoughtful and interesting. She could be close-friend caliber if she'd open up more.

Feelings burst from me to cement our bond before I could think twice: *Friendship. Trust. Happiness.* The emotions soaked right through the wall I knew Mia still had firmly in place. I bit back a yelp and shut off the feelings I'd sent on accident. I imagined padlocking them in my heart. If Mia suspected I was manipulating her, it'd be game over.

Mia relaxed her death grip on the books and said, "Thanks. I wish I could show you around my old home like you've taken me around here. Maybe someday."

A touch of Texas heat whispered past me, dry and hot. On my *skin.* Oh man. If I got the physical sensations from someone's emotional memory now, too, that could get really awkward, really fast.

Things just kept getting messier. My gift was acting like an overexcited Saint Bernard, charging down the street, dragging me behind barely clinging to its leash.

I smiled without missing a beat, despite my thundering pulse. "No problem. See you tonight. And fair warning, even with this project, Mr. B will have a killer exam. Maybe we could study for that, too, sometime."

"Okay, then. Sure," Mia said, more warmly. We headed home together.

But there had still been no laughter.

 193

16

At Charlie's, Mia and I sat on one side of the booth facing Josh on the other.

Josh said, "Thinking about getting the supreme pizza. Any votes?"

"It's delish," I confirmed.

Mia pressed her lips tight. "I'm not ordering anything. But I did have some ideas for this project."

Josh followed her lead and jumped right into business, which was a nice thing to do, but still. I wanted to clonk their heads together. How could I make romantic sparks from Mia's suggestion of Nelson Mandela?

Mia had everything locked down except a bit of nerves. Josh wasn't shoving his emotions on me, either, but if he did, no doubt he'd be all reds and yellows and sparkly gold. No moody grays on him, thank goodness.

I suggested we study Coco Chanel but got vetoed by Mia immediately. Josh listened respectfully to both of us, asking good questions.

Fiddling with the peanuts on the table, I made up my mind. Mia was going to find herself enjoying a bit of a thrill. Feeling bold, even brash. Taking risks would feel adventurous, not dangerous. Insecurity and fear would have no seats in the house.

Forget Operation Cupid. This was Operation Love Doctor, with surgical precision. I sent my gift floating like fog to surround Mia. *Confidence. Hope. Trust. Boldness.* Positive emotions rained all over the girl, who sat straighter. Her eyes twinkled. For good measure, I sent a sprinkle of it Josh's way too, though he needed no help in the confidence department. I couldn't even tell a difference.

I could *feel* the ice block around Mia's heart melting, from either the warmth of Josh's attention or the empathy at work. I pumped up my gift a little more.

Josh leaned forward, completely earnest. "I think we should do our project on Cecilia Payne, the woman who first realized the sun was mostly made of hydrogen. Did you know her boss blew her off as nuts but then published a paper saying the same thing five years later? But it was still her discovery that changed science, even if she didn't get proper credit."

I clapped my hands. "That's a brilliant idea. I'm in. Forgot Coco Chanel. Well, no one should ever forget Coco. But let's do our project on Cecilia Payne."

"That was my mother's name. Cecilia," Mia said.

I braced for an explosion of pain, but Mia kept things together, even offering an authentic, if sad, smile.

"That settles it, then!" Josh said. "Let's do this. Women need more shout-outs in the sciences."

How could Mia resist him? Answer: she couldn't. Her eyes didn't leave his face. And both their hearts were no doubt speeding like a relapsed shopaholic on her way to the mall.

As we ate—supreme pizza for the win—we chatted about plans for Thanksgiving break, and Mia didn't steer the conversation back to schoolwork. Josh described how hard the practices had been for their winter dance recital, and Mia listened with stars in her eyes. I felt a little starry-eyed myself.

"If I end up in the hospital, I hope you'll come visit me," he joked, looking right at Mia, but he didn't sound ha-ha at all.

I excused myself from the table to grab some napkins. I could probably push them into going to the dance right now, but ... If I played up their obvious interest with my gift, maybe it wouldn't last, like how my mother's mood faded. Better to be a little more patient. Their brains were obviously churning out all the right chemicals on their own.

After grabbing a mountain of napkins, I took my time easing back to the table. Josh's hair slid across his forehead as he scribbled more notes. Nerves rushed across the room to me. Then Mia reached over and pushed the lock of hair to the side for him.

His cheeks flushed, but he smiled. Mia did, too. Then she looked away, fidgeting with her sweater. But her smile remained.

Everything was perfect.

Falling for Josh would steamroll Mia's tricky wall in no time, especially if I kept the girl feeling confident and carefree. And with luck, Avery's bad vision would disappear faster than the pizza off Josh's plate.

But the sort-of couple hadn't agreed to go to the dance together yet, and I wasn't taking any chances. The two of them needed to be head over heels, at least until after the deadline. Math wasn't my thing, but the equation seemed straightforward:

$$Date + Dance = Distraction + Delight =$$
$$Delay\ or\ Dismantling\ of\ Danger.$$

Ten days until the day.

Time for Part B to commence. I texted Avery under the table: *Call me.*

When my phone buzzed a minute later, I stepped away from the two almost-lovebirds.

"'Sup?" Avery said, voice muffled, a sound I'd heard times beyond counting.

"Haven't I told you to keep those pins out of your mouth? You could swallow them!"

"Give it a rest, Grandma. If you want your ratty yet gorgeous dress for Electra done on time for your talent show dealio next week, you'll hush." But a sprinkling of tiny clinks followed, and her voice was clear when she spoke again. "Now, aren't you supposed to be arranging for hearts to fall tonight?"

"That's why I'm calling. Genius plan happening here. If I have to leave because of an emergency, they'd be forced to stay here together now and talk alone, right?"

"Theoretically. What makes you think Mia won't take off right after you?"

"I have my ways, my pretty, oh yes. You wait and see."

"Fine. Honestly, I'm feeling a little down anyway. Weird dreams last night, stuff that makes me wonder if my visions are taking over my subconscious now, too."

"Are you kidding? I require an update."

"Come on over, then. I've got chocolate."

I sighed with satisfaction and hurried over to the table, schooling my expression into one of concern.

"Is everything okay?" Mia asked.

"Avery asked me to come over. She sounds pretty upset, so I think I'm going to have to bail on you guys. That's okay, right? I'll research Cecilia tonight and bring the notes to class tomorrow."

"Well—" Mia began, blinking rapidly. Anxiety rolled from her like an approaching storm. Mia wasn't actually scared of Josh, though, or I would never leave them alone. Mia was scared of the way she felt around him. She preferred to suffer needlessly rather than move on and be happy. Big difference.

"Of course," Josh said. "I'll make sure Mia gets home safely. Whenever she's ready to go."

Bless his heart. He was almost too good to be true.

"Thanks! I'll see you guys tomorrow." I ignored Mia's widened eyes. It was time for the girl to jump in the pool. The one-toe-at-a-time business wasn't working.

"So what's got my girl upset? Do I need to take Todd down?" I asked, slamming my fist into my palm over and over like a cartoon baseball player.

Avery laughed darkly, curled under her covers. "Hardly. Though he's still an idiot."

"No debate here."

"But he's a really cute idiot." Avery sighed.

"Would you actually go to the dance with him if he asked?"

She turned red. "It doesn't matter. I heard he's asking Veronica West. But I don't want to go with another guy."

A sharp spike of pain zipped along my spine, startling me. Never had Avery spilled a drop of emotion. She must be hurting more than she'd shown.

"Oh, Avery, I'm sorry. We'll go together," I promised. "We can even match: an angel and devil are easy to pull off last minute. It's not like I have a date, either."

"So Ethan's being dumb, too?"

"Maybe it's something in the water. Now, what else is going on? It's not just Todd."

"It's nice to be known. I had another vision, a new one, but I didn't understand it at all. It was impossible.

But horrible."

"And?"

"In this vision, you and Mia kept merging into one person, and *that* was the person who brought the FBI on us. We were all locked away from our families, with tubes sending something into our blood. Or maybe they were taking ours. I couldn't see clearly enough."

I propped my chin on my hands. "In this new vision, was I using my gift to project stuff?"

"Yeah, why?"

"I managed to use it on Mia for the first time today. I was going to tell you when I got back. What are the odds of that coincidence? You having a new vision with me and Mia the day I manage to soften her up. She and Josh were actually flirting—major progress."

"I know I told you to use your gift to get the job done, but something's definitely off. I think you need to cool it for a bit. At least the projection part."

"Tick tock, tick tock, Avery. Halloween is a week from Saturday, and I've finally got a tool that can fix this."

"Unless it turns out you trigger the threat now."

"That doesn't make sense, though. If my gift makes her relaxed and happy, why would she cause some problem that would draw attention to us? It could do wonders for Mia. Nothing else is working." I pointed at Avery. "You know what Mr. Beller says: Do it right or get off the stage. And maybe your vision was just an anxiety dream."

Avery chewed on her bottom lip. "Fine. But tell me if your gift does anything else new, okay? Maybe it'll change the vision and the future."

"It did sort of fritz out once in the hall, actually, with a moment of blankness. I think I've just been overworking it, but I gotta say, the moment of silence? Pretty nice."

"Okay, keep me posted if anything else happens. And be subtle, okay?"

"Me? Always." I flipped my hair like a supermodel, and Avery giggled. Life suddenly felt much more normal.

Avery shook off her covers and rummaged in her sewing corner, pulling out a tattered white thing. "Now, how about you try on this dress? I hope you're ready to look unhinged. Electra took the grieving thing to a whole new level."

Slipping on the Greek-styled, artfully destroyed dress, I preened in front of the mirror. "Avery, you're the best. Oh my gosh, can you imagine how amazing my performance would be if I used my projection on the whole audience at the show? I bet I could now. It's a whole new world."

"Don't you even think about it! You just said you'd be subtle! People will notice something like that, no doubt, and you'll be locked in a science lab in an orange jumpsuit for the next twenty years. And no one should ever have to wear a jumpsuit. Don't borrow trouble, okay? It seems to find you plenty enough as it is."

And wasn't that the truth.

EVER hopeful, on Thursday's walk to school, I asked Avery, "How's your third eye doing this morning, Fortune Teller?"

We were running late, so our pace was fast. At least the morning air was crisp and cool, that perfect stage in October when the Texas heat had finally surrendered the earliest mornings to autumn.

Avery snorted. "Believe me, if I could pluck it out, I would. Did you see Mia this morning? Why didn't she walk with us? Was she mad you left her with Josh?"

I kicked at a pen abandoned on the sidewalk and scowled. "I saw her heading out when I took out the trash this morning. She said she was going in early for some art thing. She asked about you, actually. I told her you were fine. She didn't seem mad, but she didn't seem happy, either, so I guess the good mood effects didn't last. Ethan's the same way, so I think it has to do with what kind of mental blocks someone has. The effects only stick around on people without blocks, and even then it fades eventually."

"Maybe Mia's an emotional ninja."

I snorted. "Whatever the deal is, I'm still pressing forward with the old-fashioned way of developing friends, too."

"You mean sharing all your chocolate?" Avery wiggled her fingers in a gimme motion.

I smacked her hand away. "Seriously. She's hard to help, but I like her."

"Me, too." Avery sighed. "I wish we didn't have to worry about her, you know, destroying our lives."

"Maybe after the dance, it'll be like none of this ever happened."

"And is she going to the dance yet?"

"So far, no, but it's getting closer."

"Then you'd better get your gift on lock," was all Avery murmured. Her eyes were focused across the street. Anger and hurt crossed her face like shadows. I followed her gaze and landed on Todd.

I let out a gusty sigh. For heaven's sake. Well, I couldn't fix Mia's pain yet, but I could do something about my BFF's. If Todd came crawling back, it shouldn't take long for a smart girl like Avery to figure out he wasn't worth the heartache.

It was probably just the forbidden fruit effect, the psychology of unavailability. It all went back to brain chemistry, really—people's dopamine levels went up when they had to wait for what they wanted. Once they got it, their interest often faded. Sounded like the perfect shortcut to set Avery free. Righteous rejection of her ex would also offer a flood of feel-good hormones, too. By the end of the weekend, at the latest, Avery would be back to normal.

Narrowing my eyes, I turned my gift on the most undeserving of menfolk. *Nostalgia. Love.* I pushed hard—and he spun like a puppet and crossed the street to us. He dropped to one knee in front of Avery, adoration gleaming in his eyes.

I murmured, "I'll, uh, keep walking."

I could still hear his words as I hoofed it away.

"Avery. I'm so sorry. I shouldn't have broken up with you. I was an idiot."

Oh man, oh man. My heart raced. I'd really overdone

it. Surely Avery would know and be so, so mad. She'd take it as a pity offering. And if anyone did *not* need pity, it was Avery.

But at the sound of a squeal, I turned around despite myself. Avery had thrown herself into Todd's arms, a beaming smile on her face. *What?* She was forgiving him right away? And Avery was supposed to be the genius among us.

Some things were beyond understanding, but if it made my friend happy, it was worth messing with Todd a bit. Of course, I wouldn't mention what I'd done. No need for that. Admittedly, interfering was perhaps a wee bit unethical, but Todd deserved it.

And Avery deserved happiness.

And it felt *so good* to make her happy.

There was only one person whose happiness would feel even better.

Thursday after school, I set the stage carefully. My dad had a late class tonight, but this time I would stay subtle anyway. Like a river, slowly wearing down the banks of the river bed.

My mother sat in the living room on the couch,

reading a magazine. She didn't even look up when I stood in the doorway.

You love us. You are happy. Content. Your life is perfect exactly as it is. I floated the feelings out like a gentle cloud, letting my mother breathe it in while I myself didn't breathe at all. My mother laid down the magazine and stood up.

By the time my father arrived, a homemade dinner was on the table, including an apple pie. The house smelled like cinnamon and spice. A smiling wife greeted him with a kiss. He raised his eyebrows at me, and I shrugged innocently. He didn't need to know what I'd done. Ignorance was bliss and all that. It was an act of mercy on all of us.

And if I planned to repeat it daily, it was only to relieve my mother of the terrible burden of resentment and anger. No one wanted to live like that. For heaven's sake, my mother was practically singing and dancing now.

My dad didn't ask me flat-out if I'd changed my mother's feelings again, and I very carefully didn't offer the information. The good feelings in the apartment smelled better than the homemade apple pie. Making my mom happy was the best thing I had ever done.

Now I just had to take care of Mia.

Fridays always had an abundance of good feels, but today everyone felt happy. Well, except one person.

At the end of the hallway, Darla stared in her locker with a giant scowl on her face. The scowl taunted me, since I knew for a fact Darla had passed the looming science test.

Normally, I would have all my feelers out like a quivering ant, reading the girl's heart, primed to make a call, set up a date, help with homework, whatever it took. Now? I could simply push happiness into the girl. But first, I wanted to know what part of my plan went off the rails. Live and learn. "What's up, Darla? No frowns on Friday!"

"My mom wants to move me to honors science."

"That's great!" I cheered.

Darla rolled her eyes.

"Uh, it's not?"

Darla slammed her locker door. "It's not."

"But you aced your test! You knew that stuff!" I protested.

A sly look came over Darla's face.

"You did know the stuff, right?"

 209

"Parker, come on."

"What does that mean?" The blazing success of my week began to curdle.

"You have to ask?"

"You … cheated?"

"Give me a break. I'm too good to waste my time, and too good to get caught. Aaron asked me to the movies, so I used a shortcut to get what I wanted."

A shortcut? "But—but you wanted to do better in class—"

Darla gave a harsh bark of laughter. "I *wanted* to get out of trouble. And I was fine once I got that A. But if they move me up, I'll have to work harder *and* I won't be with Aaron. No thanks, know what I mean?"

I really didn't. I stood there, the empath, flat-footed and speechless.

Aaron strode up. "How's my girl?"

"Great!" Darla smiled. "Later, Parks."

I gulped. What had I done wrong? I bit my lip and pondered as I ran to class. Luckily, it seemed to be an isolated weirdness. Maybe I hadn't been specific enough on what I'd sent. Or maybe Darla was someone who could resist my projection like Mia.

Too bad for Darla, but I didn't have time or energy

to correct the unwanted side effect. I still had to rain confidence and trust on Mia, happiness and contentedness on my mother, keep Todd interested in Avery, and there were still plenty of others with needs, too. I pushed Darla from my mind. Some people were just destined to be mysterious. But Mia couldn't be one of them.

At lunch, I sat next to Ethan, who was first at the table for once. Self-torture, maybe, but delicious nonetheless.

"How's the new awesomeness going?" he whispered. A package of ketchup skittered across the table and tore itself open. I grabbed it, trying to put a warning in my eyes.

"Great, mostly. But Darla had a strange reaction to my gift. Not sure what to think."

"You'll figure it out."

"Do you still feel good after we're done practicing? Does it stick?" I leaned in close to him, his nearness making my heart race. Thank heavens I was the empath, not him.

"No, it fades when you're done. Of course, I always have some of my shields up."

"But you feel normal later?"

"Well, I still feel happy, but I think that's just 'cause

we have such a good time together."

Tingles raced through me, and I licked my lips. Maybe this was the time to tell him how I really felt. That I loved hanging out with him, too, more than anything …

He continued, "I'm really glad we're friends, Parkuor."

I swallowed the words I'd been about to say, like gulping down a big chunk of dry toast. "Yeah, me, too," I managed.

He was really glad we were *friends*?

When Mia arrived, I scooted away from Ethan to make room, glad for some space between us. The others of our crew must have been busy for lunch today, so it was just our tiny group of three. I ate quickly and quietly, my taco turning into a brick in my belly. Ethan asked Mia about school stuff; she answered with an unusual amount of honesty. But then again, Ethan often disarmed people, especially girls. That stupid smile did it every time.

He went to grab another taco, and Mia murmured to me, "He can't keep his eyes off you."

I startled. "Really?"

"All the time. I think he really likes you."

"Sure. As a friend." I tried to not sound as sour as I felt.

"Um. No, I don't think so. Not the way he stares at you when you're not looking."

"You're serious?" My pulse sped up with fresh hope.

"I'd never lie to you like that," Mia said gravely. "You're my friend."

I nodded, pushing away the guilt that pinched a bit at her words.

Ethan was already heading back to the table. I let my dimples peek out a bit, wishing I dared flirt more. Just in case Mia might be right. But even if she was, for now I had to focus on someone else's love life.

"Well, speaking of staring, Josh sure was looking at you at Charlie's. Well, since he first met you. I've heard he's turned down two girls to the dance." I nudged Mia with my shoulder.

"I'm not interested in going to the dance." Mia's tone said the conversation should be over.

"I still don't see why not. He's gorgeous."

"Gorgeous, huh?" Ethan said, sitting back down. "Sounds like you're talking about me. What did I miss?"

"The Josh in your math class, the new guy. He's in our history class and wants to take Mia to the dance."

"And she looks so thrilled about it," Ethan noted.

Mia said, "He transferred into our class a few weeks ago. I barely know him."

"Well, with our project, we'll all get to know each other

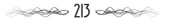

really well. Super awesome!" I chirped. "Right, Ethan?"

Ethan clapped his hands in a slow, sardonic clap. My tray jiggled a little on the table, all by its little ol' self, and my hands slapped down on the sides of the tray. Hard. I sent a forced smile at Ethan and rolled my eyes toward Mia. He laughed.

"Wasn't he going to eat lunch with you sometime soon?" I asked Mia.

Mia's huffed a loud sigh and pushed around the rubbery refried beans on her plate. "I've got to go."

"Don't," I said, placing my hand on Mia's arm. "Stay. I'm sorry. I won't keep asking about him, promise." I couldn't afford to alienate Mia now, plus I always hated upsetting anyone. My gig was the opposite. I sent a burst of feeling, trying to tie words to it: *I should sit down. I'm making too big a deal out of this. Parker's a friend. I trust her.*

I focused harder than a gymnast attempting a triple back-handspring for the first time. My brain seemed to twist and a huge wave of adrenaline hit me, like someone had punched the boost button on my gift.

Mia plopped back down into her seat. *It worked.* Holy cow. I was hard-pressed not to pump my fist. Ethan raised his eyebrows, probably at my enormous grin. I wondered if this was how he felt when he used his gift.

Instead of being drained by my projection or afraid of it, I simmered with the same rush I got on stage, without the hard work of a performance. I'd just leveled up.

Mia tucked a stray lock of dark hair behind her ear, looking a bit dazed.

"Painting going okay?" I asked her, striving to find a topic unrelated to Josh. Romance was only one part of life, after all, even if it was tons of fun. And art was definitely one of Mia's gifts.

"It's alright. I love the freedom they give us here."

"I saw there's a great competition coming up in town. You should enter."

A sudden split of pain made me fumble my fork. Mia squeezed her eyes shut for a moment before locking her gaze on her tray.

Forget the art thing. Two strikes was enough. A third might bench me the rest of the game. "Never mind. Sorry. I know art is private and all that. No worries," I babbled, trying to push through the lingering stings of grief. Why was I doing this to myself again? Oh, right. Our entire future.

"No, it's just … I'm having some trouble with my project. It's upsetting."

Yeah, and Niagara Falls was a babbling brook. Maybe

it was just as well Mia was so repressed. I wouldn't be able to breathe if all those feelings hit me at once, probably a full 10 on the Pain Emo-scale. Something big was under there. I needed to know—was it the loss of Mia's mother? That seemed so long ago. The thing with that guy Mark? But he looked so mean. Or was it something else entirely?

I squeezed Mia's arm and said, "I know! Let's have a slumber party! You, me, and Avery!"

It'd be a perfect way for us to spend time with Mia when her defenses were lower. Strategy was my middle name. Next to Fun.

I sent a mix of feelings to Mia: *homesickness, wistfulness, eagerness.* It felt like hot chocolate swirling through me, thick and rich.

Ethan watched me with narrowed eyes. What was his deal? It wasn't like he didn't know what was up.

"Uh, I don't know, Parker," Mia said. "I'm still behind on my art project, and I've got an essay to do."

Apparently, the girl was on some kind of emotional diet. Nothing.

"Come on, Mia! It'll be a blast! Let's do it! Tomorrow night!" My excitement surged down my arm, jumping into Mia.

Mia sat up straighter, eyes warming. "You know, now

that I think about it … That sounds like a good idea. Saturday works. In fact, it sounds great!"

Ethan dragged his finger across his neck, casually, but a clear signal. Whoops. If *Ethan* thought I should knock it off, I'd better.

I let go of Mia's arm, imagining the emotions tapering off like a wispy cloud dissipating.

A few minutes later, Mia left the table to stop by her locker on the way to history class, shaking her head. Her gaze was turned inward, like she was examining a puzzle.

"Think you went a bit overboard?" Ethan whispered. "You've gotten really good at sneaking past my shielding. You might turn a plain brain like her into putty with power like that."

"Look, if a girl has a heart like a rock, you've got to hit it a little harder to open it up."

"Remind me never to get on your bad side," Ethan said. He was smiling, but his eyes didn't have their usual sparkle.

True, I'd probably overplayed my hand, but I was running out of time. The Halloween dance was next week. With the art contest still off the menu, we were stuck with the Dance and Dude plan. It was time to giggle and gossip over boys. It was a cliché for a reason. It worked. This weekend could be the key.

THE sleepover had to go perfectly. My place was ideal, since Mom was so cooperative these days. Exhaustion mixed with constant exposure to my new skills meant Mia might finally accept her new friends and home. Avery would be there as wingman, and I had new strength and energy on hand. If this worked, Mia would be happier, and my friends and I would be safe. Win-win.

The two thumps on the door meant Avery had arrived on time.

"Did you get the chocolates?" I demanded.

"Need you ask?" She held forth a box of Belgian chocolates, perfect works of art with pink flowers painted atop their sleek dark shells.

I clapped my hands. "And I've got the popcorn and the makeup!"

"You cannot be serious about doing a makeup thing." Avery swept into my bedroom and flopped on the bed. She wore her newest favorite pajamas, black covered with colorful dots that upon closer inspection were tiny unicorns pooping rainbows.

"We need something fun and distracting," I explained. "I can't deal with a tidal wave of gloom all night, and I'll influence her better if she's relaxed. So we'll giggle and paint our nails. Get over it."

Avery sighed but didn't argue.

Someone knocked on the door. "She's here!" I squealed. Geez, I was already acting the part. The thought made me giggle.

Then the Black Pit of Despair walked into the room. Whatever happiness Mia had felt the day before had been swallowed by sadness once again.

For once, I had zero guilt or fear about pushing good vibes into her. This was mercy, just like with my mom. I let it loose, like lifting a barrier on a dam to let the water rush into a dry river bed.

Mia shuddered. Then she blinked slowly, and a smile bloomed on her face. The difference was shocking. A pretty girl became drop-dead gorgeous.

Avery whistled. "There's too much awesomeness in this room right now! Haha!" She gave me a hard jab in the ribs.

I barely felt the prod. The power running through me felt new, different even than the rush at lunch. After all the exercise I'd gotten, maybe my gift really was stronger now. This was like a herd of wild mustangs stampeding through my blood stream. I grew dizzy with it and tightened the reins. Who knew what would happen if I overwhelmed one person with too much emotion? The worst I'd had to deal with before was fighting off everyone else's issues.

Avery gave me a strange look, her brow furrowing.

"What? Do I have something in my teeth?"

"Nothing. It's nothing. Later."

I debated trying to get a hint, but then Mia said, "Oh my gosh, are those Belgian chocolates?"

My laugh was only slightly forced. "I knew we were destined to be friends. If you let me do your nails this fabulous shade of emerald, I'll know it for sure." I held up the bottle and wiggled it.

"Ooh, it looks like shamrocks!" Mia said. "Sure! Ireland's on my list of countries to visit one day."

"Really?" I guided Mia to the chair and pulled out the polish. "You've got a list?"

I set to work on Mia's right hand while Avery started painting Mia's toenails a glittering sapphire.

"Definitely. Ireland, Scotland, England. Well, actually, pretty much everywhere. I love the idea of walking through ancient history."

Avery said, "As long as you do it without wearing white tennis shoes. Americans have a bad style rep overseas."

Mia smiled. "I promise."

I shifted to the other hand and sent a small pulse of relaxation through our touching fingertips. Just a small one, nice and easy. "What kind of history do you like?"

Mia leaned back in her chair. "All of it. The Sumerians, the Mayans. Egypt and the Pharaohs. The Greeks, of course. But the Vikings are my favorite right now."

"Vikings? Like, with the horned hats and all the swords?"

"They were warriors, yeah, but they didn't actually wear horns on their hats like the cartoons."

"I never knew that," I said, finishing Mia's last finger-nail. "Voila! Green's good on you. It spices things up a bit, too."

Mia held out her hands and admired them. "Thanks! What about you? I see you more like a cotton candy pink shade. No, wait." She looked closer at me. "Magenta. That's you, Parker. And Avery, you should go with this metallic silver. It suits you."

Avery and I exchanged a smiling glance. Mia had selected two of our favorites.

"Impressive!" I said. "Let's do it!"

By the time all the nails were shiny, though, Mia was back to one-word answers. Dang. She shook off my influence almost as fast as Ethan.

"Oops, there's one last part of the manicure!" I spread some scented lotion on Mia's hands and turned up the power again, until Mia was hopped up on as much enthusiasm and relaxation that I could squeeze through those shields while staying subtle.

Avery held up *Roman Holiday* with Audrey Hepburn. "Ladies—let's watch a classic."

"I love Audrey Hepburn," I said. "Always gorgeous and kind, but strong. My hero."

Mia smiled broadly, sniffing at the lotion. "Me, too. Did you know she won an Oscar for her performance in this?"

"Her first big role, too," I said.

"Really?" Avery flipped the DVD case over to read the back.

Mia continued, "Yep. She wasn't even in the top billing of the credits at first, but Gregory Peck called his agent after he'd been working with her and said, 'Listen, her name needs to be above the title with mine,' and his agent said, 'You can't do that,' and he said, 'Oh yes I can. This girl's going to win the Oscar her first time out.' And she did!"

I gave a dreamy sigh. "Gregory Peck."

"A prince among men," Avery agreed.

I asked, "Rome on your list, too, Mia?"

"Near the top."

I gave a thumbs-up. Avery and I settled on either side of Mia and kicked back to relax and renovate one sad girl's heart and mind.

Hours later, amid crumbs of cake, chocolate smudges, and popcorn kernels, the three of us lay sprawled on the carpet. Four candles sent steady warmth into the dim room, the vanilla scent soothing. I wished we could all go to sleep. Mia had smiled tonight more than usual, but each time I'd stopped projecting, she went back to her usual wary expression within half an hour. And she hadn't relaxed enough to laugh at all. I kept the good feelings flowing, though.

"Everything going okay? Anyone need more brownies? They're homemade!" My mom called through the door.

"We're good, Mom, thanks!"

"She seems … really happy these days," Avery noted. I ignored the raised eyebrow.

"It's sweet, the way your parents act together," Mia said.

I almost preened but caught myself. "Tomorrow's their anniversary, actually. I was going to make them dinner, but I don't think burnt toast is a good anniversary meal."

"I could help you." Mia's offer was almost inaudible.

"Seriously?" I sat up, half my hair falling out of its fish-tail braid. Mia had tried her best at the makeover bit, but beauty skills weren't her gift. But it seemed she had other, hidden talents.

"You can cook?" Avery looked impressed. I sure was. The stove evaded my skill set.

Mia's cheeks turned rosy. "Well, after my mom passed away, I basically took over the house stuff."

"You were nine." I stated the obvious. At nine, *I* couldn't have made a boiled egg. Of course, I practically still couldn't, but that was different. Nine years old?

Mia shrugged. "It wasn't like I had any little brothers or sisters to care for, so I just took over the cleaning and cooking." She examined her hands. A faint scent of lemon cleanser misted me, tangled with grief the shade of storm clouds.

"Well, I'd love the help, thanks!" I drew my friend back to the much-happier present. "Any ideas?"

"Vegetarian or carnivore?"

"Definitely meat-eaters."

Mia tapped a finger on her lip. "Roast chicken is easy but looks impressive. Roast potatoes, baby carrots in butter sauce, maybe a salad? And French bread."

Avery patted her stomach. "Get that in my belly now!"

"That sounds awesome," I agreed. "Whatever we choose, it can't be too complicated. If I'm even near the stove for too long, it might explode. It hates me."

Mia smiled, and it transformed her face. It was easy to imagine what she could have looked like, could be like again, if things had been different for her. If she were happier.

Time to push a little more.

 225

I said, "I appreciate it *sooo* much. It'll mean a lot to my parents. They've had some problems, but I know they really love each other. So, here's a question for both of you. Truth time."

Tension snaked back in through Mia's shoulders.

"Have you ever really, really liked someone? Loved them, even?"

Mia froze, and I was struck by a whip of pain, followed by the image of that Mark guy laughing in a hateful way. A flash of bright light shuttered the memory from my mind.

I blinked away the memory, struggling to stay in the present.

"Why, are *you* in love, Parker?" Avery gave a knowing glance.

Heat flooded my face unexpectedly. Apparently, Avery had an agenda of her own.

"Who, me?" I tried to play it off. Kinda failed.

Mia snorted. "Doesn't everyone know it's Ethan?"

"Everyone except Ethan!" Avery said.

"Guys can be dumb." Mia nodded.

"Amen to that, sistah," Avery said, clinking an imaginary cup with Mia, and then sang, "Parker and Ethan, sitting in a tree—"

I threw a pillow at her face. Avery burst into giggles,

and Mia almost did. So close, so close! I yanked Mia's pillow away, making sure my hand grazed hers. I sent my gift pouring through our brief connection. Discreetness could take a back seat. *Trust. Happiness. Openness.*

"And you?" I turned the tables on Mia. "I won't ask about the guy I swore not to, but no doubt you've had a boyfriend before. Just look at you!"

Mia wrinkled her nose, turning toward the mirror by the bed. In the flickering light, her reflection looked like a ghost, half there. Her dark eyes were immense, and a shadow fell across her face. Mia traced one cheekbone with her fingers, smile fading. She ran her hands through her hair and the tips clung to her, crackling with static.

Her hand shook.

A shockwave of sharp pain flooded from her, and I flinched.

"Uh, Mia, it's okay. You don't have to say anything," Avery said, patting Mia's hand.

A sudden gust of wind blew through the room. The candles went out, and Avery shrieked. Fear slipped past Mia's walls again, slapping me hard, and carried with it the smell—and fear—of thunderstorms.

I ran to the door and flipped the light switch, squinting at the sudden brightness, looking automatically to the window. Mia stood beside it, a blank expression on her face.

Mia said, "It was open, a bit. I closed it and pulled the drapes. In case a storm's coming." Her voice sounded almost mechanical. No shaking now. She was stone still.

I checked the rest of the windows, which were firmly shut and locked. "Weird. I don't know how I missed that, but thanks for fixing it. It looks okay out there for now, but you never know in Texas. I'd hate to wake up soaked from rain."

Avery eyed Mia closely but gave me a tiny shrug.

"I'm getting really tired," Mia said.

Sadness rose in me like a tide, but it wasn't mine. Poor Mia—she was truly hurting. "We can go to bed, no problem."

"Aww, come on! Things were just getting good!" Avery said. "Parker here was going to confess all her secrets."

Mia's lips mashed into a tight line. "Maybe another time, sorry!" She crawled into her sleeping bag and faced away from us.

One good thing was that an exhausted Mia would probably send out fewer emotional jolts. The gaping maw of her gloom was stealing my pep. I wracked my brain for another shortcut to toss into Mia's Happiness

Prescription but came up with a big fat goose egg. Hopefully cooking dinner with her tomorrow would open up some new avenues. The future wasn't going to change itself. I needed to make some real progress ASAP.

"I think she's already asleep," I said. "Who falls asleep at a slumber party at 11 p.m.?"

"A girl who's seriously worn out. Look at her, Parks. Did you get any new feelings?"

I frowned. "Just more of the same. I saw a flash of the same guy. Mark What's-his-face."

"Abels."

"Whatever. He was laughing in a mean way, like before. Do you think it's weird she's the only one who's pushed images to me? It's probably because all her emotion is jammed packed in there, ready to explode."

"Maybe. But I bet now that your gift's gotten stronger, you could do it with more people. Be careful, Parker. You're playing on a whole new field."

I shook my head. "Maybe. But I've got to tell you. Yesterday, at lunch? I projected and made her sit back down. Like, I made her do what I wanted."

Avery said in a neutral voice, "And what do you think

about that?"

I hesitated before answering. Making people feel what I wanted was seductive. But controlling their actions could become addictive. I thought back to my dad's warning. My empathy had gone from a cute kitten to a roaring lion.

"It feels … powerful. I'm being careful, I promise."

Avery stared at me for long enough without blinking that it seemed a vision had gripped her. But then she shook her head like a dog after a bath. "Well, keep us posted. Tomorrow sounds promising. But I have to ask … Do you think you could control us that way? The Fab Four?"

"First of all, I would never do that."

"I know. I trust you, one hundred percent. But could you?" Avery held my gaze.

"I don't think so. I've spent a lot of time lately with Ethan, pushing good stuff into him, and he can definitely resist me if he tries at all. I still can't read him past his full shields, not that I'd do something like that anyway, or ever try to control him. Because eww."

"Speaking of our favorite telekinetic, I've noticed Ethan's been getting a little free and easy with his gift. A little chair moving here. A little catching of the dropped fork there. Are you guys in some sort of contest for who can use their gift the most or something?" Avery picked through the popcorn bowl for any last remains of actual popped corn among the kernels.

Ethan had always been a bit on the wild side, using his telekinesis to help a skateboard trick reach a new height, for example. Or to shake pecans down off a too-high branch. But he'd been using it more and more often, even in public.

"I've noticed that, too," I admitted. "I don't know why he's taking so many risks."

"Maybe he's growing stronger, like you."

I glanced at Sleeping Beauty. "I'm not strong enough to make her stay happy and distracted. And I can't be with her 24/7."

"And I still can't see exactly what goes down at the dance. I've even searched the future. I've used freakin' Tarot cards, Parker. I've read my own stupid tea leaves. Nothing."

No one hated the tools of the witchy world more than Avery. They flew in the face of her trust in science, but desperation was biting at all of us, it seemed.

I sucked on my bottom lip, staring at the sleeping lump that was Mia. It was true the world wasn't easy for anyone, but could this quiet, sad girl actually do something to put me and my friends in danger?

I felt squishy about it but decided I'd send confidence and trust into Mia while she slept tonight. Maybe projecting into her subconscious would stick better. It felt too questionable even to mention to Avery, given our little chat just now. But this was an emergency. I closed my eyes and settled back into my sleeping bag to get to work.

In the morning, Mia woke up with a smile and stretched. "What a beautiful day, isn't it?"

"Yes, it sure is," I said with relief. Dang, it felt good to be an empath. Being able to help others was the best. And there was nothing I wouldn't do to help my friends.

19

DURING the rest of Sunday, my mom was a domestic goddess, anniversary or no anniversary. She sang along to old Madonna songs and danced to the country music station while cleaning the whole apartment.

I said, "Don't forget, Mom, I've got something special planned tonight for your anniversary."

Mom beamed. "That's right! How lovely!"

With a deep feeling of satisfaction, I nudged her out of the kitchen. "Why don't you and Dad take a break? Go on a walk together? I've got dinner covered."

Mia arrived right on time, bearing groceries.

"Mia! I thought we'd run to the store together. You didn't have to do this!"

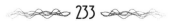

Mia blew a strand of hair out of her face. "Here, take this bag. It's no big thing. My aunt had to go by the store anyway. I figured, why not get your stuff while we were there? You've been so great to me. I wanted to do something nice for you."

Warmth tangled with guilt. "Hey, you don't owe me anything." Mia may have started off as a project, but she'd become a real friend, at least on my side.

"I know. It's not about owing. It's about wanting to give," Mia said with a hesitant smile.

This was her gift of friendship. She was finally, finally stepping toward me.

I gave her a hug and squeezed. "Thanks, Mia. For real."

Over the next hour, Mia taught me how to clean a chicken, rub on spices, roast potatoes, and make my own salad dressing.

"I had no idea cooking was so hard!" I said, opening a window. I was sweating, and my makeup had been perfection this morning.

Mia had tied her hair back and wore an actual apron. "This is nothing. Wait until I teach you how to bake an apple pie from scratch."

I sighed at the homey image. My mother had recently

taken up baking again but only under my influence. Mia had a lot of hidden skills.

"And here." From her bag, Mia pulled out a vase with a single red rose. "For their love."

"It's beautiful. Perfect. Thank you so much." It was such a sweet gesture. My eyes stung.

Mia's gaze lingered on the rose. It didn't take a psychic ability to see Mia was a romantic who longed for love and acceptance. I'd make sure she got some.

Monday morning, I woke to my mother's homemade pancakes. My father kissed my mom on the cheek before he left for work, and birdsong seemed to burst from the trees in perfect accord with my heart.

For the first time, Mia actually walked to school with me and Avery without any prompting.

"How was the dinner?" Mia asked. She sounded more upbeat. It was only a matter of time now before she'd even laugh, I was sure.

"It went perfectly, thank you! My mom nearly fell out of her chair when she took a bite of those potatoes. I had to confess you helped me. Now they'll want you to come over all the time."

"No kidding," Avery announced. "Anyone who can help Parker cook a decent meal deserves a medal."

A broad smile wreathed Mia's face. It was like spring had finally broken through winter. There was still room to grow—plenty of it—but now, finally, bursts of sunny happiness mixed with her routine gray cloud of depression. This was the week Avery's vision was going to change. I could feel it.

I sauntered into the school, for once not caring at all about Monday blues. They couldn't touch me now. I threw my gift around like I was handing out candy. A girl at her locker was moping over the loss of a friendship. I waved my hand—BOOM. Happy girl. Down the hall, I passed by a shy boy sweating over a crush. SLAM. He felt ten-feet tall once I left his side. Another guy couldn't think straight after staying up late all weekend—SWISH. He was suddenly elated, full of energy.

I felt like there should be a personal soundtrack playing everywhere I went. I couldn't wait to do my Electra monologue for the talent show tryouts after school on Friday. Right now, the way I felt, I'd be at the top of my game for any show.

"Catch ya later," Mia said at her English class.

I replied, "I'll save you a spot at lunch. But hey, don't

forget we need to find a time to meet with Josh for our project."

A voice came from behind us. "Making plans again, Parker?"

Mia paused, brow furrowing, looking past me to the speaker.

I turned, confused by the spattering of rage across my skin. "Hey, Darla."

"You just always gotta have your sticky fingers all over everything, don't you?" Darla lifted one corner of her lip in a sneer.

"I don't know what you're talking about." I felt the problem, though: betrayal, bitterness, distrust. Could Darla have somehow figured out the truth?

"Yeah right. Someone told Dr. O'Malley I cheated in science, and now I'm back to an F. It sounds like exactly the thing you'd do, always sticking your nose where it doesn't belong. And you were so shocked when I told you, too—I don't know why I thought you'd keep your mouth shut."

I shook my head, relieved at the mundane problem. "I don't know who busted you, but it wasn't me. Believe me—I have zero interest in getting you in trouble." That would seriously hurt. In fact, right now, waves of disgust and anger were turning my stomach. The emotional stench of rotting garbage drifted through the air.

"Whatever. It doesn't matter. Aaron's getting me away from this hole once he graduates." Darla looked at Mia. "Just watch it with this girl. Parker's sneakier than she looks. She's the mastermind of rumors and set-ups. Ask anyone."

I fought a blush. "If I have a rep, it's for helping people out when they need it."

"Or even when they don't," Darla snorted.

Mia's jaw dropped. "Hey. She's been a good friend to me."

I nearly dropped my own jaw. Mia was speaking up on my behalf?

"You should ask yourself, new girl, what's in it for Parker if she's spending time with you. She doesn't do anything for just one reason."

Darla was hitting too close to home in this particular instance. My hands grew slick, and I quickly said, "We're working on a class assignment, not that it matters to you. You don't have Mr. Bransford for history."

"That's right. I'm in dummy history class. Not honors, not for history and definitely not in science." She flipped her middle finger at me and flounced off.

"That's not what I ..." I drifted off as Darla rounded the corner. "Meant."

"What's her problem?" Mia snapped.

I am, I thought. It may have started with good intentions, but the end results spoke for themselves. I'd tried to make Darla a successful student, but when all those good juice vibes soaked into her, it looked like she'd used them for a different purpose. And someone must have noticed Darla's sudden and abnormally high grade. A good cheater would at least know not to make it so obvious. I rolled my eyes.

"I tried to help her pass her science class. It, uh, didn't work, but I swear I didn't rat her out." I kept it vague. It wasn't like I could mention my psychic magic wand.

"Of course you didn't. And she's the one who chose to cheat anyway. Don't worry about her. I've got your back."

That was the best thing I'd heard in weeks. It almost made the whole mess with Darla worth it.

The sleepover seemed to have been a turning point for our relationship, cemented by working together for the dinner. Mia waited to walk to school with me on Tuesday, and when I suggested she sign up for the local art club, she did.

Mia, Josh, and I met on Tuesday and Thursday to

work on our project. Mia was already a different girl around Josh now. Good ol' hormones at work. The old Mia held her body stiff, as if prepared to take a hit. This Mia leaned forward and met everyone's eyes. She even smiled. Admittedly, Josh and Mia hadn't agreed to go to the dance together yet, but I felt sure I could carry off a last-minute win.

Friday was my last chance to get the girl ready to have a blast at the dance on Saturday.

I whistled to myself on my way to the lunchroom on Friday afternoon. It was orange chicken day again, my fav. And this afternoon I'd dominate my talent show audition. Mine was right after school. Ethan's band was the last on the scheduled list, and I planned to stick around for it. Watching Ethan drum was always good. Plus, the whole Fab Four was together for lunch. The best part of the day.

To make things even better, at lunch Mia shocked my hot pink socks off by walking up with Josh already in tow. "Hey everyone. I invited Josh to sit with us, okay?"

I nearly spit out my sweet tea but managed to wave a wild hello.

My subconscious manipulation at the sleepover must have worked, along with the real-life friendship finally blooming this week. Good thing, since this was down to the wire for changing the future. The two of them sat side by side across the table from me.

Everyone stand back, I thought to myself. *This party is officially started.*

"O. M. G. Could they be any cuter?" I whispered to Ethan, on my left.

"Scale it back, chica, or you're gonna blow your cover," he said around his straw.

I hid my delighted grin. My mood was so high, I was probably sparkling. But still. It couldn't be going any better if I'd directed it.

And okay, yeah, I sort of had. I'd pretty much kicked Mia's reservations to the curb, pumped her full of happiness, and set them up to see each other daily, but the rest, the attraction, that was all them. Well, okay, maybe I provided some time alone, too, but really, I'd just made their real feelings harder to ignore.

There wasn't any ignoring going on now. Every once in a while, a pulse of nerves or excitement or even desire radiated from Mia, skating along my skin like electricity. And every time, it pumped up my mood, like a race car revving its engines with nowhere to go.

Finally, finally, things were looking up. Just in time.

Paper skeletons danced from the ceilings, and bats hung from doorways, ready for the dance tomorrow.

Deep down, I'd been nervous I was going to fall on my face after all, failing everyone depending on me to fix the future by fixing Mia. But after today, doubt was just a lame old town in the rear-view mirror. Projection was the shortest shortcut I'd ever used.

"Josh, where did you say you were from?" I asked, determined to use my limited time wisely.

"Maine." He took a sip from his water. "Texas is way better."

"Seriously? I heard it's beautiful up there." And it explained why he wore shorts in fifty degree weather.

He shrugged. "Sure, if you like ten feet of snow in the winter."

I shuddered. "No thanks. Winter here gets plenty cold for me." I nudged Mia. "North Texas probably feels like the North Pole compared to the swamp of Houston, too."

"Hmm. It's been different, for sure."

"Miss your friends back home?" Josh asked Mia. "I don't hear you talk about them."

Mia frowned. I wanted to kick him. That was not a romantic topic.

"I didn't have many friends. So, no, not really."

Mia's mood was sinking faster than the *Titanic*. No way. Not today.

I fed Mia excitement and delight without hesitation, but what we really needed was a fun fabulous distraction ASAP before this plan went belly up. Something exciting, something happy—"Oh my gosh! I have the best idea! You guys *both* have to come to our group birthday party in a couple of weeks, promise?"

"It's your birthday soon?" Mia looked up and smiled. The faint scent of scorched Earth thankfully faded. "Happy birthday! Mine's in two weeks, too. I'll be fourteen."

"Us, too!" I grinned. That had been a close call. "Our birthdays are in the same week. How cool is that? You should be a part of our party!"

Josh laughed. "A part of your party. Nice."

"Who else is having a birthday?" Mia asked. "There can't be that many people here with the same birthday week."

"Oh, you've met them." I pointed around the table at the Fab Four. "All of us have our birthdays within a few days of each other. It's kinda how we met."

My intuition began to fidget. Something inside me was rising to the surface of my mind like a screaming banshee. "You said you were born here, right?" The comment, tossed out so casually by Mia weeks ago, came back with a sudden rush.

"What?" Mia asked. Her fork was poised over her rice.

Eating was the last thing on my mind. Right now, the ground was shaking under my feet.

"Born. Here. You were, right?"

"Uh, yeah. But we moved almost right away."

A spiraling shock numbed my lips. Mia had been born here. In November, the same week the four of us had been born. She was an only child. She could have been born from the same fertility drug trial.

STUNNED, I cut my gaze to Avery's. Avery wasn't paying attention—she was actually blowing a kiss to Todd, who sat with his football buddies. I stepped on her foot and widened my eyes in silent question. Avery gave a tiny shrug. She'd missed the whole bit. Deshawn and Ethan were focused on their Chinese food, apparently confident in my ability to carry this off on my own, but Josh … He was all in on the conversation. Yet he still had no emotions radiating. His face showed nothing but polite interest in the shared birthday week.

Coincidence. It had to be. It didn't mean Mia had been conceived at the fertility clinic. Plenty of other kids had been born then, perfectly fine and normal. Really, what were the odds? But I had to keep fishing. All the records were destroyed, so … It was possible. "And you don't have any brothers or sisters, you said?"

"No." Mia smiled sadly. "My mom wanted a house full of children, but I was the only one she had. Well, the one who lived."

Discomfort and loss suddenly beat against my skin, a brief flutter before it disappeared as usual. "Oh, Mia. I'm so sorry to hear that. You lost your mom *and* a brother or sister?"

Good gracious, how much loss could one girl take?

Josh shifted forward in his seat, and his long legs pressed against mine under the little table. Before I could respond, he reached to Mia and tenderly placed a hand on her arm. I froze. He was such a gentleman, he'd move if I told him I was being squished. No way would I risk interrupting his sweet offer of comfort to Mia.

Mia shook her head. "Sort of. I had a twin. Twins are hard on a body, you know, and something was wrong with him. They never told me what, but he didn't make it at birth. And then my mom was never quite healthy again."

"That's heartbreaking," Josh said quietly. "I'm sorry."

Avery was finally paying attention again, thankfully.

"Yeah, that sounds really hard." The others murmured their sympathy.

"Thanks," Mia replied.

That story made every moment of suffering in my life look like a trip to an amusement park. I was thankful Mia's powerful block had silenced any angst just now.

But this had to be the deal. Mia must have been born through the same fertility trial we had, causing the loss of her twin and eventually, her mother ... and the creation of a psychic gift inside her. It had to be.

The vision said Mia was going to expose us as psychics—because Mia was one of us.

If her gift was revealed, no matter what it was, people would search for others. That would be the trigger. But if I just came out and said, "Hey, Mia, are you psychic too?" and was wrong? There'd be no reason for Mia not to tell on us. Even if she didn't believe, she could tell someone like Dr. O that I needed mental help. Or someone else could overhear and expose us.

"Could it be?" I whispered to myself, lips barely moving.

Deshawn said, "Low odds."

"What?" Mia said.

The hair at the base of my neck stood on end. Why

on Earth did he answer my whisper in public? Josh and Mia were too close.

Deshawn said, "I meant twins. Low odds, right?"

He looked at me and shook his head. The words were for me, not for Mia. He'd used his gift to hear my quiet mutter and was answering: he didn't think Mia was one of us. At least one of the others was connecting the same dots. Deshawn was the quietest but also the best listener of the four of us, in every sense of the word.

Mia said, "I guess. That was a long time ago. Don't worry about me. I'm fine."

Which was a big fat lie.

I didn't have much time. If Mia was gifted and became furious, who knew what would happen? She must not have any training or support. We could help her with that. We'd have to. Maybe my ability wouldn't even work to calm down the kind of major meltdown Avery predicted. Not if Mia was gifted, too.

Grief made people do strange things. Like happiness, it flooded neurochemicals through the brain, too—but not pleasant ones. Grief spun up fight-or-flight hormones like cortisol that put the body in a state of stress. Most people eventually coped, but with prolonged sadness came a dangerous downward spiral that needed serious disruption. And disruption was my middle name.

I tried to send a flurry of emotion to Mia: *confidence, boldness ... life goes on ... hope, joy.*

But Mia continued to sit there, and her mouth did not open. Nothing. She wasn't giving any hints, so I tried an X-ray and failed. That block was impressive. Maybe she even had some level of real shields. If she were really one of us, it would explain so much.

Avery carefully began talking about school work, blah blah blah, and Deshawn chimed in. Soon Mia had joined in on the debate on Mr. Bransford's choice of projects. Josh sat back, eating his rice with a spoon. The intensity of the prior moment faded from the table, but not from inside me.

"Excuse me a minute," I said, sliding away from the crowded table. The hike across the cafeteria to the dessert line gave me space to calm down and focus. I could do this. I had to.

As I returned to the table with a bowl of pudding, I pushed out a shockwave of emotion, funneling it straight toward Mia: open-minded willingness to try new things, excitement at possibilities, confidence that pummeled fear into nothingness.

Ethan was energetically describing the songs his

band was going to perform at the dance. Perfect.

I plopped onto my chair and said, "You know, Mia, I really think you should go to the dance tomorrow night. You don't want to miss Ethan's band, and it's going to be such a great time. Dances may not be your favorite thing, but you should embrace life. Love it, live it, and all that. We'll all be there with you."

Meanwhile, I kept channeling cooperation and confidence at her.

Mia blinked. "I do like to dance sometimes."

"And Josh is a dancer," Avery said, looking nervous but game.

"Right!" As if I'd forgotten. "Josh, have a date yet?"

He stared at me long enough for Ethan to look sharply at him. "I don't. But if Mia doesn't want to go with me, that's okay—"

"No. I do," Mia blurted. "Want to go to the dance. With you, I mean." She blushed. "If you want to go with me."

Josh said, "I'd be an idiot not to. And I'm no fool." He met my eyes again. "Though some people might think otherwise."

I stopped cold. I could see the question marks hovering above everyone's heads. Maybe I'd been too obvious with the pushing, and Josh had guessed something was up?

I smiled sweetly. Time for the dumb blond act. "I've worked with you in class. I know you're plenty smart. So, you guys have to think of fantastic matching costumes."

Josh said, "It's a little late for that, isn't it?"

"How about something from the drama department? I can make any last-minute adjustments so they'll fit right," Avery offered.

I clapped my hands. "Brilliant! Ooh, last year they did *A Midsummer Night's Dream*! You guys could be Titania and Oberon! I've seen those costumes in the back still."

Josh pursed his lips. "You promise everyone dresses up for this thing? Because if I come as the king of the fairies and everyone else is in jeans—"

"Promise. Right, Avery?"

Avery nodded. "Definitely. Oberon's costume was pretty simple."

"Oberon's the king of the fairies?" Ethan asked Josh.

Josh shrugged, the movement a bit jerky. "There's a ballet version of *A Midsummer Night's Dream*. My old studio company performed it."

"Cool. Learn something new every day." Ethan went back to eating.

Josh relaxed. He must really have taken some crap

 251

from macho jerks in the past.

"Everyone's dressing up!" I dragged us back on topic. "I'm a little devil, and Avery's going to be an angel." The angel's dress, sewn by Avery herself, was gorgeously elegant. And my short red devil number might even make Ethan wish he'd said yes.

Avery suddenly scrunched her face apologetically. "Actually, I'm sorry, Parker ... Todd wanted us to go together as matching zombies. I forgot to tell you. We'll be from the 1950s with a poodle skirt for me and the waxed hair for him, but all zombied up. Isn't that cute?"

"Adorable." My chicken sat like a lump in my stomach. So much for Todd and Avery lasting just a weekend. Avery's feelings for him were deeper than I'd understood.

"That's okay, right?" Avery's brow wrinkled in distress. "He's taking me out to dinner before the dance. You can keep both the other costumes."

"Of course! Y'all should definitely match. It's totally fine," I assured her. And it was. It had to be. And I had bigger issues to deal with anyway.

After the longest ten minutes of my life spent chattering inanely like a squirrel, finally Josh stood to walk Mia to her locker.

"We'll see you in class, Parker!" Mia's face was lit

from within. I didn't think all that glow had come from my projection, either.

As soon as they were out of earshot, Avery said, "You did it! Awesome!"

"Uh, yeah. But did you catch the other part? We just heard the biggest news of the century, and I had to keep it to myself. I thought I might have a heart attack."

Avery looked blank, as did Ethan. Deshawn was the only one who nodded.

Whispering quickly, I reported my suspicion about Mia being psychic. "It all makes sense! And then we could tell her about our awesomeness, too—she could really be one of us!"

The others had their doubts.

"Lots of folks are born in November," Deshawn said. "Our town's small, but plenty of babies are born every year."

"But the thing with her twin? Fertility treatments raise the chances of multiples!"

"People can have naturally conceived twins, too, even if the odds are lower," Avery said. "Besides, I didn't see her doing anything, you know, *awesome* in my vision, Parker. Not once, in all those visions."

"You didn't see much specific at all. And what about

that weird moment at the sleepover? With the window shutting? That was bizarre, right? What was that?"

"You think I'd see her blowing up the gym then, don't you? Instead, I see her crying."

"Fine. Can you at least listen in on stuff, Deshawn, over with the university profs? See if they mention any of the trials?"

"Sure thing. And I'll keep listening in on Dr. O while I'm at it."

"Perfect!"

And in the meantime, I would focus on making sure Mia had the most fun at the best dance in the history of our school. The pressure would be off by tomorrow night. Thank Heaven.

My shiny optimism ran smack into a wall after school. I walked past the office on my way to the talent show tryouts, and Dr. O'Malley stepped into the hall as if she'd been waiting.

Every hair on my arms stood on end.

"You've been very busy these days. I barely see you, even as an office aide. How's life treating you?" Dr. O'Malley asked. Her smile was cold and flat.

"Fantastic," I replied lightly and tried to slide by. Don't mess with a rattle snake, that's what my daddy would say.

Dr. O stepped to block me. "I've been wondering if everything is okay with your new friend, Mia. She still doesn't seem very happy here."

"I don't know what you mean."

"I think you do. As her friend, if she's shared any secrets that put anyone at risk, I hope you'd tell an adult. I'm here to help."

My blood ran to ice at the emphasis put on *secrets*. The woman definitely knew something. But what? She couldn't possibly know about our Fab Four's awesomeness. Was she hinting about Mia's ex-boyfriend being in a coma? That was none of the woman's concern. No way would Dr. O drag poor Mia through that again. No one would.

"Nope. No secrets here." I spoke firmly and turned to walk away, hiding my shivers. I'd go around the long way.

"Actually, everyone has secrets. But the truly dangerous ones always have a way of getting out. Your father would agree."

My jaw dropped. Thank goodness I was facing the other way. Even great actresses slipped sometimes.

"Given his profession, I mean," Dr. O'Malley added.

Was she being coy? She sounded calm, even reasonable, but her wording held a veiled threat. Intentional? Unintentional? Too hard to tell. Too dangerous to risk.

In a panic, I spun to face the counselor and pushed a wave of emotion before I could stop myself, one that crashed straight through the woman's tough mental block. *Dull, dull, dull. You want to do something else now. You find this whole topic boring and ridiculous. Who cares?*

It was easy, too easy. The mental skill that had stretched like an underused muscle just two weeks ago now rippled from me without hesitation. I said, "You shouldn't believe gossip. Mia's fine. We all are. I've got to go now."

Dr. O'Malley stood with her jaw slightly loose like she'd lost her train of thought. Which she had, thanks to me.

My head began to ache as I took off toward the auditorium. What had I done? I would have to watch myself closer than ever. And my dad and the others had to know: Dr. O was way too close to the truth. And I was closer to controlling people with my gift ... but I wasn't ready to share that part. Not even with my best friends. Not yet.

THE talent show tryouts were a welcome break from everything with Mia and creepy Dr. O'Malley. I'd tell my crew what Dr. O said, but right now I wanted to focus on the audition. Some people had a comfort food during difficult times. While I loved me a big bowl of mac and cheese, nothing calmed me like the stage.

I waited. The person scheduled before me was Kayla. Listening to her screechy voice, I regretted influencing her to sign up. Not every dream should be followed, apparently. After that performance, no doubt the snickers of the kids waiting in the wings would haunt the poor girl for weeks. I shifted uncomfortably.

Kayla staggered off the stage, probably to go cry. I would've sent soothing vibes, but there wasn't any time.

I'd just have to fix things later. I was up.

The heat of the spotlight warmed my skin, but the house lights were on, too. I could easily see the adults in the front row. The talent show judges consisted of four teachers, including Mr. Beller. Perfect. My drama teacher would really appreciate this performance. Today, my gift hummed under my skin like an electric line waiting to be plugged in. Reading the audience cues would be easier than ever. Too bad I couldn't use my projection. It would've been an amazing addition to my acting arsenal.

I announced, "For my audition, I'll be performing a monologue from *Electra*. In this scene, Electra believes her beloved brother has died while trying and failing to avenge their father's death. I've adapted it to modern English."

I composed myself. I needed to *be* Electra. Living in fury for years, desiring revenge, but heartbroken again now. Alone.

The tremble in my heart told me I was ready.

"*Aaaahhhh!*" I let out an agonized cry that shattered the silence and brought goose bumps to my own skin. "My brother! Dead? Please, don't let it be true. Oh, Orestes, brother mine. You've left me, as our father did, and now I'm all alone."

I pulled at my hair and fell to my knees. "Our mother scorned your death, Orestes! They laughed. How can I bear it? I'll be a slave to that selfish women who birthed us both and murdered our father!"

A mother who wished her daughter had never been born ... that was something I understood. Wrapping that hurt around me, I wailed, rocking back and forth. I sank into it. Emotions surged in me, wild and hot. I screamed again, thinking of my mother's bitterness filling the house for years, sour like rotten grapefruit. Pain ripped along my throat from the violence of my cry.

Deep within the world of Electra, energy pumped through me from head to toes. My light sparkle of tears became real, dripping down my cheeks. A fiery ache burned in my chest, and I could barely breathe. My own mother ... My mother hated me. My mother betrayed me.

Through the roaring in my ears, I heard crying nearby. Not mine. The sniffling and a few broken sobs came from the seats below. I was still on stage, and I was Parker Mills, not Electra. And my teachers were weeping.

I snapped back to full awareness of myself, felt my empathy pouring from me like blood from like a sliced artery. Pain was running straight from me into my teachers.

By accident.

Staggering to my feet, I immediately tried to cut off my sending. Never mind the rest of the monologue—the show would have to end here. My chest still heaved from the emotional riptide. It was hard to pull back my power. Those real emotions beckoned to be released like rain bulging in a heavy cloud. It'd feel so good to let them go.

With trembling hands, I imagined a waterfall, washing away all the emotion coating me. But for every bit that washed way, another took its place, bouncing back from the emotions the teachers were sending to me, like one giant feedback loop. I couldn't stop it. Several kids poked their heads from around the curtain where they'd been waiting their turns.

Forget the waterfall. Thinking of Ethan's best shield, I slammed down a steel wall between myself and everyone else. I put a thousand rivets in that sucker, and finally, finally, the storm of emotions cut off from both directions.

The sobs quieted, the sniffles stopped. I jumped down off the stage, a hot lump of dread in my stomach as I hurried toward my teachers. The whispers of the students waiting in the wings onstage grew louder. I couldn't believe I'd lost control like that. It was definitely not subtle.

Worse, I'd never sent unhappiness into anyone before. I'd inflicted harm. Guilt seared. My gift had never felt so dangerous. Hopefully they'd forget this experience as quickly as my mother always did. The other students weren't hit with the emotional sending, at least.

While the other teachers blew their noses and wiped their eyes, Mr. Beller jumped out of his seat. I rushed to meet him so we were far enough from the base of the stage to keep curious classmates from overhearing. Fury radiated from his stiff shoulders, and I added a few more rivets to my mental shield and added a waterfall to boot. No way did I want to feel *that*.

"What was that, Parker?"

"It's a, uh, great play, you know, really, uh, powerful," I stuttered.

He glared at me. "No, you did something. Something was different—"

If he talked about this around Dr. O …

Suppressing a sigh, I set to work. *Happiness. Peace.* "Of course not. That doesn't even make sense. I'm just doing my best to sweep everyone off their feet." *Everything's okay.*

He blinked. "You sure?"

"Totally." I shoved hard, blasting him and the other teachers. *Happy time. Be unconcerned.*

"You're a fantastic actress, Parker," he chirped. "You'll definitely be in the talent show. I can't wait to see your auditions for the spring play!"

Nausea twisted my gut, but I summoned a smile. Despite tying my gift down with triple knots after that major screwup, fear and suffering still lingered against my senses, wafting through the now-cheerful mood like the stench of a burnt bottom crust on a beautiful pie.

My teacher added, "Make sure you keep up the hard work, hear me?"

"I hear you. Loud and clear."

Way too loud and clear. What was going on?

It took a lot for something to register on my weird-o-meter, but today's audition had done it, especially on top of the run-in with Dr. O. I needed to talk to someone, a friend I could trust a hundred percent with something like this. I had to come clean. Avery was already gone for the day, so Ethan was the next logical option. I'd just have to keep my gift and heart firmly in check.

But it was going to be tough. He was drumming

right now, warming up for their tryout. Ethan on drums played ghost notes on my heart. One of these days, he might hear them.

First, though, I'd pass the news about Dr. O to Deshawn. We needed his extendable ears on max. Thinking through his schedule, I cut through the courtyard on my way to the band practice rooms. Beyond the cobblestoned square, a few members of the track team were stretching out in the shady grass. Easily picking out Deshawn's tall frame in the team's hideous yellow and white shorts, I waved at him until he looked over. In an exaggerated gesture, I held my hand up as if telling him to call me. He nodded.

I murmured aloud, pretending to talk to myself as I continued on my way. "Dr. O's definitely onto something. She asked about Mia's happiness and hinted at the dangers of secrets, basically said my dad ought to know better. I don't know what else we can do, but keep an extra-close ear on her, okay?"

I casually glanced over at him. He lifted his arm and gave a thumbs-up from his straddle stretch position. Man, psychic gifts really saved time. He'd pass the news to Avery if he saw her first, too, and probably his parents, too, which was comforting.

With that critical duty discharged, now I could talk to Ethan. Carefully.

Descending down the stairs to the basement area of the school, I wrinkled my nose at the sharp scent of brass and polish mixed with old sweat and powder. My head, growing worse by the second since the incident, began to thump along with the rhythm of Ethan's drumming.

The pulsing beat came from the farthest practice cubicle. The door hung open. Of course it did. The bass rattled my chest, forcing my breath to come at the rhythm he dictated. He was always good, but I'd never heard him play such a complex rhythm before. Lordy, but that boy could drum.

I peeked around the doorframe.

Ethan was pounding away on the drums, eyes closed. His whole body moved with the beat, shoulders and arms showing finely developed muscles. His dark hair was ruffled, and sweat left dark patches on his blue T-shirt. He looked good. Reeaally good. Four sticks were practically blurring in their speed—

Wait—four?

I gasped.

Two in his hands, ruthlessly slamming against the snare drum … and two in the air, tapping against the cymbal. On their own. No hands attached.

The floating drum sticks paused in their rhythm to spin three times in rapid succession before dropping right back into the driving beat.

"Ethan!"

The beat went silent, and his eyes popped open. The air still vibrated. I stepped in the room and slammed the door shut behind me, shaking.

"Well, Parkour," Ethan drawled, two drum sticks spinning again next to his head, two in his hands. "If you wanted to be alone, all you had to do was ask."

"You think this is funny? What's wrong with you?"

"I'm so wrong, I'm right." He laughed. "Nah, I wanted to practice fine-tuning my gift. Doing pretty good, too, huh?" He sent the drum sticks spinning faster.

"That's awesome. It is. But you could have been caught—Dr. O's getting nosier—"

"Chill out, Parker. No one comes down here after school on Fridays, not even the teachers. We're not up for tryouts for another hour, so the guys went home to grab some food first. How'd it go for you?"

"You're not changing the subject, Ethan Jae-Sun Kwon. Things would suck if we were outted. And that's right where you're headed. I just told Deshawn to zero in on Dr. O even more. She was hinting about people with dangerous secrets." I grabbed the floating sticks.

He waved his hands dismissively, stepping around the drum set to me. He snapped his gum, and cinnamon wafted past. "Then he's got us covered. Look, you're the one who inspired me, working so hard on your gift. You of all people should understand the need to practice." His voice went low and husky.

His reference to our many practice sessions made me shiver. There was something so … intense about sharing emotions the way we'd been doing. But never real feelings. Not yet. I couldn't afford the distraction. Neither could he, apparently. He needed more focus, not less.

"I'm only stretching myself like this because Avery said it'd be all over if I didn't."

"Gotta keep up with my Parkour, don't you think?" He toweled off his sweaty neck and face, leaving his hair even more tousled.

My Parkour.

My blood fizzed with lightness from those two tiny words. He probably didn't mean anything by them, though. Certainly, he leaned against the wall with a casualness I wasn't feeling.

"Has Mia chilled enough to laugh yet? Or kissed ol'

Twinkle Toes?"

"Not yet."

"So what if you get caught making Mia feel things she wouldn't, knowing things about her you shouldn't?" He looked at me with calculation in his eyes. "Any one of us could bring down the whole house of cards if we aren't careful."

"But that's exactly why I'm working so hard. So, you'll be safe. I won't let anything happen to you." My voice came out fiercer than intended.

We held each other's gaze for a long moment.

"I believe you. I trust you with my life, you know?" he said.

My cheeks grew warm. He looked so serious all of a sudden. Maybe this was the moment. He'd forget about performing with his band at the dance—he'd want to be with me most of all.

He said briskly, "So, you didn't come down here to scold me. You look like you don't feel so great. You said Dr. O might have learned more?"

And just like that, he dropped back into the old-best-friend mode, as if his statement hadn't had that extra-special lining. But I knew it had. Hadn't it? For a half second, I debated even giving him a little push. Given the wild moment on stage, I could probably get past his full shields if I tried hard enough. A moment of boldness might be all he needed … but no. I didn't want anything from Ethan that he didn't freely offer.

I sighed. "I actually don't feel good at all. I almost forgot, what with your insanity and all. I had the weirdest thing happen during tryouts just now."

He collapsed in the chair next to his drum set. "Do tell."

"Well, I was doing that monologue from Electra, where she thinks her brother's been killed, right? And I was super into it. Like, really, a shining moment. But then all four adults watching me burst into tears! I'm talking, really crying. I don't think it touched the students waiting their turn in the wings, but those poor teachers were seriously sad. I know I'm good, but Ethan, this wasn't my acting. This was my gift. It blew out like some sort of explosion when I was in the scene, and I couldn't stop it right away. It's getting stronger. Way stronger."

"That's good, right? Why are you so worried?"

I gulped and barely whispered, "But I didn't do it on purpose. I didn't even notice at first."

That was the most disturbing part. I'd been so caught up in the moment, I hadn't even sensed my gift reaching out to anyone. I hadn't even known I was projecting. I'd just felt powerful.

"And my drama teacher was so freaked out I … I did it again, to make him calm down. I just kept piling on emotions like when you try to fix a bad makeup job with more makeup but you only make it worse."

People would be up in arms if they knew what I could do now. Being able to X-ray hearts was bad enough, but controlling them? Maybe Mia would find out and tell—maybe that was how she ended up ruining our lives.

"Maybe it was a fluke," Ethan suggested.

"Then I got this killer headache afterwards."

"Okay, maybe a super weirdo fluke. But even so, if anyone can figure this out, you can. Maybe back off for a while. Stick to what you know best. Be the Love Doctor. You've sure got things down in that department." Ethan tossed the drum sticks in his bag and stood with a groan. "I've been in here for ages. Want to mock the other talent show contestants with me until the band's up?"

I pondered for exactly three-fourths of a second. Ethan was dangerous to my heart, but right now, I could really use his company. He made me laugh and trust myself. I only hoped I did the same for him. "You're on. But you're buying me a lemonade from the machine."

He pretended to be stabbed in the heart, and

I laughed. The tension I'd been holding since my performance leached away. It was only a fluke. I'd been focusing so hard on Mia's feelings, I'd forgotten to keep my own emotions under wraps. Maybe all these pent-up feelings for Ethan were messing with me, too. I'd just have to watch myself more carefully.

I squared my shoulders. Even if Dr. O had suspicions, she didn't have any proof. She couldn't do anything, not as long as we were careful. My gift might be getting a bit wild right now, but the real danger in the vision was Mia. And I would make sure Mia was too happy to destroy any lives at the Halloween dance.

22

SATURDAY was unusually hot for Halloween, even for Texas. I spent the morning in the gym, arranging punch tables and chairs around the room.

Avery shook out her arms and groaned. "I think I just hung my two thousandth balloon."

"But it's looking good, yeah?"

We watched the committee worker bees in action. "It looks perfect," Avery said, but she wasn't smiling.

"Okay, spit it out. What now?"

"This is how it looked in my vision, Parker. Down to the jack-o'-lanterns in the corners."

"Should we ditch the pumpkins, then?"

Avery sighed. "I saw something new last night.

271

Something I don't know how to tell you."

A lump formed in my belly and grew. Avery wouldn't look at me. "Go on."

"The vision—well, it changed finally."

"Get out! Shouldn't that be good news?"

Avery shook her head. "You came tonight dressed in your cute devil outfit. And at first everything was fine. But then you did something to Mia—I'm not sure what—and the next thing in the vision, the whole gym is collapsing, and kids are screaming and the lights go out, and it clicks to the same old vision, where we're locked in lab cages. You did something, Parker. To Mia. And everything blows up in our faces."

"You're saying *I'm* the reason we get caught?"

"I'm saying something's changed. What Dr. O told you this time was scary, but she's hinted like that before. I don't think that was a big enough change to cause a new vision. What's different since yesterday?"

I thought back to my talent show audition, that rush of power spilling over. "Uh, well, my gift is a maybe little out of control in the projection department."

Avery narrowed her eyes. "Tell me."

"You have to see it to believe it. Watch."

The DJ was testing out the sound system with a

groovy dance beat. I sent my gift into the kids near the speakers and filled them with playfulness. They dropped their tape rolls and crepe paper streamers on the floor and began to dance, even though they were bad at it. Really bad.

"Whoa, you just did that to them?"

"Yep. If I change their mood enough, it changes their behavior. My gift's felt different since that day I made Mia agree to the sleepover, but yesterday, I used it on Dr. O to make her lose interest when she got too snoopy, and then on some teachers without meaning to."

"You used it on Dr. O? And other teachers?" Avery hissed. "No wonder the vision changed. That's huge, Parker. Were you even going to tell me that part?" Hurt shone in her eyes.

"I was! I just did. But afterwards, you weren't around and Ethan was, so we chatted and he convinced me I was over-reacting. But now that you've told me the vision changed ..."

"Yeah. Mia's close to being triggered. Maybe you're right, and she *is* gifted. Whatever her deal is, I don't think you should use your gift at all tonight. Looking at those poor saps over there, I'm thinking you shouldn't project ever, even after the dance."

Heat scorched across my face, and I crossed my arms. "I've helped a lot of people."

"No doubt, and with your parents happy now, I'm sure it feels great. But didn't you say Darla freaked out? And then there was Kayla's talent show fiasco. I heard about it from five people this morning. It must've been really awful."

"It was an unfortunate experience for all of us." Thinking about that performance still made me squirm.

"So, stick to the old tried and true methods. Mia's already going with Josh, so maybe all you have to do is make sure they dance and have fun. A first kiss would be good, too."

"No pressure or anything," I muttered.

"I'm serious!"

"I know! And I'll do my best to stick with the regular shortcuts."

Dr. O was on the chaperone list, so it was just as well if I didn't use my projection, but I wasn't ready to promise anything. It took away my biggest weapon, my last resort to keep Mia calm if worst came to worst.

I groaned and mentally prepared for working through the best party of the year.

"Thriller" by Michael Jackson blared out. It echoed

hauntingly. Nice. I gave the DJ a thumbs-up. The kids wooted and kept dancing, and I realized I'd never stopped my projection. I cut it off, sharp as a knife's edge.

One kid bumped Elizabeth. She staggered into Rodney and suddenly, all the kids were pushing and shoving. Voices rose, name-calling grew. "Stop it!" "Klutz!"

"What the—" Avery began.

Then Elizabeth punched Alex, and a heap of bodies fell in a writhing mass of fighting.

I stood with my jaw open. I was the only one who knew that the fighting began just after I stopped sending playful happiness. Maybe Avery had a point about sticking with tools we actually understood.

Teachers started handing out detentions, and the fistfight settled down fast. I heaved a sigh of relief. The negative side effect wasn't long-lasting, at least. And if Mia was going to have one like that, she surely already would have. And Ethan, too. Their shields probably protected them. But better not to take any more chances.

"It's going to be fine, Avery. Trust me."

"I do."

I thought of how I'd set Avery up with Todd again. My stomach twisted. Well, too late now.

 275

"Meet me at the punch table when y'all get there to check in. And have fun tonight with Todd," I said when we headed home, trying to make the best of it.

Avery looked suspicious, but a delighted smile broke through anyway. "I will!"

I had ensured it already. One night of happiness guaranteed, for everyone but me. If I couldn't have the best night ever, at least the ones I loved would.

A few hours later, two outfits lay on my bed: one angel, one devil. The devil was perfect for grabbing Ethan's attention with a high skirt—as high as I was ever allowed—and sparkling red horns. He'd no doubt make a bad pun about me having a devilish smile, which added potential flirting opportunities. But the angel costume was beautiful. Elegant.

The angel dress would've been perfect for Avery, and the two of us would have been adorable as a set. I didn't regret my friend's happiness, or anyone else's for that matter. I wished, though, that I could just focus on having fun myself sometimes. Taking care of everyone was getting old. I touched the slippery satin fabric of the devil costume and sighed.

Maybe it hadn't been such a smart move on my part to push Todd's feelings. In fact, he might break up with Avery *again* after I stopped interfering. I'd been so sure Avery would've seen through him by now, but she seemed as enamored as ever. I counted back to the last time I'd refreshed Todd's emotions and realized my influence might not last the night. I broke into a sweat.

"Knock, knock," my dad said from the doorway. "Why the long face, kiddo?" He sat down on the bed next to me.

"Just trying to figure out … the right and wrong of stuff."

"Heavy stuff for a party night."

"Unfortunately."

He chuckled lightly. "Well, I wanted to tell you how proud I am of you. I know going to the dance alone isn't what you wanted, but I'm glad you're going to support your friends. Since you're on the committee, it's important that you're there."

"I know I've got to be there, but I'm afraid the dance will be really awful for a few friends and I'm not sure how—or how much—to help. Especially without using my gift."

He grew serious. "Don't feel bad about your friends

277

floundering around like the rest of the world does. It's the only way for people to grow."

"If you say so."

"I do. Messing with people's moods would definitely bring its own set of problems."

Maybe in some cases it already had, I admitted. But I wished I could tell him that he was wrong, at least with Mom. Our home life was still like a fairy tale. A mother who sang while she cooked, a father who beamed when he got home. I was determined to maintain that particular situation. My father seemed to believe that the changes stemmed from that one unintended projection but had continued to improve naturally, without further influence. I felt it was kinder to let him think so.

"Is this a dad-and-daughter conversation only?" Mom poked her head through the open door.

"Of course not." My dad's smile could light up the sky. My mood rose at the sight.

My mom said, "Good! Because check this out!"

She pulled out a feathered mask and slid it over her face. "It's Mardi Gras!"

"Uh, Mom, that's not tonight?" Maybe too much projection was making my mom's mind slip after all? But just to make sure they had a good time tonight, I sent a tiny trickle of happiness into her. The tiniest. Hardly anything at all. Just to be safe.

Mom giggled. "For our dance costumes. Here, honey." She handed Dad a mask, too.

I goggled. "What?"

"Didn't your mother tell you?" he said. "We're chaperones tonight. They were short on numbers, so I volunteered us." He pulled on the mask and posed with spirit fingers.

"Great." I groaned.

My parents both laughed.

"Don't worry," said Mom. "We'll pretend we don't even know you."

"See you there!" Dad kissed my cheek and searched my eyes. He whispered, "Whatever's bothering you, I know you'll make the right decision. I believe in you."

With those soft words, arrows straight into my heart, my parents left me alone to choose between being an angel or a devil.

Really, there was no choice. In Avery's new horrible vision, I was wearing the devil costume when I somehow ruined our lives. Every decision had the potential to affect the future. I held the angel costume up to myself in the mirror. It washed me out and did nothing for my blond hair and pale skin.

But symbolism mattered. No more emotional manipulation. The angel costume would remind me, keep me on my good-girl toes. I'd only project if it was an emergency. I promised myself I'd even confess to Avery what I'd done—tomorrow. Tonight had to be about saving us from whatever Mia would do if she refused to let go of the past and face her future.

I reached for the halo. It sat a bit crooked on my head, but that seemed about right.

23

MUSIC filled the air like fog, snaking through the roiling crowds of kids and stiff-necked chaperones. Emotions were even thicker, a surging ocean for me to swim through. My ears ached from the DJ's blaring speakers, but my heart ached more from the clashing emotions: fear, humiliation, heartbreak, lust, hope, mindless elation. The moods ran the gamut and swirled into a sort of emo-soupy-sludge, making me dizzy.

I leaned against the punch table and kept my eyes open for a redhead in 1950s zombie attire. Couldn't be more than one. I focused on building a waterfall that constantly washed over me. It muted the emotional noise some but not enough. Perhaps I should have spent the last two weeks learning to silence all emotions around me instead of projecting. I pressed my fingers to my temples and promised to get right on that. Maybe Ethan would help me out.

I craned my neck to get a glimpse of him and his band, Kinetic Threat, setting up on stage. They'd play after the DJ warmed up the room. The goober could've taken me to the dance, if he'd really wanted. But no, I had to stand here waiting, alone.

"Hey, Parker!" Darla waved from across the room, one arm wrapped around Aaron. "Great party!"

Startled, I waved back. Talk about a mood switch, but at least Darla was happy again. Hopefully the bad effects would stay gone.

"Thanks!"

Darla was right about the party. Our team had knocked this dance out of the park. The dark room was dotted with green glowing lamps and glow sticks taped under the tables. The strobe lights of the DJ gave the room an eerie feel, like an old movie set. The music pulsed in my throat, forcing my foot to tap to the beat. And my awesome classmates had gone all out with the costumes. I grinned, pride pushing aside my pity party.

Pirates and elves and vampires danced to the beat. Deshawn, despite his protests, had even thrown on a doctor's coat and his dad's stethoscope. He was helping the band with their equipment. Ethan wore his band T-shirt, which totally didn't count as a costume, but before I could march over there and chew him out, I noticed something glittering in his hair. I looked closer: little devil horns poked up through his spiky hair.

My breath caught short, knees going a bit weak. Had he remembered what my costume was going to be? Had he meant to match?

Even the teachers had gotten into the spirit, so my parents weren't the only adults dressed up, at least. My mother was the only adult getting her groove on, though, in the middle of the dance floor. She did another spin, sending her skirt flying high. I cringed. Holy cheesesticks. Maybe that last little hit of happy today had been too much. But before I could focus enough to send some calm in its place, Mia and Josh arrived.

They looked like a perfect match, equally gorgeous. A long, tulle skirt hung from Mia's hips to her knees, with a tightly fitted white bodice that showed off the smooth brown skin of her shoulders. Her black hair flowed down her back in waves, adorned with red and yellow flowers. She looked simply magical.

Josh sent a flash of heat through the room all by his

lone self. I fanned myself in response. His costume was simple, but the black pants paired with a loose white tunic shirt and forest green vest worked on him. He wore a crown of autumn leaves and a deep green cloak swished in pace with his long strides. They both walked with the grace of fairy royalty.

I let out a wolf whistle, and Mia turned to search me out. The grin Mia gave bolstered my sagging confidence.

"You. Look. Amazing," I said, running over to them. "I'm so glad you're here!"

"I'll get us something to drink. Want anything, Parker?" Josh asked.

"Such a gentleman. No, I'm good, but thanks. The punch table is right over there."

Josh nodded his thanks and left us alone.

Mia asked, "Ethan's already on stage with his band?"

"Yeah. They'll be playing soon. He hasn't even said hello."

"Then he's an idiot, because you look incredible, too."

I glanced down at the long white dress. My angel wings had bumped a few people, but I liked the way they glittered. "Thanks."

Mia reached over and straightened the halo. "There. Now you're perfect."

Josh had completed his mission, drinks in hands. We both turned to watch his approach.

"He seems pretty perfect, too," I murmured. "It's good y'all found each other."

Mia blushed with a smile. "Yeah. I'm glad you pushed me to get to know him better. I wouldn't be here without you."

The sweet words triggered a flash of guilt. Mia seemed so happy now ... but only because I forced her to be. What if the happy couple fell apart the way Darla did or the kids during setup? But my mom was still okay. I held onto that like a lifeline. And Ethan, too.

I kept my tone light. "I think you'd have managed fine without me."

Avery walked up, Todd in tow. "Wow, Parker. I'm glad you went with the angel costume. Girl, you look divine."

"We're all kinds of gorgeous here, I guess."

Avery managed to look stylish even with her red hair half-falling out from its bun, topped with a tiara. Her poodle skirt was ripped and covered with fake blood, and black circles smudged under her eyes, but no amount of bad makeup could cover up her happy glow.

"You make a great zombie," I told her, "but I can't believe you went with messy hair when you could have worn this."

"Not just any zombie," Todd pointed out. "She's a 1950s zombie homecoming queen."

I pursed my lips. "Of course she is."

Mia said, "You make adorable zombies."

"Brains!" Todd tugged Avery toward the food table.

"See you later!" she called, waving.

"Yeah. Later," I said. The words got swallowed by the noise as Ethan's band took the stage, but I couldn't take the time to watch. Not yet.

Josh had already pulled Mia onto the dance floor. I shook off the embarrassment of my mother, my loneliness about Avery, my guilt about Mia. I focused like a laser, to make sure this night ended well.

At first, it seemed all was perfect ... almost. The happy couple danced, but they didn't kiss. They smiled shyly but didn't laugh. I looked at Avery with a question mark in my eyes, but Avery shook her head and shrugged her shoulders. Nothing had changed yet.

Deshawn came by and offered a cup of punch. "You look a little worn down for an angel."

I gulped the cold drink. "Thanks, Doctor Deshawn. I don't understand what's taking so long. Look at them. They're perfect."

"How things look and how they are aren't always the same."

"What are they talking about?"

He shook his head. "Nope. No way. I'll listen in on Dr. O and scientist-talk, but those two right there? Sorry, Mood Ring. But from what I'm seeing, you'd better hope our man over there busts out some smooth moves fast."

"Anything new from Dr. O?"

"She's been on the phone a lot, yeah. Talking about projects I don't understand, but something sounded off. We've got to cross the finish line tonight."

"Doing my best."

"I know. We all are. I'll keep you posted if I hear anything from Counselor Creeptastic."

The time grew later. Ethan's band sounded fantastic, doing mostly covers. They took a short break—too short to even find him in the crowd—and soon claimed the stage again. Their lead singer, Luke, was doing a great job, but to me, it was always Ethan's band, no matter who was on lead mic.

Luke shouted, "Hey everyone. Let's get this party lit! This next song is an original, written by our very own Ethan Kwon!" The crowd yelled and gathered around the stage. I bit the inside of my cheek in frustration. Josh and Mia needed a slow song, but I knew this set—we wouldn't get a slow number until near the end.

Ethan caught my eye and winked. Then he called out, "One, two, three, four!"

He began a driving beat, and I burst into full-body goose bumps. Kids screamed and began to dance, not so much with each other but as a crowd.

I couldn't take my eyes off Ethan. His spiky black hair grew wilder as his body swayed to the beat, his expression fierce. He'd lost the horns somewhere along the way, but he didn't need them to look devilish, not with a smile like his. He'd developed a light sheen of sweat along his arms as he worked. The deep bass of the drum sent thunderbolts through me.

In the bridge of the next song—another original— he paused while Luke sang a haunting melody a capella. He sounded good, but he didn't light up the stage like Ethan did.

I wove my way closer and caught Ethan's eye. "You are amazing," I mouthed. He would assume I meant the playing, but really, he was flat-out amazing in every way. He held my gaze, his chest heaving as he waited for his cue, and for one second, it felt like we were alone in the whole room. Buzzing filled my mind.

Thoughts of watching out for Mia, for my mother, for Avery ... Everything faded away, until the only thing left was the glowing spotlight on Ethan Kwon, a best friend since forever, crush for years. And he didn't know. How could he? I hid my emotions as carefully as he did. He hadn't taken me to the dance, but there'd been a good reason. And I'd acted like it didn't matter. He wasn't the empath. I needed to tell him my real feelings.

I'd tell him. Tonight. Just like all the other kids who'd offered up their hearts on the sacrificial table of the school dance, for better or worse. Regular people didn't get to read hearts before deciding what to do. They had to venture forth into the wild unknown. Maybe the risk is what made it all worthwhile.

I pressed closer to the stage and moved toward the right, so I could get an unobstructed view of my boy. He was really pounding on the drums now, eyes closed, completely caught up in the music. It gave me shivers. *He* gave me shivers.

His drum sticks were mere blurs, his feet dancing on the pedals ... I focused on those pedals. I counted them. The hi-hat pedal had no foot pressing on it, but the cymbals were clanging away anyway. He was using his gift to make them move.

Heat flowed over me, and I glanced around at the crowd. Dr. O'Malley stood by the entrance, scanning the room. Ethan's feet weren't visible from the front, thank God, but from the side, someone else might notice. Luckily, a mosh pit had formed in the middle of the gym, and not even Avery was paying attention to Ethan's antics amid the chaos.

I sent a jolt of good mood vibes to him—a kind of knock on his door. He almost missed a beat but looked over at me, furrowing his brow.

"Knock it off!" I said, knowing he'd read my lips. I mimed the hi-hat cymbals hitting together and wiggled my finger at him firmly. He rolled his eyes, but the cymbals went still.

I let out a sigh of relief, but the mere fact he'd done it made me tremble. What if he did something worse? I narrowed my eyes at him, and he laughed.

Well, crap.

KINETIC THREAT

finally moved into their slower ballad of the set without any incidences. There was little chance of any drum stick dilemma with a pace like that, at least. Kids paired up, and I looked around. Everyone I knew had a partner for the dance floor. Except me. Parker Mills, a two-time winner of the Ms. Divine Pecan Pageant. *Unbelievable.* Even Deshawn, so committed to staying single, was dancing with Belinda Trudeau.

Well. That was okay. It helped me focus on Mia and Josh. They were in each other's arms at last. Nathan the guitarist had his instrument wailing, slow and lilting. Mia and Josh moved slowly round and round, his hands on her hips, her hands on his shoulders. The dim lighting made it hard to read their expressions.

Time for a progress report. Given their distance from me, I'd get a wider reception than I preferred, but an X-ray wouldn't affect anyone but me. It was fair game. I opened my shielding and stumbled a little at the rush. Hearts and roses practically floated in the air from the combined euphoria of the couples in the room. It was downright intoxicating, despite the discord of jealousy and loneliness woven throughout like a descant in a minor key. But Mia and Josh were still closed to me.

It didn't matter. It was obvious to anyone with eyeballs in their head that Mia liked him but was too afraid to let him closer. It was equally clear he was a good guy who'd never press her beyond her comfort zone. Normally, that'd be lovely, and they could take their sweet time. But the clock would be striking metaphorical midnight soon, and if something good didn't happen for Mia, the vision could still happen. Projecting on Mia was a no-go, but Avery hadn't said anything about using it on someone else. Someone like Josh.

More sparkling zings of interest and delight brushed past me from all directions. If he felt anything like what half the room felt, he'd have to try for a kiss soon. It wouldn't take much to tip him over, and there were plenty of dim areas for a little private moment. And granted, Josh had been pretty much a solid wall, but I was so much more powerful now. All's well that ends well, or so Shakespeare said. One little emotional push toward Josh could fix the future. And bending the rules was one of my specialties.

Don't be afraid to kiss her, I sent to Josh. It was all emotions, not words, just shy of a command. I dug up handfuls of boldness and threw it at him, balancing it with a dash of respectful concern. Of course, he already had that in spades. A turtle could move faster than him.

Avery whispered something to Todd and hurried over to get a drink. "Hey there, hope you're having a good time," she gushed, and stepped on my toes. Hard. And the girl had on steel-tipped saddle shoes.

"Owwww," I squeaked. Avery cut her eyes to the side, leading my gaze back to Josh. He was looking over at us now, staring at me, not Mia, eyebrows drawn into a dark V. Was he baffled? Maybe even irritated? Whatever. I was overdoing it if a non-gifted could sense my toying. Avery was casually shaking her head as if listening to the music, but I got the message.

Dr. O was standing across the gym, eyes on us. On me. My breath froze. Fear surged through me, and my manic excitement vanished, leaving me in a cold sweat. Reality returned with a hard slap to the face. What on Earth was I thinking, using my gift after the obvious mess at auditions yesterday? And the fistfight this morning?

I gulped and turned off the fountain of love sparks. I bricked up my shielding. The party punch curdled in my stomach, my sparkling mood snuffed out in a heartbeat like the burnt husks of firecrackers. Once the overwhelming love vibes faded from my senses and the thrill of matchmaking was crushed by fear, I saw Mia and Josh with new eyes.

I saw myself with new eyes.

In the not-too-distant past, I would have said the ends justified the means when it came to protecting my friends. But now … no. I would read a heart if I had to, but I wouldn't use my projection anymore. Not on anyone. Not even my mother. That last thought brought a small pinch to my heart, but I squashed it ruthlessly.

With even Ethan acting weird now, directing my gift at people seemed fraught with unexpected danger, like a minefield in a mini-golf course. Projecting had turned me from the Herald of Happiness to the Queen of Mayhem. And really, maybe it was time to reconsider *all* my shortcuts, psychic or not. Interfering in people's lives had consequences, no matter how well it was done.

Mia and Josh genuinely liked each other. What if I messed it all up? Maybe that was why Avery's vision had me in the demon outfit, triggering Mia's breakdown.

Besides, the dance was almost over, and there'd been no sign that a dangerous secret had slipped out of Mia yet. No risk of danger, no risk of being found out, assuming Ethan kept his gift under wraps. If anyone, I was the one out of control, but I'd grabbed back the reins in time.

Maybe Avery's vision had already been altered. A girl could hope.

The song slipped into another ballad. Avery turned to find Todd in the crowd. I heard the sharp intake of breath before a jab of pain broke loose from Avery's heart, slicing at my own. I spun.

Todd was dancing with Veronica West.

They were pressed cheek to cheek, bliss written plain on their faces. They couldn't get any closer if Todd were ironed on her. Avery turned slowly to me. Her eyes were narrow.

"Tell me you didn't make him take me to the dance, Parker. Tell me you didn't influence him."

My whole face and neck grew hot. Next to the white

angel dress, I'd look scarlet.

I grabbed Avery's shoulders. "I'm sorry. It was an impulse, and then you were so happy—"

"Stop. Just stop. I'm so mad I can't even talk to you right now. You can take your happy plan for me and shove it." Avery spun to go and looked back over her shoulder. "Who are you, even? I don't think I know you anymore."

It felt like the ground was falling away from me. *Avery,* I wanted to cry out. But I couldn't. My tongue wasn't working. My head was aching. But Josh and Mia were still dancing. Still dancing. There was still hope.

I didn't send any emotions to them. But I begged them in my mind. *Please, come on! Come on!*

Josh ran his hand down Mia's hair, and she looked up. *Yes,* I thought.

Mia offered a tremulous smile, meeting Josh's eyes, so very dark in the shadows. Bright flashing lights shimmered along his blond hair.

Their movements slowed.

Perfect, perfect, I thought, my lips dry.

Josh lowered his head, tilting to one side.

Oh my gosh. Please please.

Mia lifted her chin.

Yes!

Mia froze.

What?

Mia backed up, shaking her head.

No. Oh no, no, no.

And Mia ran. Ran from the dance floor like Cinderella, leaving her handsome prince alone in the swirling spotlights.

Mia's pain was a sudden shockwave for me, even through my shielding. My head bowed under the weight of it. It was like a stadium full of people roaring. The flickering lights didn't hide the tears gathered in Mia's eyes as she shoved past on the way out of the gym.

This was my fault. I had to fix it, but I wasn't sure how.

Thunder rolled through the room. Real thunder, the loud crackling kind that meant a severe storm was on its way. My head snapped up. Mia's path out the side door would take her directly to the courtyard, outdoors without any cover.

I took off, pushing past bobbing dancers. With each touch, emotions slammed into me, my shields shattered from Mia's extreme pain and fear. Pleasure, disappointment, jealousy, hopefulness. A new emotion took the lead with each contact. The wild whiplash of emotions had me staggering.

I yanked open the door. A gust of chilly wind blew my halo right off. "Mia!"

The wind was already howling. Inside the gym, heat lifted from the crowd like lazy smoke from candles, but outside, the temperature was dropping fast. Texas weather didn't mess around.

"Mia!" I called again, gathering my skirt to run. At least it wasn't raining yet.

"Don't." A voice behind me was firm and insistent.

I spun to see Josh looking out the door, eyes searching.

"Don't?" I asked, disbelief pitching my voice higher than usual.

"Don't go after her. She needs a break, okay?"

"You don't understand. She's afraid of thunderstorms. She went this way, but it leads outside to the courtyard— not safe in a storm."

"I'll go find her."

"But I want to help—"

"But you're *not* helping, don't you get that yet?"

The words silenced me like nothing else could have.

I backed away from the door, and Josh ran down the sidewalk. His cloak flew sideways, catching on the waist-high bushes, and he tore it off without pausing. His crown of leaves tumbled away.

Dazed, I turned to face the heat and the noise of the gym. Deshawn was watching by the punch bowl, eyes sharp—probably listening in. Ethan was still on stage, but he was watching me too. His eyes tracked mine, and I had no smile to offer. No cute flirty move to give. Not now.

I wasn't helping.

No, it couldn't be right. Josh didn't understand. I dragged the thought around me like a comforting blanket. If he knew the truth, he wouldn't have said such a thing. He didn't know what I'd really been up to, how hard I'd worked to set Mia free from fear and guilt. That Mia was truly my friend.

I turned to go back outside. I was going to follow Mia no matter what. Josh didn't know anything.

I was stopped by my mother's hand on my shoulder. "Parker."

The Mardi Gras mask was gone. My mother's face was crumpled into an earnest expression. "Listen, honey, I've been thinking, I love to dance. I simply love it, and I realized that's what I need to do."

"What?" The music was too loud. I must have heard wrong.

"I need to move to Las Vegas, honey. I'm going to be a showgirl! Isn't that fantastic? I'll miss you and your father, but I told him, and he says he understands. So, I'm leaving tomorrow."

The lights swooping around the dance floor seemed to carry me off with them.

"You're ... leaving us? To be a *showgirl*?"

"I'm sorry. But yes, I'm leaving. Tonight, in fact." Her eyes were lit from within by a feverish gleam.

"Tonight?" My voice was dull. Numbness stole through me.

"YOLO, isn't that what the kids say? I've got to go pack, but you'll have to visit me a lot, okay? I've got to follow my dreams and my passions. That's what you're always saying! And you're right, I see that now. Being happy is the most important thing."

Was it? For an empath, it had always seemed so. Yet somehow, at this moment, I thought I'd never been more wrong in my life.

25

I ran to the quietest spot I could find. In the peaceful darkness of the library, I peeled off my wings, left them on the floor. I wouldn't be needing them anymore. I laid my head against the study table and flopped my arms out like a doll's. The tabletop was cool against my cheek. Messing with people's feelings had never been so easy, and yet everything else was so hard.

"I don't think osmosis works for learning stuff, you know," a familiar voice said. "You've got to actually read the books, not just be near them."

Wearily, I lifted my head and stuck my tongue out at Ethan. He flipped on the low lights behind the main desk. His eyes twinkled, and he walked with more pep than a whole cheer squad at Homecoming.

"God, don't you ever get tired?" I said. "You've been working hard up there. You sound great, by the way."

"Thanks. We took a set break. Deshawn listened in on the thing with your mom. That really sucks. And we both saw Mia running out. He's keeping an eye and ear on the gym. Where did Avery go?"

He rubbed my shoulders, and I sighed. "You have until forever to stop doing that. Avery, well, I don't know. She's mad at me."

His fingers stilled for a moment. "Why?"

"I screwed up. Can we leave it at that?"

"If it helps."

"I don't know what'll help. She's mad, Mia ran off, and Josh told me I wasn't helping. And my mom. Well. You heard from Deshawn. Her leaving will kill my dad." My voice cracked.

"I'm sorry, Parker. I am." His fingers were strong, pushing away the aches and pain. He leaned over me, to put more pressure on my shoulders, and his body brushed against mine.

My eyes fluttered shut. Our end goal for the night still mattered, but I just couldn't get back on the field right away. Please no. Not yet. All I wanted was to curl against Ethan, lean against him, forget everything else.

His hands slid up along my neck. My heart, bruised as it was, jumped hard at his touch. Heat crackled inside me and spread like wildfire. He was the only one who made me tremble. These feelings would never go away. I didn't want them to.

I'd dug myself a deep hole with my friends by trying to manipulate every situation instead of just being honest. I'd done the same thing with Ethan. Flirting. Laughing. But never laying my real feelings on the table, never taking risks. I was tired of pretending. I licked my lips.

"It's not just about Mia. Or Avery. Or even my mom."

"What else is it?"

I couldn't give myself all the courage I'd been pumping into Mia, but I forced the words out anyway. "I wanted you to take me to the dance, you idiot."

His hands froze. I twisted around and looked up at him. His head tilted to one side, a little furrow between his brows.

"You mean you wanted a date?"

I sighed, stood to face him, and took one of his hands. "No, dummy. I didn't want *a* date. I wanted you."

I could prove it. If I simply let my gift go.

Swallowing hard, I opened my shielding. But instead of projecting a fabricated emotion, I let him feel the truth inside me. The years of affection, the confusion, the yearning—I let it all shine. My heart was under an X-ray for the first time, my more-than-friendship feelings exploding right into him. Our gazes latched, and I didn't look away.

"Parker?" he said in a strangled voice, one hand tight in mine, the other clenched against his chest.

I wished his own feelings were on display. He was probably horrified. Like his sister had a thing for him. Gross.

Just let the Earth swallow me now.

"Never mind. Forget it." I let go of his hand. So much for courage. Friendship was better than nothing. I struggled to put those feelings back under wraps, but it was like trying to hold down a tidal wave. Some happiness guru I was.

"Parker," he said again, his voice different.

Tendrils of happiness floated from him, cobwebs of pleasure brushing along my skin, followed by electrical stings of … excitement? And a rush of heart-filled caring. For me. For *me.*

From Ethan.

It all rained over me, like standing in a downpour of love. My exhaustion was swept away.

 304

I whispered, "Where are your shields?"

"I dropped them." He took hold of my shoulders.

"Why?"

"Because for an empath, you're awfully blind sometimes."

And then he kissed me.

I did feel blind. I'd imagined this kiss too many times to count, but reality was a thousand times better. His lips fit perfectly against mine, warm and soft. His arms were tight around me. I leaned into him and let it all go.

Forget my quest to save us all. Forget my mother's rejection. Forget that my friendships were in smoldering ruins. Forget everything but Ethan, his heart beating with mine. I felt lighter than air.

The top of my head bumped into something. Confused, I looked up and gasped. We were eight feet high, heads brushing the ceiling, legs tangled.

"Ethan! We're floating," I burst out with a laugh.

"It's the way you make me feel," he murmured, and I thought I might explode with happiness.

Then a hand grabbed my ankle, and the golden bloom of emotions around me cut off into sudden silence. I plunged to the ground, landing in a heap with Ethan.

"Good God, you're like a thermonuclear explosion in

 305

here. Do you want everyone to know you're psychically gifted? Do you have any idea what would happen if people found out? Get a grip, for Christ's sake."

Rubbing my sore elbow, I blearily squinted at the interloper.

White blond hair. Dark brown eyes. Glaring daggers that should have pierced me with agony, especially with my shield scattered to the four corners of the earth. But I felt nothing.

Holy Buddha on a stick.

"Josh?"

Just Josh. But not so "just" after all. He'd neutralized Ethan's powerful gift and my own with a touch with some kind of psychic gift of his own.

Maybe the problem that was going to set Mia off had nothing to do with me.

He looked scornfully down at me. "I thought you knew better than this. Whatever. Looks like you get another chance to help. She pushed me away, and her gift's getting out of control. Like, right now."

Chills raced down my skin. "So she *is* psychic!"

"And I thought you were supposed to be sensitive to people."

"But how do you know—"

"We don't have time for this right now. Mia's out there, really upset. She needs her friend, not Parker the Psychic. Your gift isn't what you think anyway."

Thunder boomed again at that moment. The lights flickered.

"Wait a minute," I said. Memories flickered through my mind: The wind whipping Mia's hair across her face at the stargazing party. The sudden storm during the art portfolio discussion. The candle blowing out from the gust of wind at the slumber party, not an open window at all. Mia's terror of thunderstorms and obsession with painting them.

"Oh my God." I stopped cold. "She can control the weather."

"She can *influence* the weather. Right now, her control is pretty much gone," Josh snapped. Thunder rolled through the air again.

"But you could stop her, shut down her gift! That's what you do, right?"

"Yeah, if I could touch her, but she wouldn't let me near her. The wind kept pushing me away. She needs someone she trusts. That's you, Parker. Even if you don't deserve it."

"I do care for her. I promise. I was only trying to help,"

I said. Ethan touched my hand.

Josh nodded, but his eyes went unfocused like Avery's during a vision. "God—I can see her now. Her gift's spiraling. It's so strong."

"Good thing we've got you, then," I said. "Lead us to her, and I'll do what I can."

We set off down the hall, Ethan jogging behind us. "No wonder we didn't guess about you," he said to Josh. "You probably don't seem gifted unless you're stopping a power."

Josh spoke quickly, clearly distracted by whatever psychic fireworks he was sensing. "I've always thought it was a matter of balance. Natural laws and all. A powerful psychic balanced by, well, me. I can see other people's gifts and turn them off with my touch. And I can sense when other people use a psychic ability, like a radar. It's how I found you guys here, and how I'm seeing Mia."

"Handy," Ethan said. "But how—"

Deshawn waved from the doorway at the opposite end of the breezeway near the main gym entrance. "Your break's over," he called, voice echoing against the brick walls of the building.

Ethan stopped, looking torn.

"Go," Josh demanded. "Keep everyone busy and

entertained. Play so loud no one will hear if a tornado is blowing through."

"Could that happen?"

Josh pressed his lips grimly. "It might."

"I have lots more questions for you later, after the dance."

"Sure. Assuming there is a later."

"Be safe," Ethan told me, with a quick caress along my cheek before taking off to join Deshawn. My skin tingling, I followed after Josh.

We left the protection of the building at the main back exit, stepping into the middle of the breezeway that ran along the length of the school. Wind whistled between the tall columns of the narrow, covered corridor.

"Are there more of us where you're from?" I asked. We headed toward the open courtyard.

"There's ten of us at my old school. My mom and I came looking for others, thinking there would be safety in numbers. There was a weird drug used in a fertility treatment trial—"

"Wait, what?" I stumbled but kept going.

He glanced at me. "Long story. Listen, you can read people's emotions easy, I bet, but when you project, you're doing something else. I don't know what exactly, but it's not really empathy. It's like you're making them crazy. When I thought empathy was all you were using, I wasn't worried. Mia's got strong natural shields; I can see them. But this other thing you do—it breaks past shields and wreaks havoc. I didn't understand it until tonight when you tried to use it on me full-blast, or I would have warned you."

I screeched to a halt and grabbed his arm. "What? But I'm making people happy! Setting them free from fear!"

"No, I think you're setting them free from a sense of responsibility. We all have certain rules we play by, but you're making people rip up the rulebook. I'm a psychic sinkhole, so it doesn't affect me, but for everyone else— you're creating chaos."

"No!" I protested. "I, I can't—my gift can't be doing anything like that."

"Your gift is probably what made Ethan use his gift like that today—such a bad move. Can't you see how the people you project on start to lose their inhibitions? Your gift is why Mia's so close to exposing us."

"I just hoped that if she felt confident enough to go out with you, she'd be too sidetracked by all the romance to cause problems tonight."

He quirked his lips, but sadness hid in the back of his

eyes. "Guess I wasn't enough of a distraction. And here I hoped she actually liked me."

"Oh, she does—"

He lifted a hand to cut me off. "Doesn't matter. And that's up to her to tell me, if she ever does. Show us a little respect."

"I do respect you! And Mia!"

"Then let us deal with our own problems."

Ouch. I'd never thought of it like that before. Josh was on a roll.

"It's not just you, anyway. I didn't help the situation, either. I knew she was nervous. I shouldn't have tried to kiss her, but I—well." He sighed. "Anyway, deep down, I think she's tired of hiding, tired of being scared. We all get that way sometimes, right?"

I gulped hard. "Maybe."

Rain began to fall, spraying sideways under the narrow roof. I shivered.

"Definitely," he corrected. "Mia's not a bad person; she's just hurting. We should've given her more time and space. If you use your projection on her again, she might snap."

My mother's bizarre decision to take off to Vegas came to mind. "I believe you. Is Mia still in the courtyard?"

His eyes grew unfocused again. "Yes."

"I've got this. Okay. Avery's a precog—you probably knew that." I rolled my eyes at his nod. "Grab her and find out if she sees the future changing yet."

But Avery was already running down the breezeway toward us from the gym, zombie hair wildly flapping, saddle shoes clomping.

"Ethan told us about Josh and said you might need more back-up," she panted.

I grabbed her in a tight hug. "I'm so sorry about Todd. I didn't know what I was doing, and it was wrong and—"

Avery held me back by the shoulders. "We'll deal with that later. Listen to me. The future's close to shifting now. She needs you."

"I'm afraid." I spoke softly. "Her pain's going to be torture—and I can't even stop her with my projection if she gets out of hand. What if I make things even worse?" My throat grew tight.

Avery said, "I'm sorry, but you don't have time for a freak out. Ethan has the perfect view of the gym from the stage, and Deshawn's eavesdropping on just about everyone, ready to come up with a distraction if he has to. I'll look into the future while you do your thing with Mia. You can do this."

Lightning crawled across the sky.

"Make it or break it time, Parker," Avery said.

I lifted my chin and nodded. "Okay then. Let's go."

ETHAN'S band was slaying it in the gym, so no one else roamed the breezeways. Hopefully the rain would keep people out of the courtyard, too. We flat-out ran, and I considered all my available options:

- Sweet talk Mia into rejoining the dance like nothing had happened? Too late in the game and insulting to boot. The girl was too smart for that.
- Lie to Mia to keep her happy? Nope. Lying had already caused too much trouble.
- Tell Mia the truth and get her on our side? Mia was, after all, one of us. But if she suddenly turned into a weather goddess and caused a big scene, people would come running.

We turned the corner at the end of the building and ran down the last short breezeway. The courtyard came into view, and a bolt of lightning hit a tree nearby. A deafening crack followed immediately, rattling the drain pipe above our heads.

"She's in the courtyard." Josh gestured at the end of the breezeway. "Out there."

I swallowed hard. "That's my cue. If she can't shut it down herself, I'll bring her to you, but only if she agrees."

Avery said, "Good luck, Parks. We'll wait here, watching for anyone coming this way."

I hesitated. "In case things go bad out there, I really am sorry, Avery, for what I did. I love you. You know that, right?"

"I know it." Avery tugged on my fluttering sleeve. "I'm still mad, but I love you, too, you idiot. You're no angel, but you aren't the devil. You've got this."

Maybe. Either way, I would do my best for my friends. All of them.

Mia sat on one of the stone benches scattered about the cobblestoned courtyard. A high wall of white rocks anchored the back of the courtyard, and half-walls edged the rest of the courtyard except for two exits. I usually loved the arrangement, but today it felt like a prison. The empty flagpole rope in the center of the space clanged morosely with each gust, and the trees around the square bowed and shimmied.

The rain had already turned Mia's dark hair into a tangled mass of black cobwebs, the cheery flowers gone. Her tulle skirt hung as heavy as her mood.

I shifted my feet back and forth. The poor girl looked crushed. "Mia?"

She jumped up. "Who's there?"

I lifted both hands and stepped into the soft glow of the courtyard lights. "It's just me." Just me. No gift. No games. I'd have to be enough on my own. "I saw you run away from Josh."

Mia looked away. Her body jerked as if she were choking back a sob.

My body ached in response. I couldn't focus enough to block out Mia's pain, but that was okay. I let it come, lace through my veins. I didn't try to fix things or sugarcoat anything. Not this time.

"Listen, I really screwed up," I said. "I meant the best for you, but I'm sorry I pushed Josh on you. It was too much."

Mia shook her head. "It's not your fault."

"Well, it kinda is. It's hard to explain. I thought you guys would be so good together, and I didn't listen when you showed you weren't interested. I'm so sorry."

"I'm the one who agreed to come to the dance with him. I shouldn't have, but I couldn't seem to help myself." She sighed.

"About that. Yeah, that's what I mean when I said it's my fault. You really couldn't help yourself. Bear with me here. There's no way to make this sound less weird, so here goes: I can sense emotions from people, psychically." I left out the emotional manipulation part for now. I'd start with the easy part, work my way to the rest.

"Wh-what?" Mia shook her head. "Don't tease me. Not today."

I said, "I wouldn't do that to you. I'm your friend. But I'm also an empath, Mia. I've been able to sense people's emotions since I was little. Not all the time, but a lot."

"You … You're saying you can actually feel what I'm feeling?" Mia looked like she might vomit.

Not the response I had anticipated. If Josh somehow wrong about Mia being gifted, if our instincts were off—

I spoke faster. "Well, no, not from you all that much.

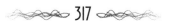

You have a natural ability to block me. It's why I suspected that you have a psychic ability, too. You do, don't you, Mia? You don't have to pretend anymore. We don't have to have any secrets from each other!"

The lights flickered around the courtyard. The sallow fluorescent lighting buzzed and hummed.

A wedge of fear spiked through the air. It tasted bitter, an aspirin dissolving on my tongue. A thrumming noise rode along the feeling, too, a deep growl, laced with panic. Like a cornered animal. Oh yeah, Mia was psychic, no doubt, and knew she was busted. She just needed to know she was safe, too.

I pressed forward, blinking against the icy rain still pouring down. It surrounded us like a cold curtain. My angel dress clung to my skin. "You're able to influence weather, Mia, which is amazing. You can learn to control it. You're not alone, and we can watch each other's backs. This is a good thing, I promise."

Mia's jaw clamped shut. Static rose in the air, and the top layers of her tulle skirt floated up a few inches from the electrical charge, fanning the skirt into a misty bell-shape. Another unexpected response. As an empath, I was batting zero.

Mia's voice was low, harsh. It didn't sound like her at

all. "You promise? After you've been lying to me all this time? Snooping on me?"

A quick sharp lash of betrayal cut at me, followed by fear ... loneliness ... and was that despair?

"No, Mia, please, I only wanted to help you feel better. And sometimes I really can't help sensing stuff. I thought you and Josh would be happy together, so I sort of encouraged things in that direction. And okay, at first I did it so you wouldn't expose us. Avery had this vision you somehow were going to push us out of hiding and it was bad—"

"Oh, Avery, too? Great! Great!" Mia began pacing, pulling her hair.

"But that's what I'm saying. You don't have to hide from us. We can help—"

"You and I are nothing alike. *Nothing.* I'm not like any of you." Her words were carved out of ice.

"Hey, whoa there, it's okay!" I raised my hands in a pose of surrender. My teeth chattered. "Look, we're not splashing it on the news. Our parents know, but no one else does. We're going to keep it that way. You're safe."

I tried to keep my voice casual, though it felt like knitting while the house was burning down. "But if you make a big scene, there will be people who will want to study our powers. You're putting us all in danger right now, but we'll be okay if we go home right now."

"No. Right now, I need to know who else already knows about me." Mia glared and braced her legs, crossing her arms. Girl wasn't going anywhere, and the dance would be ending soon.

I gritted my teeth. It'd be faster to play along than try to convince her to move. "Only a few know, but we all have gifts, too. Deshawn can hear people from far away, Avery gets visions of the possible future, and Ethan is a telekinetic. In fact," I rambled, "even Josh is psychic, and he's managed to stay completely under the radar until today."

Mia's head jerked up, her eyes wide. Everything grew still. Droplets of rain clung to her dress and hair, refracting the lights above. The harsh buzzing of the fluorescent lights grew louder under the sound of the rain. She licked her lips and whispered, "J-Josh? He's psychic, too?"

Not him! On a whip of pain, I heard the words as clearly as if Mia had wailed them.

"Looks that way," I said, trying to sound calm. "You have even more in common—"

I never got to finish my sentence. Mia backed toward the exit of the courtyard, holding up her hands.

"No. No, no, no," she chanted.

The pressure in the air began to plummet. My ears popped. Images flooded my mind, quick flashes one after another: Mia's mother, Mark, her mother again. Mark, Josh, Mark, Josh. The boys' faces blurred together until they were impossible to tell apart.

My stomach turned like I was on a tilt-a-whirl gone out of control.

Mia muttered, "It was all a trick. He lied, too. Josh never cared about me. Just like *him*." Frost formed along the edge of the sidewalk, crackling and hissing.

"No!" I pushed away the images and raised my voice to be heard over a new wail of wind. "Believe me, Josh really likes you!!"

"Liar! You knew about Mark! You knew about me this whole time—" Mia's words spiraled into a shriek. Tiny jagged lights flickered along the ground at her feet.

Fury flickered against my skin now and a feeling that was close to obsession, but different. Maybe this was what madness felt like. I fought to strengthen my shielding. This wasn't just a sad, scared girl worried about discovery. There was a whole lotta something else going on.

The wind rose, blowing my wet hair back from

my face. My nose was numb. A few loose courtyard cobblestones jittered as the gusts picked up speed. The flag pole rope clanged louder against the metal post.

"Calm down," I yelled over the howling winds, struggling to stabilize my footing.

"Stay away from me!" Mia screamed. Her fingers spread wide. Soaker hoses lining the grounds roiled like a nest of snakes and burst, *bam, bam, bam,* spraying us with icy water.

I ducked, covering my head with a yelp. Daggers of rage and betrayal stabbed at me. Mia's emotional storm was even more powerful than the one she'd created from the air.

Mia narrowed her eyes at the water spray arcing through the courtyard. She lifted a finger, and the droplets turned to tiny frozen chunks that clattered on the tile.

God Almighty, Mia had made hail. If anyone was looking for evidence of paranormal activity, an extremely localized ice storm on an otherwise ordinary Halloween night would definitely qualify. I didn't wonder anymore why Mia kept her gift under lock and key.

But I didn't run. "Mia, stop," I urged. "Please, it's important that you stop this."

Mia answered in a faint voice, as if she were sleep-walking.

"Why should I?"

My scalp crawled. "So they can't lock us up and study us like animals."

"But if you're dangerous enough, they won't be able to take you," Mia said. Her tone grew rougher. Angrier. "Aren't you tired of pretending to be less than you are?" Still heartbroken, but resentment was rushing in to fill the hollow space inside.

"I don't pretend anything. We just keep certain things to ourselves so we can live a normal life."

Grief mixed with a dark satisfaction coated me like sticky sap. The desire for revenge tasted bittersweet.

My hands turned icy, and I backed two steps away.

Mia put her hands on her cheeks and shook her head. "No. Why am I saying these things?" The swirling winds sputtered.

"Because of me." I took a deep breath. If I was ever going to earn back Mia's trust, it was time to come clean, confess the worst of the worst. This would either go very well—or horribly. But I had to take the gamble.

"Here's the truth, all of it. Recently, I haven't just been able to sense moods. I've been able to change them. And I've been using my gift to change your mood. To make you feel happier."

Mia looked like I had punched her in the gut. "You … what?"

I swallowed heavily. "Yeah. It's really bad, I know, but I swear I meant well. I just wanted to make you feel better, but I'm never doing that again. Ever. The thing is, when I was trying to lift your mood, I didn't know my ability has some major glitches."

"Glitches. Messing with my feelings had some … *glitches*?" Righteous rage blossomed on Mia's face, dancing over my skin like fire.

I flinched. "Yeah, see, we all have emotions we never act on, but I've been setting them loose on accident. It's like I opened the cage door on your deepest wants and fears and locked up your gatekeeper. Not to mention that I ran right over you when you didn't want to go out with Josh in the first place. I've screwed up lately, and I totally own that. I hope you can forgive me one day. But we need to stop all the psychic stuff right now, before anyone sees. Josh can help you. He can stop gifts."

Another wash of anger flared from her, slicing into my mind with words lined with bitterness and self-loathing. Words that sounded nothing like Mia.

Yes, let's find Josh, the voice whispered. *Maybe the liar needs to learn a lesson.*

"No," Mia moaned in answer to the silent thoughts. "Leave him alone."

I spoke carefully, slowly. "If you can't shut down your gift on your own right now, we can get Josh. He'll help."

The sly voice came again. Goosebumps broke out across my skin.

No one can help. Everything's ruined. Why not take everyone down with me?

I was nearly flattened beneath a sudden pressure on my heart. A world's weight of grief. The wind grew even stronger.

My words could barely escape from under the pressure of her pain. "Nothing's ruined here. Nothing will be. Not me. Not the others. And not you."

My words only spurred more hopelessness from her. My last bit of patience snapped. I was stopping the insanity show. I couldn't use my projection, but if I looked deeper inside Mia than I ever had before, maybe I'd find some truth that would connect us both. It wouldn't hurt Mia, only me.

But it would hurt a lot.

27

FOR once in my life, I would embrace pain instead of fighting it. I sent a tiny tendril of my own empathy through the bars that surrounded Mia's heart and found a frightened little girl who hated herself.

You're evil, Mia. You weren't meant to exist.

Your mother died because you were cursed. Cursed from birth.

Everything you touch will die.

Mia believed every word. Why wouldn't she? No one had ever told her otherwise. In my mind's eye, a weeping nine-year-old Mia sat in the dry dirt at home, clear as a movie on a screen.

Drought had ravaged South Texas for months. Bruise-colored clouds loomed, but not a drop of rain had fallen to bring relief. Young Mia wished with all her heart for rain to nourish the flowers she'd planted on her mother's grave, and the rain had come down, mixing with her own tears. For the first time, she'd realized she was different, cursed, and she'd known right then how her father would react. She'd lose him like she lost her mother and brother. And she'd been right. Her father hated her for her strange ability, one she couldn't hide well enough. She'd been all alone.

The image faded. My heart broke. "Mia. I'm sorry."

"You're sorry," Mia repeated, eyes narrowing. "Not good enough." She lifted her hands high. Wild energy shot from her into the sky, immediately followed by a crashing boom. The sky grew darker far too fast to be natural, looking like time-lapse photography.

Rage radiated from her, coating me with burning heat and broken hope. A pulsing need to lash out filled me, her urge to take revenge and make them pay. Then maybe this pain would go away. The literal bitterness made me choke. I pushed to my feet, planning to run to Mia, but it looked hazardous to my health to get any closer.

Mia's hair stood up in an arc around her head. Her skirt swished and floated as truly befitted Queen Titania.

She raised her hands once more and lifted her face to the sky. Sparks danced around her in the air like fairies. And her hands began to glow.

G-L-O-W.

Shivers marched along my skin, but before I could think of a single word to say, lightning flickered everywhere, like live sparks in a cloud

"Oh my God." My mouth grew dry. If anyone saw this … If Dr. O'Malley showed up … Were there any school security cameras? Maybe the icy rain and huge electrical charges would ruin any video captured.

A bolt of lightning hit the ground in front of Mia. Sparks flew, thunder cracked, and I screamed.

Josh stumbled into the courtyard from the breezeway. "Mia! Stop!"

"Get back!" I shouted to him.

Mia opened her arms. A huge gust of wind roared and knocked me and Josh down. A wall of wind surrounded the courtyard, swirling, darkening.

Josh grabbed the flag pole to keep from being swept away.

"What do you know of sorrow? Of death?" Mia yelled, fury replacing the usual softness of her voice.

Die. Die. Die. Die.

The word scrolled through my mind on repeat, and my weakened shields unraveled, blown away by the strength of the emotional storm. I squeezed my eyes shut and tried to rebuild my shield. *Waterfall ... waterfall ... steel wall ...* The lightning grew all around us, wilder and broader, dancing sideways across the sky, shimmering high in the clouds.

"You think you can understand me? That you're *like* me?"

"Mia! We care for you! You've got to believe me," I cried.

Josh clung to the flag pole, his big brown eyes fixed on Mia, face pleading.

Mia pointed at the sky, and the winds screamed harder. A whirlwind gathered around her, sending leaves flying in spirals.

I frantically thought back ... How long had the effects of my gift lasted on Ethan? A couple of hours at the most, maybe. Darla's changed moods had lasted for days. I had never hit either of them with as much power as I'd been pouring on poor Mia.

I'd screwed everything up instead of fixing it. I knew that already. But now I *knew* it all the way in my bones. I really had destabilized Mia. All that pain and hurt and fear had twisted into some wild fantasy of revenge. And like all fantasies, it wouldn't deliver on its promise of satisfaction. It wouldn't bring my friend the acceptance or love she wanted. It was hopeless. The truth hit me full in the face: I'd become an instigator of chaos.

Lightning crawled along Mia's legs and reached toward her hands.

"Parker! Stop Mia now," Avery shouted. "This is it!"

One more touch of projection might destroy any chance of Mia caring about consequences at all. "I can't," I called. "Josh, make her stop!"

Josh lunged forward, reaching with one hand for Mia's wrist, the other hand still clinging to the flag pole.

Mia lit up like the fourth of July. Her hands grew incandescent.

I realized the danger as he moved. "Wait!"

Before he could touch Mia, a glowing arc of electricity jumped from Mia's hand to his, attracted to the metal he still held. He arched his back and screamed.

"No!" Mia cried.

Too late. Electrical energy coursed through him in a glowing stream, and he tilted his head back, lips drawn in a feral-looking grimace. His knees buckled. The light raced into the ground, and Josh followed its path, collapsing on the stone squares of the courtyard.

Time seemed to stand still, a snapshot of the worst moment of my life. Josh lay unmoving, his torso twisted at an odd angle. His hair was swept off his face. His eyes were closed. The sudden silence was deafening.

Then Mia's heart and mind broke, and I didn't just feel the shockwave of agony that sent me to my knees. I didn't just see memories as I had before, or even smell or taste them. My power received the cry of Mia's heart as if it were its own. Suddenly, I looked out of Mia's eyes at another time and place. I became Mia.

Mark had said to meet at his house, but he wasn't home. Had he been in an accident? He was never late. I waited, worried, confused. When he finally appeared around the corner, my heart tripped at the sight of him, as always. I crossed the lawn, thankful he was okay.

He wasn't alone, though. A girl walked with him, a girl with long legs and a rowdy laugh: Wendy Taylor, cheerleader and all-around queen. They were holding hands.

No. *My stuttering heart stopped.*

Mark looked over at me, alone. He whispered

to Wendy, who smirked and headed into the house.

He stalked over, looking down his nose at me.

Ice crept over my heart, numbed my lips. "What's going on? Why are you with her?"

"Get the hint, Mia. We're over—I don't date freaks."

"What? You said … You said you'd never known anyone like me—" I didn't understand. Couldn't.

He snorted. "That's true enough. Weird things happen around you. It's sunny out when you're happy. It rains when you're sad, even in the middle of a four-year drought. Tornadoes hit our county every November 22nd … Isn't that the day your mom died? I don't know how you do it, but you're not normal."

"That's … that's ridiculous."

"What's ridiculous is you thinking you'd get away with it forever."

My fingers tingled. The sensation spread up my arms. The stars overhead disappeared, coated with clouds. My own heart was eclipsed as suddenly as the moon by the looming clouds. Tears dripped down my cheeks, and rain began to fall from the clouds.

Mark lifted his hand. Raindrops spattered on his palm. "Exhibit A, folks. Just save the tears for when I tell everyone you're a witch or a demon or whatever you are. Pastor Nelson will lead the charge to run you and your devil voodoo out of town. This town's full of good Christian folk. Your dad won't stop them. He hates you, too."

He turned on his heel to walk away. His pale hair glinted in the lightning. Hair I'd run my hands through countless times.

I couldn't breathe. They'd kick me out for sure. But I feared scientists the most. If they *found me, they'd lock me up, study me with knives—my father had said so. The only reason he hadn't turned me in himself was fear they'd slice him up, too.*

"I thought you loved me." The words were pulled from me. I hated myself for saying it.

Mark turned to me with a sneer. "You're nothing to me. To anyone. Nothing but a mistake."

I couldn't move. Mistake. Mistake. Mistake. That's just what Dad said.

He spoke again, spitting the words like bullets: "A godawful mistake. You should have died with your mother."

Sudden fury laced my veins. In that moment, I wished Mark and I had never met. No, more than that. I wished he was dead. Dead and gone.

The volcano inside me erupted. The clouds boiled purple. My hands reached to the sky and heat flashed through me, setting my skeleton on fire before I melded into it. I couldn't stop it. The power flew right at Mark.

Lightning speared like a javelin, knocking him flat. The thundering boom left my ears ringing. I screamed at the sight of the unmoving Mark lying face-up on the ground. Was he … dead? Regret and horror swamped me like the rain that poured down.

Time snapped back into place with a sickening lurch, and I sat stunned on the ground.

Avery was checking on Josh, having run out of the breezeway to kneel beside him.

"I hurt everyone I love." Mia's words were startling clear.

"Josh is breathing!" Avery said. "I think he'll be okay."

"Liar. You just want me to come quietly with you. Too late for that."

The storm grew stronger, closer, sounding like a giant stomping across the land. A very angry giant. I thought I'd seen what Mia could do. Apparently, a windstorm with some hail and few bolts of lightning was just the preview.

Avery joined me, grabbing my hand, clammy and shaking, but firm.

"What time is it? Is the dance almost over?" I whispered to her.

"Close enough. We've got to shut her down before everyone leaves, Parks. Now."

Mia glanced over to Josh's prone body, and she bared her teeth into the storm.

Ice beat down and coated the cobblestones of the courtyard, popping like gunfire. Avery and I broke apart, scuttling under the shelter of two benches.

The pain and rage I sensed spun into a spiraling madness. One feeling bubbled up through the chaos: Mia wanted to destroy everything. It would feel good to her. Really, really good. If Mia wasn't unhinged before, she definitely was now.

This new wave of emotion scared me so badly I closed myself off with the strongest shields I'd ever built. Shoving aside grief and guilt, I pulled myself out from the bench, ignoring the mud smearing my white angel dress. Icy rain stung my cheeks.

"Mia!" I shouted, but the wind ripped my words from my mouth and flung them far away. The storm howled in my ear, as if berating me. Lightning blasted the tree twenty feet away and shook the ground. I stumbled to my feet, scraping my knees beneath the ruined gown, but I kept going, dodging a stone bench that fell backward with a clatter.

My teeth chattered. I inched past Avery's bench, using it to brace my feet. A quick glance showed Avery curled up with her eyes squeezed shut. Maybe a vision was on her again, but I couldn't wait.

Mia stood near the flagpole and Josh, ten feet away. I slipped and skidded but ran toward her anyway. The whirling wind around the edge of the courtyard picked up, darkening further, screaming in defiance.

28

I wished Mia could see how amazing she was. Lightning crawled along her skin and her dark hair whipped across her face. She looked like a fierce warrior princess, even in the dress. Maybe a fairy warrior princess.

But the Mia I knew wasn't a warrior. She had a gentle soul, a terribly wounded one.

"Mia!" I called over the storm. "Listen to me! You're a good person! You don't want to hurt anyone else!"

"I'm a murderer," Mia called back. Her voice cracked.

"It was an accident. Mark's in a coma, not dead. And you were shocked. Hurt. Angry!"

"But I thought he was dead, and for a moment, I was glad." Another crack of thunder split the air.

I winced but kept talking. "It was an accident—you

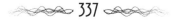

337

didn't know how to control your power, but we'll help you. We've all wanted to hurt someone, even if we don't act on those feelings. Trust me, I feel it from everyone. You're normal."

"I'll never be normal," Mia moaned, covering her hands with her face.

Near her feet, Josh stirred, murmuring softly.

I said, "Look! Josh really is okay! He's moving! I heard him say something!"

"No, it's too late." Mia's words were flat. She swayed a little like she might collapse. "I'm too dangerous. I'll always be alone."

I braced myself and slid open my shields again. Mia's pain tasted like a bloody lip, overwhelming the thirst for vengeance. "Josh can help you get control. If you'll take his hand, it'll all go away, at least for now. No one wants to hurt you. We believe in you."

The wind halted for a moment. Just a hiccup, but enough for me to gain strength.

Josh stirred again. I took five careful steps toward Mia and made my voice show my love, my worry, my stern belief in the goodness of Mia Rodriguez. "You're powerful, but you don't have to be dangerous. Josh can contain your gift, but you've got to touch him. He can't reach you."

Mia looked up. Her eyes were so bleak.

I wanted to turn away but couldn't. Wouldn't. It turned out there were worse things than sensing people's pain all the time. Causing a friend's pain was the worst feeling I'd ever had.

"It's not his responsibility to stop me," Mia said hoarsely. The wind picked back up.

"Josh, wake up!" I cried.

An invisible fist of air shoved me away, lifting me off my feet. The courtyard blurred, and I slammed against the back wall. My breath lodged in my lungs. The steady wind pinned me above the ground, leaving me dangling. I struggled to move. Mia turned her back on me, gazing down at the barely conscious Josh.

The pressure on my chest was immense, but I forced the words out. "No, it's not your fault, Mia. It's mine. I unbalanced you. Do you hear me? I thought I was helping, but I wasn't. I should have trusted you to start with. We're all in this together. Don't you see that?"

Mia finally glanced over her shoulder, and I put every drop of the compassion I felt into my eyes. Love like this was real, and my projected feelings, even when super-sized, offered only a poor substitute. How had I never understood that before?

My mind reeled, but I kept talking. "Mia, we love you. We trust you. You aren't broken, not a mistake. You're just powerful. We can help." The words blurred to a steady hum in my ears, but I kept on. Mia had to believe me.

Mia turned away, but the wind changed directions, and I slid down the wall. I gathered my courage and ran into the eye of the storm.

I reached Mia's side and staggered into a reverberating silence even as the wind shook trees around us. The stillness was shockingly loud to my battered ears, but my words stayed soft.

"Mia. Mia. We love you. Don't do this. It's okay."

I kept whispering words of comfort, of love. The winds around us slowed. The leaves stopped shredding into pieces as they flew. I could feel Mia's heart begin to thaw, like the tiniest green shoot sprouting after a hard winter.

"You don't understand," Mia said, clenching her fists. "No one knows what it's like to be different. To have your own parent hate you. To have people *fear* you."

"I do. I hurt, too, even though I don't let it show." I hugged Mia, who stood like a statue. Maybe she was afraid if she moved, she'd break.

I understood that, too. "My mom hates me. She's afraid of me, and it hurts worse than anything."

I dredged up the face-slapping moment of hearing my mother's secret thoughts—*unnatural. A mistake.* I'd tucked it safely away where I wouldn't have to think about it. Now I let the memory replay through my mind in its brutal Technicolor fullness. Instead of hiding from the pain, I leaned into it. *Feel it*, I commanded myself. *That's reality.*

Squeezing pain shook my chest, then blew outward down my arms and legs, rippling through my entire body. It was like I would fly into a hundred pieces. My legs weakened, and I locked my knees. A whimper escaped my lips. The pain ricocheted back up my spine, filling my throat, mushrooming outward, until I couldn't stop it any longer. I burst into tears, real, honest-to-goodness tears.

Sobs ripped at my throat. My tears scalded. But worse was the throbbing anguish in my chest. I'd been right: sensing someone else's grief hurt; embracing my own was even worse.

Arms still around Mia, I let my own tears pour out, too. They kept coming. And coming. Maybe they'd never stop? An ocean of hurt to be drained. Mia's sobs shook us both, years of pain saved up to share.

I held on tight, ready to stay there for as long as it took. But the harshest moments of grieving often go deep, not wide. The wildness of our pain soon left us both spent, empty and fragile like a shell after new life had begun.

Mia's weeping grew soft, and our combined heartache eased a little, enough for me to remember where we were. My own sobs faded but left my breath hitching. My head ached. My throat was raw. No doubt my face was a blotchy mess. Yet, there was a lift to my soul that I'd never experienced. And Mia had been a part of it all.

A light rain still pattered, though the hail had stopped. Only minutes had passed, but it felt like an eternity. I wiped my face with one sleeve of my dress, wiped Mia's with the other. "You're not alone. We'll take care of each other, okay?"

I looked around. Avery was pulling herself out from the bench. Thank heavens she was okay. "That includes all of us," Avery said, brushing off her hands. "We're all with you, Mia."

Mia nodded numbly but didn't speak. Tears still leaked down her face, but quiet spread out from her like a soothing balm until intelligence flooded her eyes once more.

"Thank you," Mia's words were hoarse. She looked over to Josh. "We need to get him help. They'll ask questions, but—"

Josh groaned and put his hand on his head.

"Well, thank the little baby Jesus," I said.

Mia took a trembling step toward him. She whispered, "Josh is—"

I answered, "Alive and kickin'!"

Mia took another step, and her knees gave out before she reached him. She broke down crying again. This time, relief rolled through the courtyard, flooding me with the taste of lemonade.

The remaining clouds drifted apart. As Mia wept, sparkling stars peeked through the last drops of rain. The moon broke through the clouds and sent a beam of light down to the crowded courtyard.

Josh crawled over to Mia, saying, "You're okay. We're here. I'm here. You're not alone."

He hesitated, offering his arms in a hug. After only the slightest pause, she wrapped her arms around him. The last bit of wind faded to nothing.

I plopped to the ground. Crisis averted. Barely, but I'd take it.

Avery joined me on the ground at the same time

Ethan and Deshawn ran into the courtyard. Ethan's smiling face made my eyes water up. Just a bit.

"Whoa. Looks like we're late to the party. I should've made the DJ take over sooner," Ethan said.

"Trust me, bro, it was one heck of a night," Deshawn said. "Glad I could listen from a distance. Nice work, Parker. Pain isn't so bad after all, huh?"

"Still not a favorite. But yeah. I get it."

Ethan said, "If it's any consolation, the dance was definitely a hit. People will be talking about it for weeks—for all the right reasons. No one seemed to notice anything unusual about the storm. Seemed to think it made the Halloween dance even better, actually."

I gave a tired smile. "Good. We didn't see anyone else out here, either. I think we're okay."

Mia cleared her throat and stepped away from Josh. The others drew back, as if ready for another storm to descend, but I wasn't worried. Mia had been the one to regain control on her own before Josh touched her.

I sensed Mia was still raw inside, with a lot of work left to heal from the rejection, fear, and guilt she'd carried for so long. This wouldn't be the last time such heavy tears came. But now her feet were back under her. She could hike up that steep hill with friends helping her along when she got too tired.

Mia walked to where I sat, knelt down, and hugged me. The air was calm and warming quickly. The raging emotions we'd shared had left a measure of quiet peace behind in both of us. Still pain, yes, but the beginning of acceptance.

"I'm so sorry," Mia said.

I said, "Good Lord, Mia. You don't owe any apologies. Help me up, girl. I thought I'd talk myself hoarse."

Mia began to giggle. If it was a bit hysterical, well, she'd earned it. "Only you, Parker. Only you could have kept talking that whole time."

Avery sighed. "I saw lots of different futures flash by, but the worst one vanished when you cried together. I think we're really going to be okay."

"Fantastic, but we've got to get this place cleaned up, like yesterday," Deshawn said.

Mia looked around, eyebrows raised. Stone benches were tipped over. Bushes were squashed flat. Chunks of hail still littered the ground.

"Allow me," Ethan said. Before anyone could protest, fallen branches and piles of ice were swept over the short walls and into the grass, hidden easily beneath piles of leaves. The benches slid back into place along the courtyard.

"Ethan!" I grabbed his wrist. "Oh no! My gift's making you crazy, too!"

"No, it's not. Deshawn told me what Josh said about your gift. It explains a lot, but I'm fine. I got maybe a little carried away, but my shield is seriously strong. The floating thing was a bad idea, yeah, but no more risks, promise. I'll be on watch for it, now."

"You're sure you're okay?"

Avery said, "I haven't seen any problems with him, so I think we're good."

He winked at me. "You make me crazy, but in a different kind of way." He ran his hand down my hair. I felt more thunderstruck than during the storm.

Josh faced Mia, taking her by the shoulders, face serious. Mia shrank back like she was expecting a slap.

"You—" he began.

Panic. Fear. Hope. Fear. Mia's feelings rained all over me. Again.

"—were magnificent." And he wrapped his arms around Mia in a tight hug.

Mia's relief sparkled like fireworks, and I raised my ragged shields to give them their privacy. I was really going to have to work on that. Maybe Ethan could teach me how to have super strong shields like he did. The thought of more time with him made me grin.

A thousand diamonds shone above. A falling star glittered in its arc across the sky. I wondered if Mia had done that somehow. At this point, I wouldn't put anything past the sky queen.

"I hear those sparkling lights are just bits of dust burning up," Josh told Mia with a smile.

"Someone once told me we're all made of stardust, and everything's beautiful in the right time and place. This is my time and place."

He leaned his forehead against hers, closing his eyes. A small smile played on his lips.

Voices broke through the trees, echoed through the corridors. At the other end of the school, the gym's lights flickered through the branches. The dance had ended.

I tipped my head back and looked at the moon. "We made it."

"It's not over," Deshawn warned. "Dr. O'Malley suspects something, I swear."

"Yeah, but we survived a Hurricane Goddess. We can deal with a nosy counselor, even without my projection. We've got six of us now, working together."

Josh shook his head. "There's a lot more than six of

us out there."

"We may never know how many for sure," Deshawn pointed out.

"But we know we've got each other," I said firmly.

Ethan said, "Always."

We headed toward the gym.

"Parker?" My father stood just outside the doors. Alone.

My smile faded.

"Meet you back home, okay?" he called. "Ethan's band said they need some help loading the drums out back, but this old man's gotta get home and get these dress shoes off."

"Sure, Dad. Be there soon."

My mother really had taken off. How could I have forgotten even for one second? I'd been soaking in my triumph while my dad was undoubtedly hurting right now. Even if the weird response wore off soon, my mom must have wanted to leave, deep down, or she wouldn't have taken off as soon as her inhibitions were gone. I looked back up at the sky and took a few slow breaths. The stars swam.

Ethan squeezed my hand. "I'm really sorry about your mom." He gave a quick update to the others who'd missed that particularly awful moment.

"Oh, honey. What a night you've had." Avery gave me a hug.

Mia put an arm around my shoulder. "I'm sorry. We're here for you."

I nodded. If Mia could find comfort despite her losses, so could I. But taking my own medicine had never been as easy as giving it to others.

29

My dad sat on the side of my bed as I confessed everything that happened with Mia. My gift, Josh's gift, Dr. O's hints, everything.

He kissed my cheek, eyes serious. "I nearly lost you today, my little girl."

"But I'm still here." The words came out a little squeaky.

"Thank God. It definitely puts everything in perspective. Poor Mia. I'm glad she's found friends who accept her. You're a good person, Parker."

I swallowed the lump in my throat. "Dad, I'm sorry I made Mom go away. I didn't mean to—"

He shushed me. "No. You didn't know. I'm sure you meant well, though I seem to remember telling you not

to do that again. It could have gone so much worse."

A heavy weight sank in my belly. "I know, but I hated to see you so unhappy. And Mom …"

"I understand, though we'll talk more about you breaking that promise later, when things aren't quite so raw. But as far as your undue influence on her, your mother already called from the airport, wondering what she was thinking."

"So she's coming home! Oh, thank goodness. Everything can go back to the way it was—"

But Dad shook his head. "I'm sorry, sweetie. We decided that a separation would be good anyway."

I sat bolt upright. "Dad, no!"

"Just listen," he said, holding up a hand. "You may have done the influencing, but I lied to myself about it. I knew deep down her change couldn't be real. Hear me: your gift let your mother take a step to escape an unhappy life. I wasn't strong enough to let her go, but it needed to happen. For her. And for you." His voice cracked, but he cleared his throat and remained dry-eyed. That was more than I could say.

Normally, I'd stuff down my rising tears. Seeing me in pain would hurt my dad, which in turn would hurt me more. Now, I let my disappointment drip down my cheeks.

Only a soft ache from my father's heart hinted of his own pain.

He patted my hand. "I wish she wasn't unhappy here, but she is. It's about her, not you. She'll keep your secret, but she doesn't need to live with it every day. Maybe we'll get back together eventually, but I don't want you to worry about that. No more trying to fix people, right? Not in any way."

I gave a wobbly laugh. "Right."

"One silver lining is that you guys aren't as alone anymore. Privacy is important, but I'm seeing now that you'll always be at risk, and there's safety in numbers. Maybe Mia's aunt could even handle the truth. It'd be profoundly healing for Mia."

Tears still fell, but my heart warmed. "Dr. Lopez is fantastic. I bet she'd definitely deal!"

My dad continued, "We'll talk to Josh's mother tomorrow, find out about this other group of kids, and see what we can do to arrange a meeting. I suspect there's more to each of your abilities that you haven't fully discovered. Sounds like they have some ideas. And another empath to talk to. That'd be good for you, I think."

I nodded and dried my eyes. I had the world's best dad. "Meeting another empath would be cool." Maybe they'd had better luck figuring out how to project without accidentally messing people up.

My father tucked the sheets around me like he had when I was little. I wiggled deeper into the bed and sighed.

"Night, Parker. I love you."

"Night, Dad. I love you, too. With my whole heart."

Three weeks later, Thanksgiving decorations lined the hall, and the slamming lockers and shouting voices were blissfully normal. As always, emotional pandemonium crashed through the halls, but I didn't have to fake my smile.

My shield was stronger than it used to be, thanks to frequent (and fabulous) training sessions with Ethan. Resisting the compulsion to fix people was easier if I never sensed their problems in the first place.

But sometimes, emotions still managed to sucker-punch me. Kayla was crying again, head stuffed in her locker. I didn't have to use my psychic X-ray to know it was boy trouble. Again. My specialty. But I kept on walking.

Down the hall, a boy dropped his notebook on his foot and staggered into the girl he secretly adored. It flashed right into me—the girl liked him back. But it would mean more in the long run if they figured that out for themselves. I kept walking.

I passed the giant poster I'd made for Mia, congratulating her for winning the university's annual Young Artist Show. The portrait of her mother, "Joy in the Darkness," had taken first prize.

"Hey, Parks," Avery said, coming alongside me. "Nice poster."

I preened. "Yeah, I wanted to make her feel really good."

Avery lifted one brow. "Oh?"

I nudged her shoulder. "So I made her a giant poster with glitter, silly! I'm done with projecting."

Mia was doing tons better anyway, working on her shielding and going to therapy. Random thunderstorms were no longer a risk.

I leaned close. "Or did you get another vision I need to know about?

"Nothing from the great beyond, and let's hope it stays that way."

"Wow, none? I figured with Josh's friends maybe

visiting and Dr. O being as weird as ever, you'd be flooded."

"Nope." Avery snapped her fingers once. "I've gotten almost zero since your dad taught us how to meditate better. Believe me, I couldn't be happier about that."

We headed to the lunchroom, such an easier place for me these days since hanging up my fairy godmother hat. Or crown. Tiara? Whatever.

Deshawn and Ethan were already at our table. Ethan's eyes twinkled from across the room. He blew a kiss and flashed his wicked grin. I shivered.

After hurrying through the line—orange chicken day! Score!—I slid in beside Ethan. Deshawn and Avery sat across from us. Mia and Josh joined us, too, as they did almost every day now.

"Parker, thank you for the sweet poster! I love it!" Mia said as soon as she sat down.

Josh nodded. "It's really great. Maybe you can make one for my dance studio's recital in December."

"Well, I'm no artist," I replied, "but I can glitter bomb like a pro."

Mia laughed, still a rare sound but happily becoming more common. "That art lesson offer still stands. Just say the word."

"I'll have to take you up on that one of these days. No rush, though. We've got plenty of time."

For me, taking the scenic route was proving better than expected. People's moods would probably always swirl through me in rainbow colors, but that was okay. Loving others no matter how messy life got—that was what really mattered, even when I didn't get every happy ending I hoped for. No shortcuts required.

Admittedly, certain constant refrains did still get on my nerves. Making Tina Lee stop obsessing over her hair would be fantastic, but the relief would only be temporary before chaos broke loose. Not worth it.

Not even my parent's official separation could tempt me to use my projection again. The loss of my perfect family dream stung, but it was necessary pain, like pulling a thorn from a wound. My dad and I would just have to figure things out day by day. And we would, too.

Just like everyone else.

ACKNOWLEDGEMENTS

This book has changed in so many ways with each revision over the years, it's nearly impossible to mention everyone who impacted this story along the way. However, I most assuredly owe many thanks to the following wonderful people: Jessica, Jeannine, Valerie, Jamie, Elizabeth, Matthew, Edward, Stacy, Krystal, Lara, Ann, and Carol. Several of you read this back when it had a different title, but it wouldn't be the story it is today without each of you.

Thanks to SCBWI and the Twitter writing community, always full of encouraging support. Editor Olivia Swenson helped the book shine, and CBAY Books continued the good work after picking up *Shortcuts*. I've admired CBAY since attending a SCBWI workshop in

2009 in which Madeline Smoot gave helpful feedback on my first manuscript—what a thrill to be part of her list now! Thank you, Madeline! Many thanks also to artist Jeff Crosby for the awesome title art and to Madeline for the eye-catching cover.

There are not enough words to say thank you to my husband and children, for all the help and cheerleading along the way. And thank you to my parents, sister, and mother-in-law, for always believing in me. I love you all and appreciate your steady support.

In some ways, this book is more personal than any I have written, even though I'm nothing like happy-go-lucky Parker. If you struggle with depression or feel stuck in grief, please know that a professional therapist or doctor can help. You are not alone. And if you feel compelled to rescue everyone around you, I humbly recommend reading up on codependency. The *Shortcuts* page of my website has a list of articles and resources about young people's brains and emotional health.

Thank you for reading, all of you. I'm grateful every day for the chance to tell stories to others.

Amy

ABOUT THE AUTHOR

AMY BEARCE writes fantasy and light science fiction for young readers and the young at heart. She is also a former reading teacher and school librarian. As an Army kid, she moved eight times before she was eighteen, so she feels especially fortunate to be married to her high school sweetheart. Together they're raising two daughters in San Antonio. You can find Amy online at amybearce.com.